THE SEA

RIKKE VILLADSEN

fantagraphics books

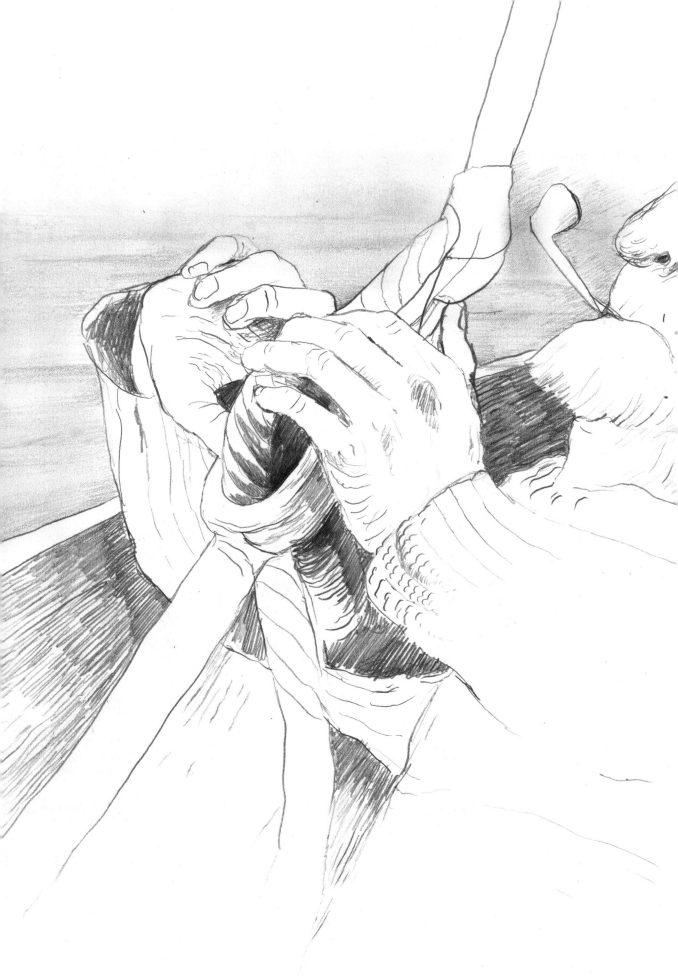

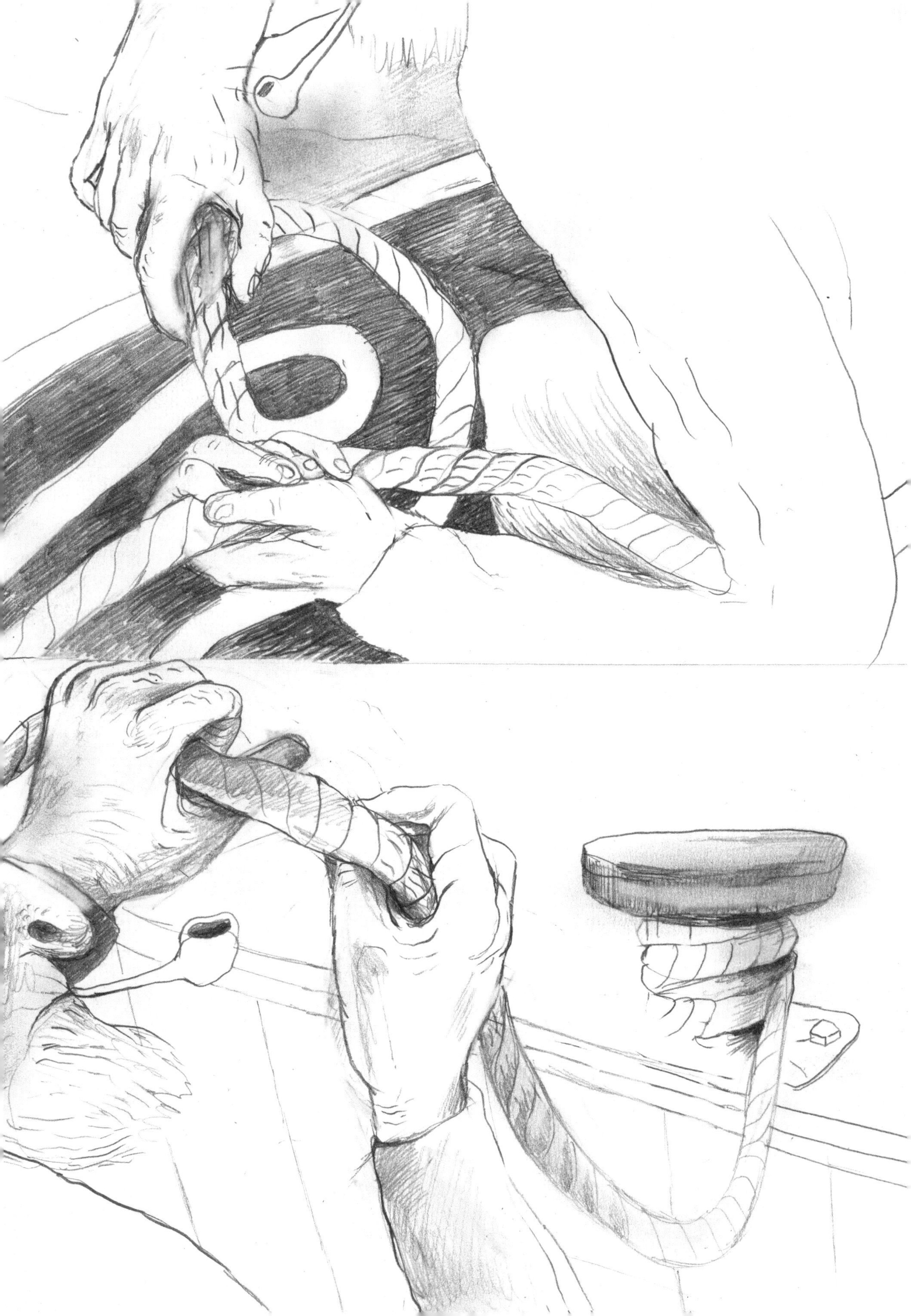

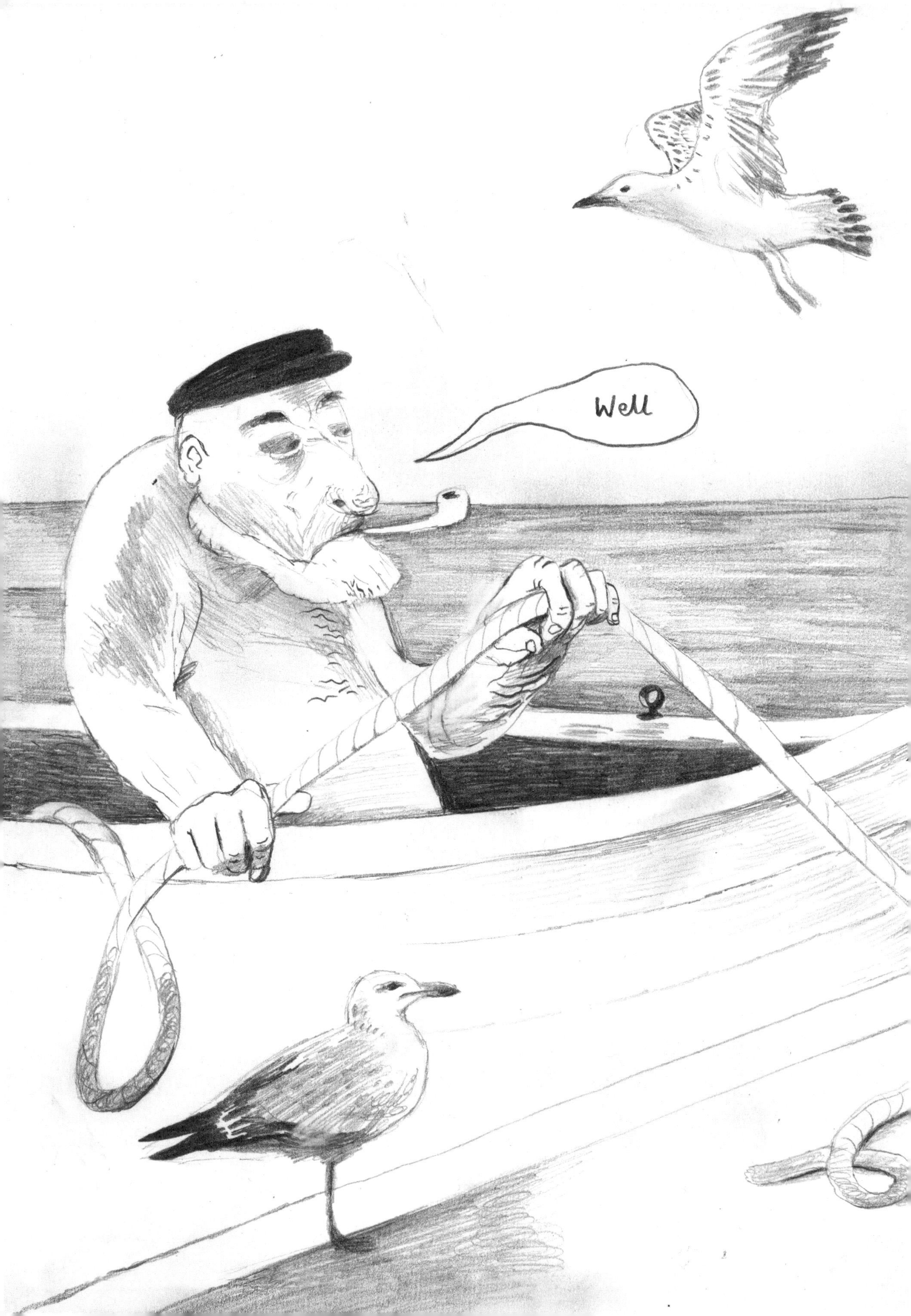
Well

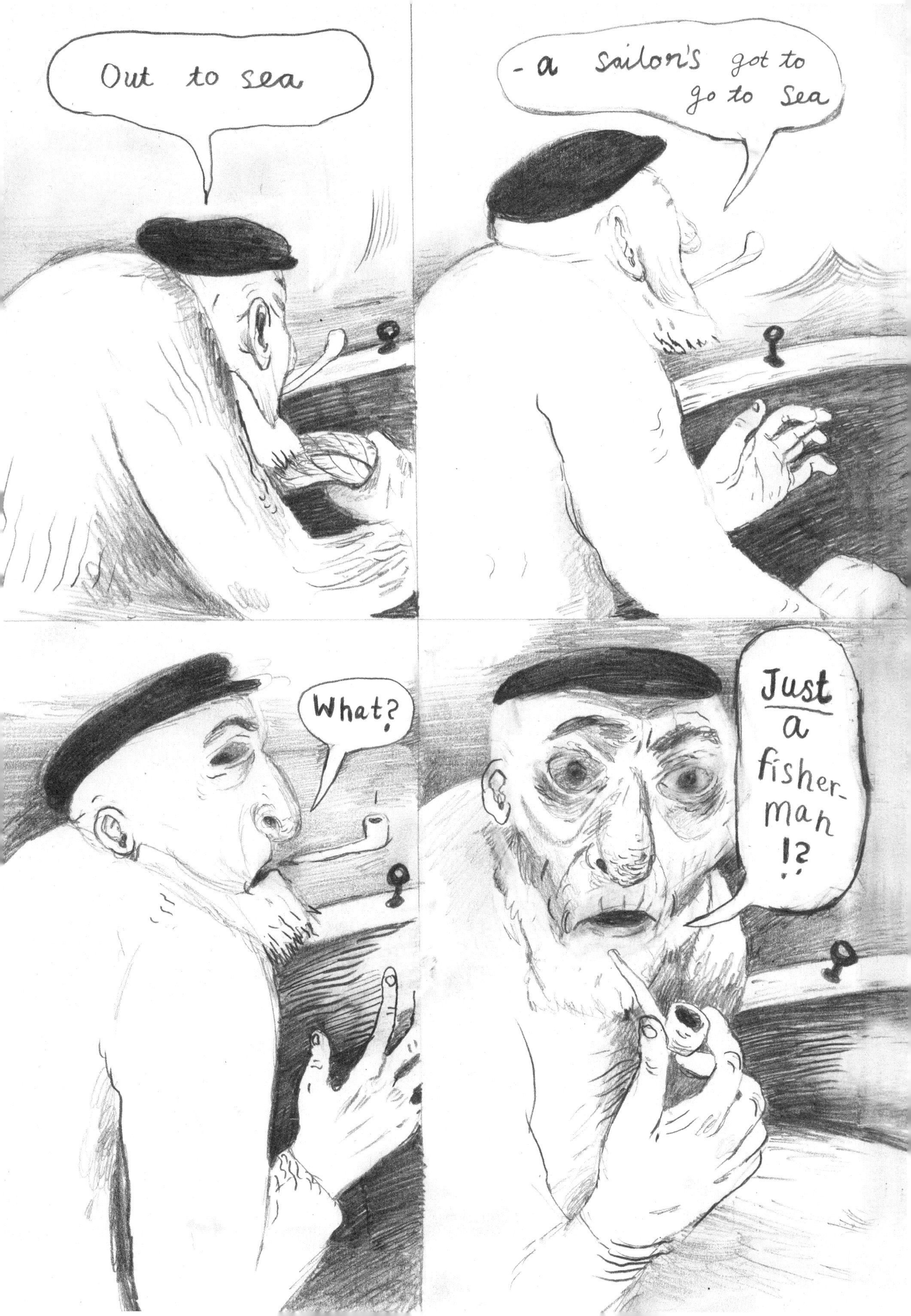
Out to sea
- a sailor's got to go to Sea
What?
Just a fisher-man !?

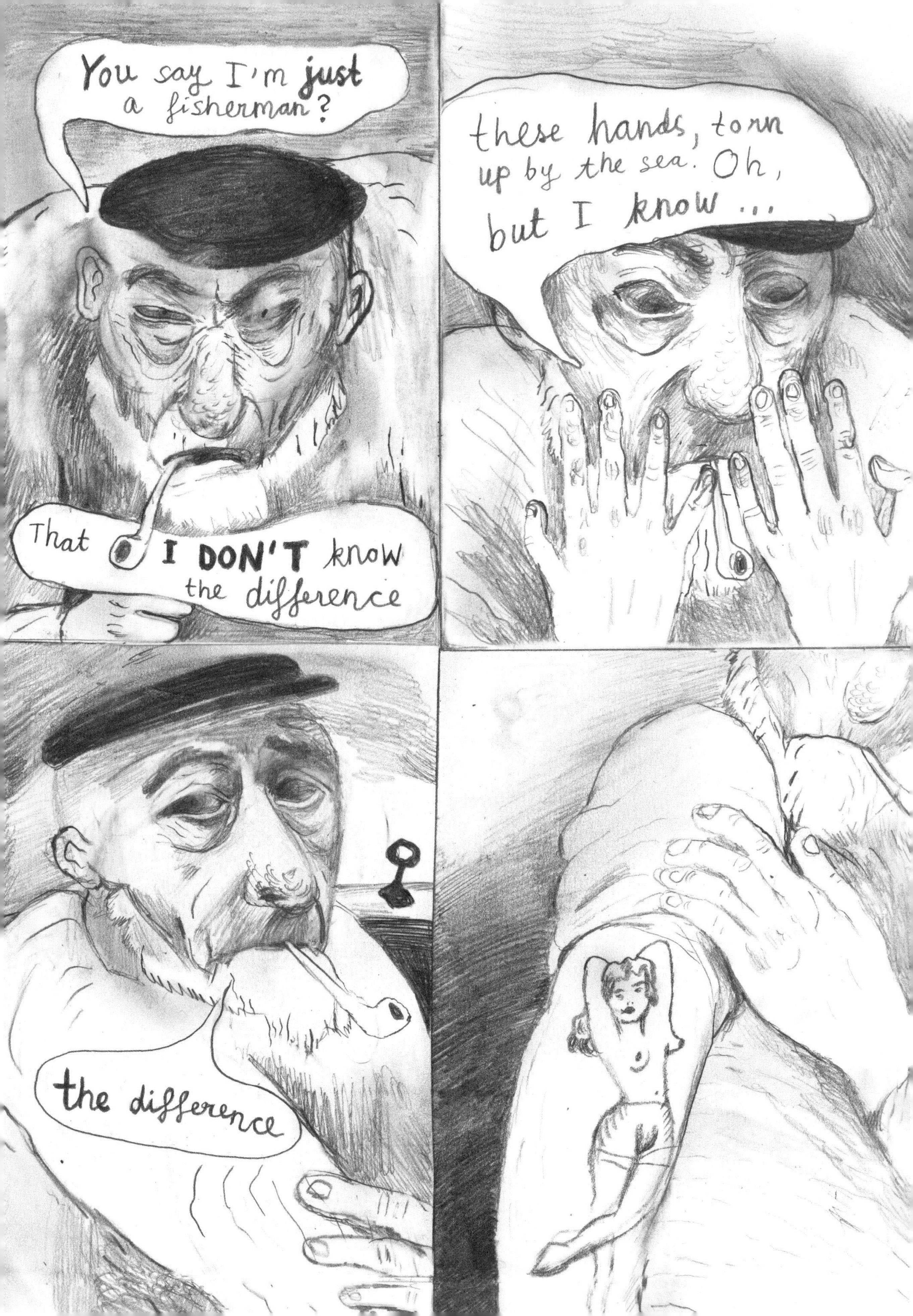
You say I'm just a fisherman?
That I DON'T know the difference
these hands, torn up by the sea. Oh, but I know ...
the difference

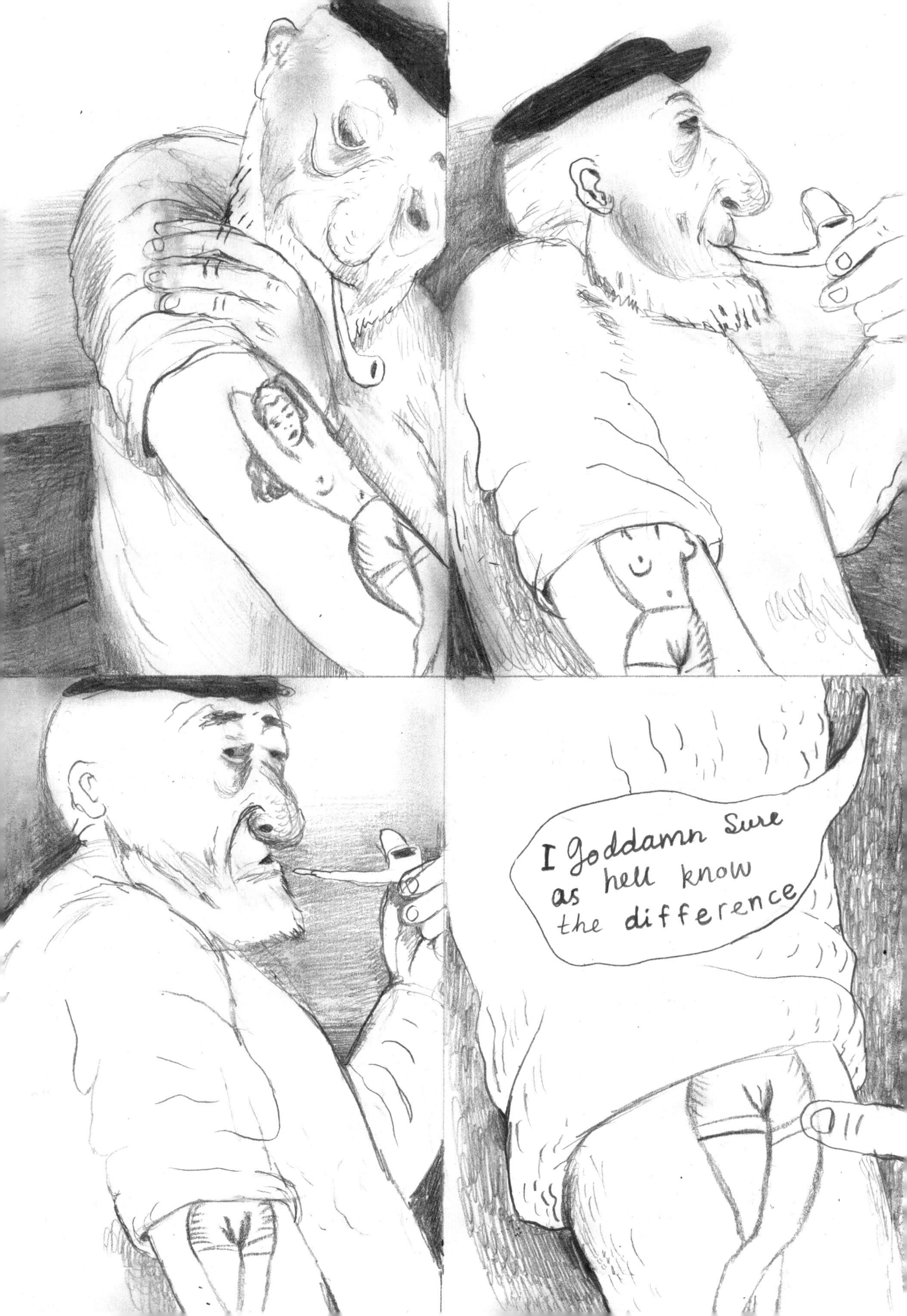
I Goddamn Sure as hell know the difference

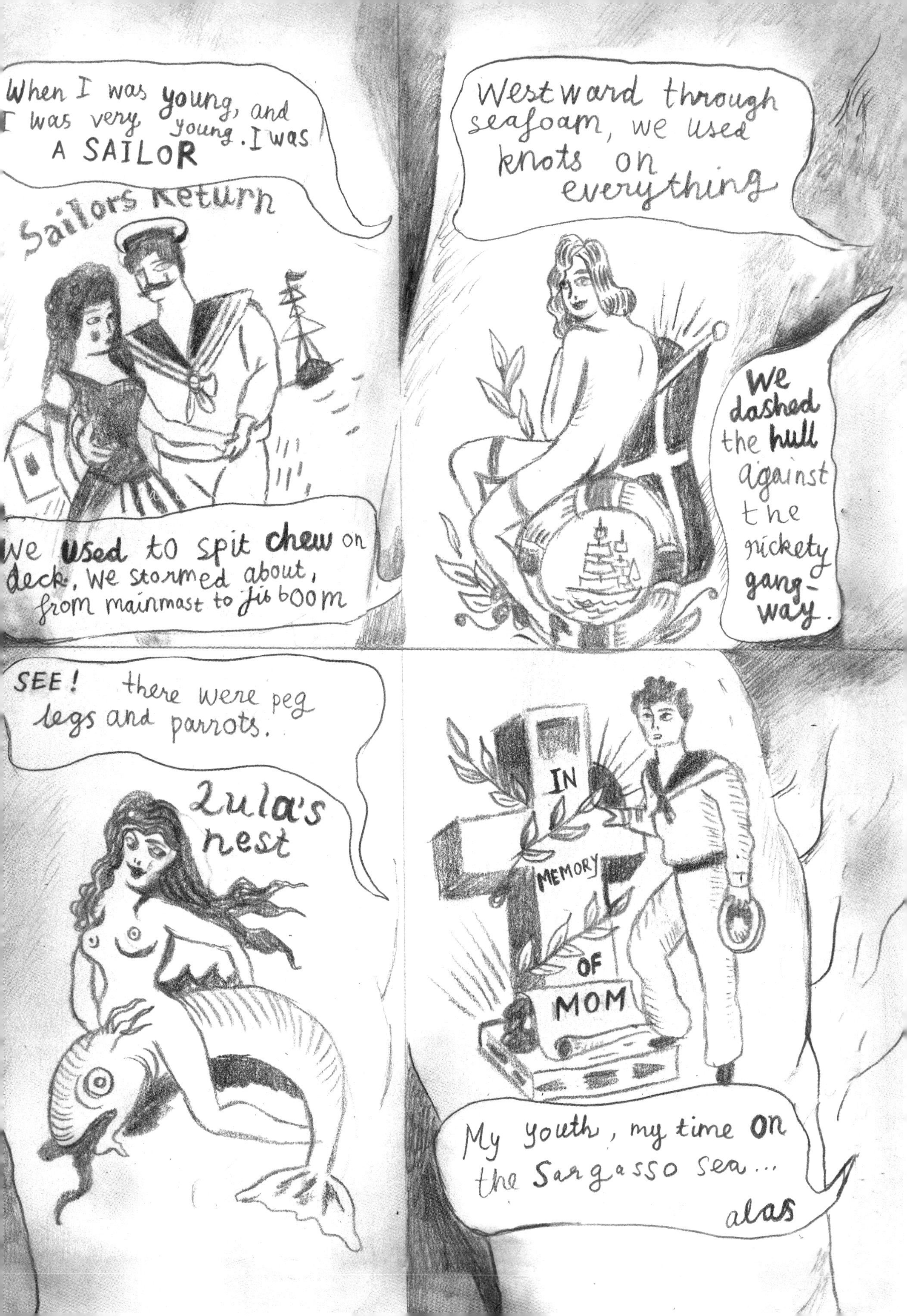
When I was young, and I was very young. I was A SAILOR
Sailors Return
We used to spit chew on deck. We stormed about, from mainmast to jib boom
Westward through seafoam, we used knots on everything
We dashed the hull against the rickety gang-way.
SEE! there were peg legs and parrots.
Zula's nest
IN MEMORY OF MOM
My youth, my time on the Sargasso sea... alas

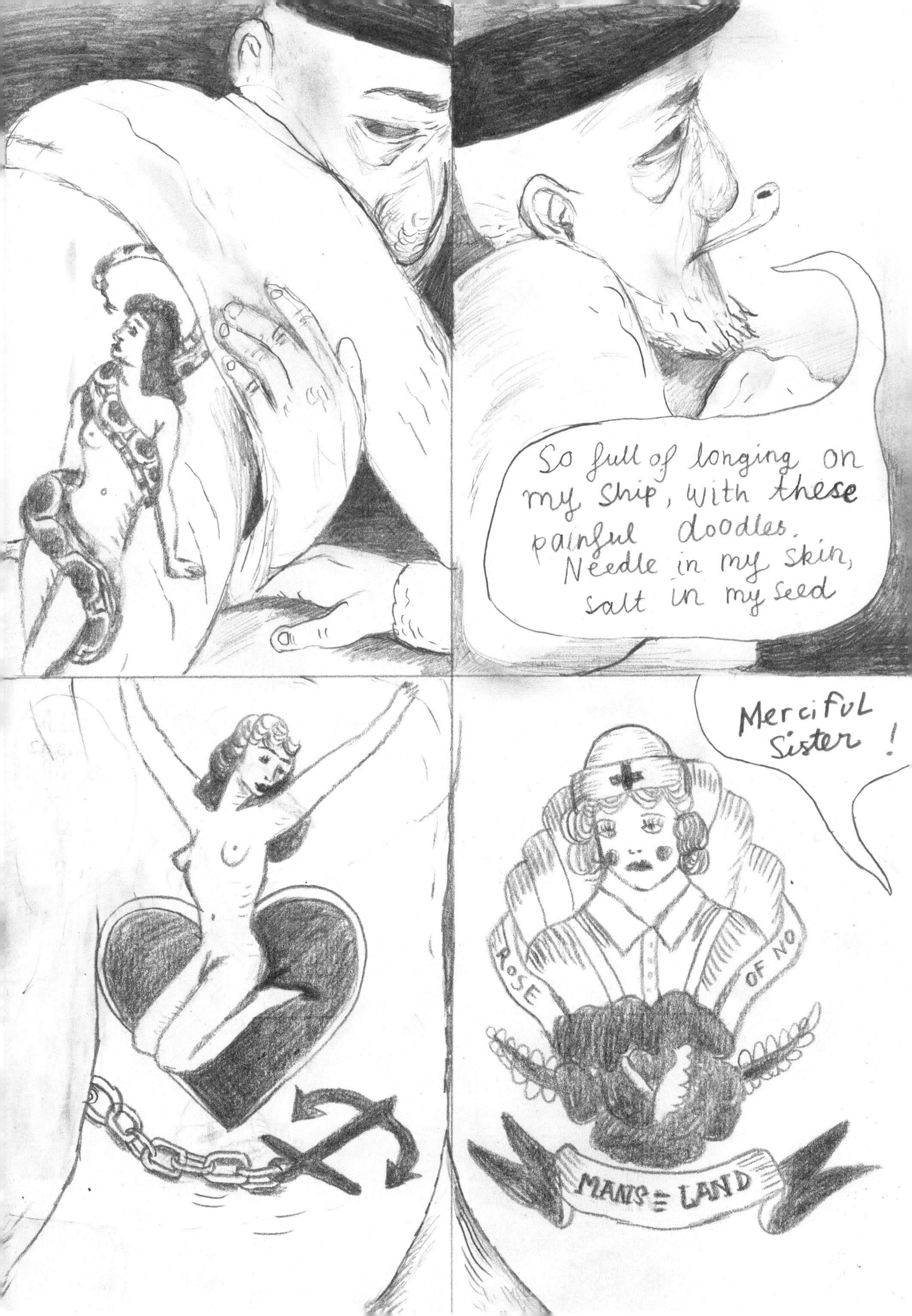
So full of longing on my ship, with these painful doodles. Needle in my skin, salt in my seed
Merciful Sister!
ROSE OF NO
MANS LAND

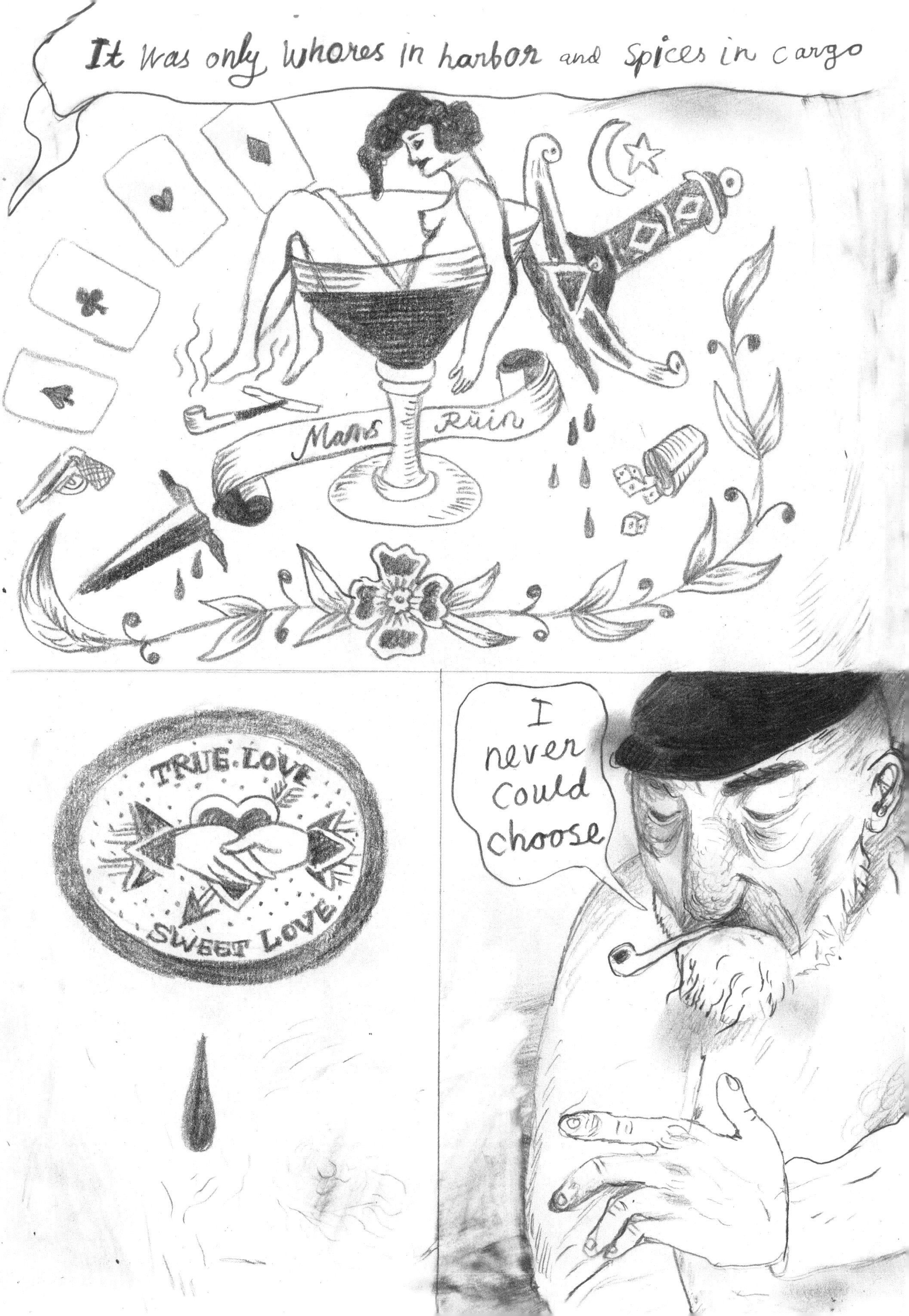
It was only whores in harbor and spices in cargo
Mans Rüin
TRUE LOVE
SWEET LOVE
I never could choose

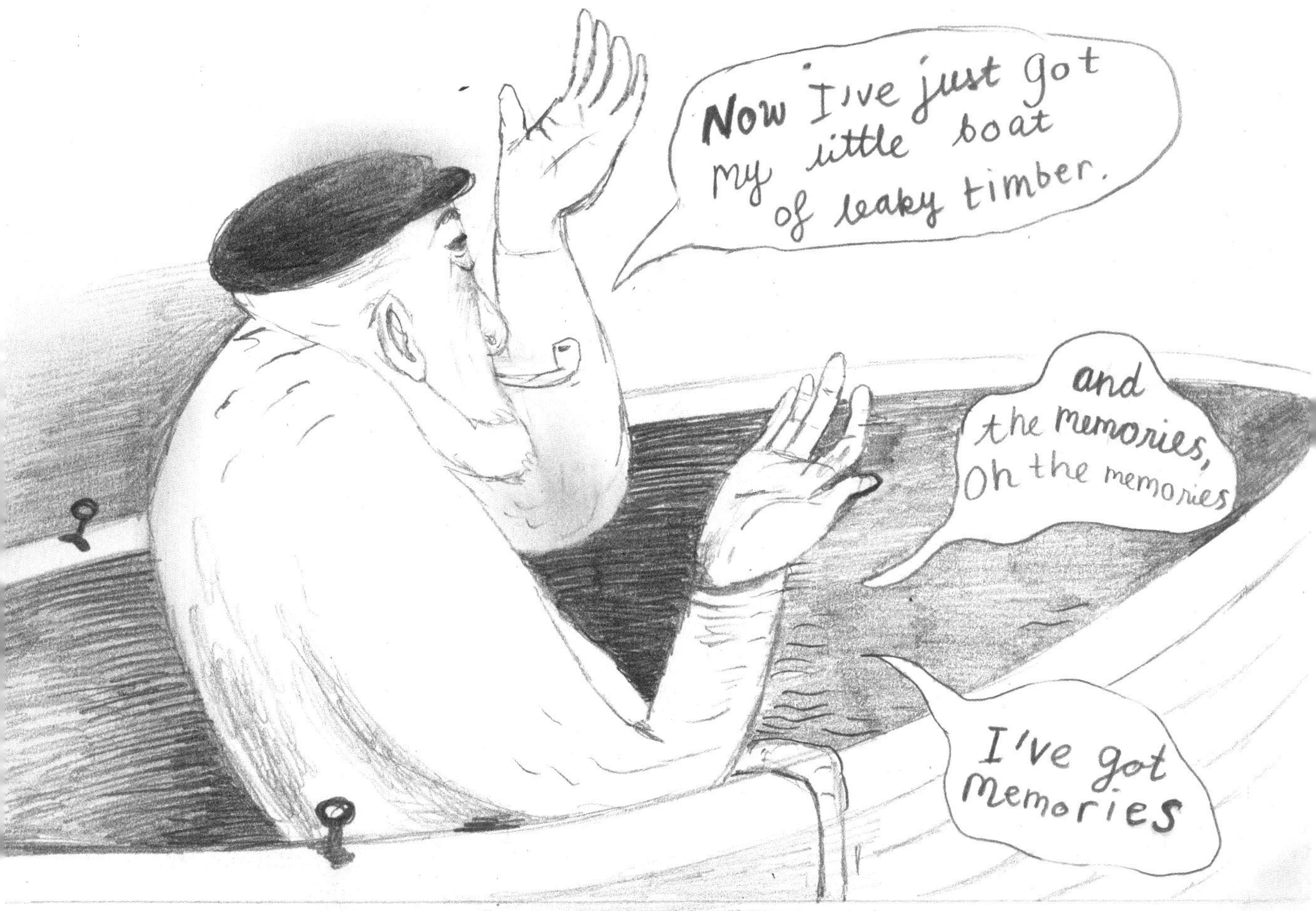
Now I've just got my little boat of leaky timber.
and the memories, Oh the memories
I've got memories

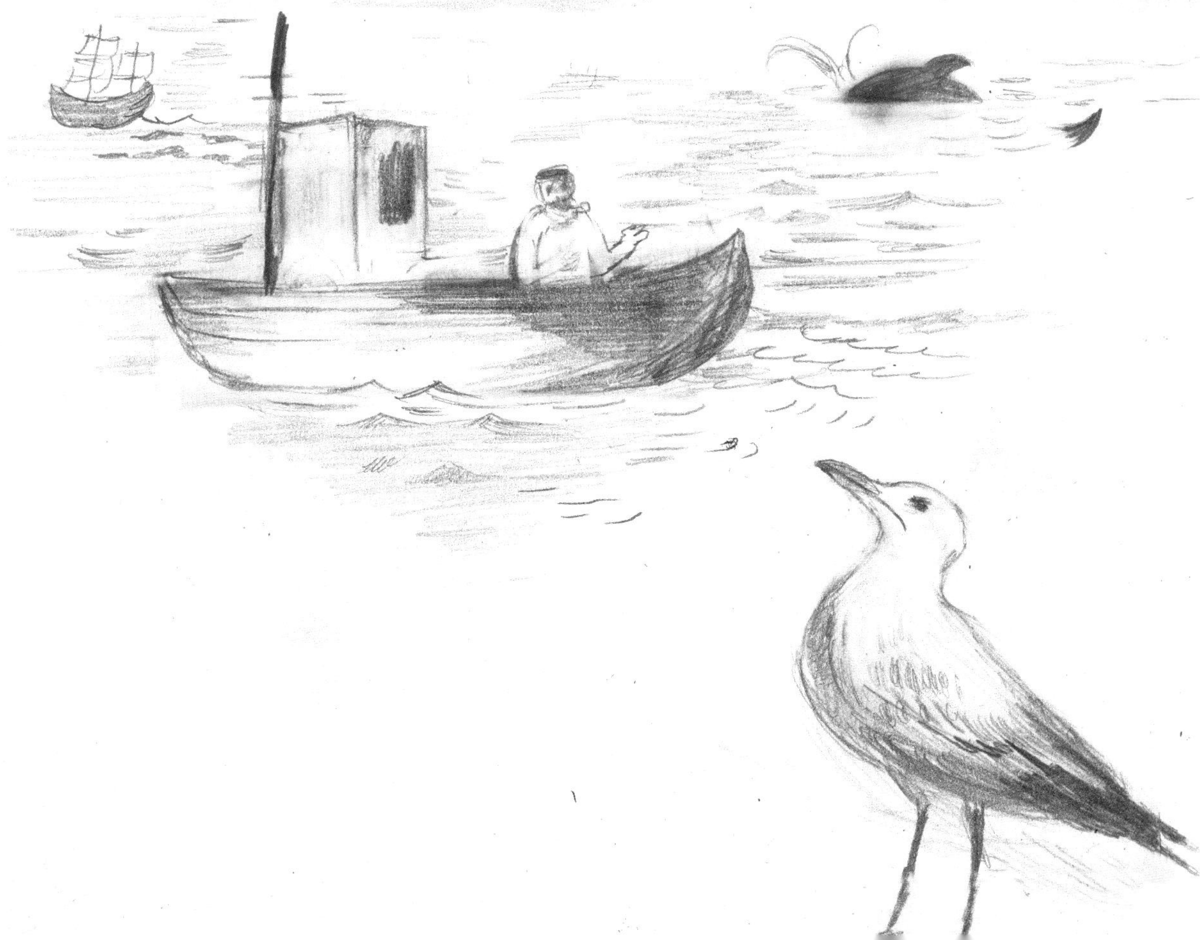

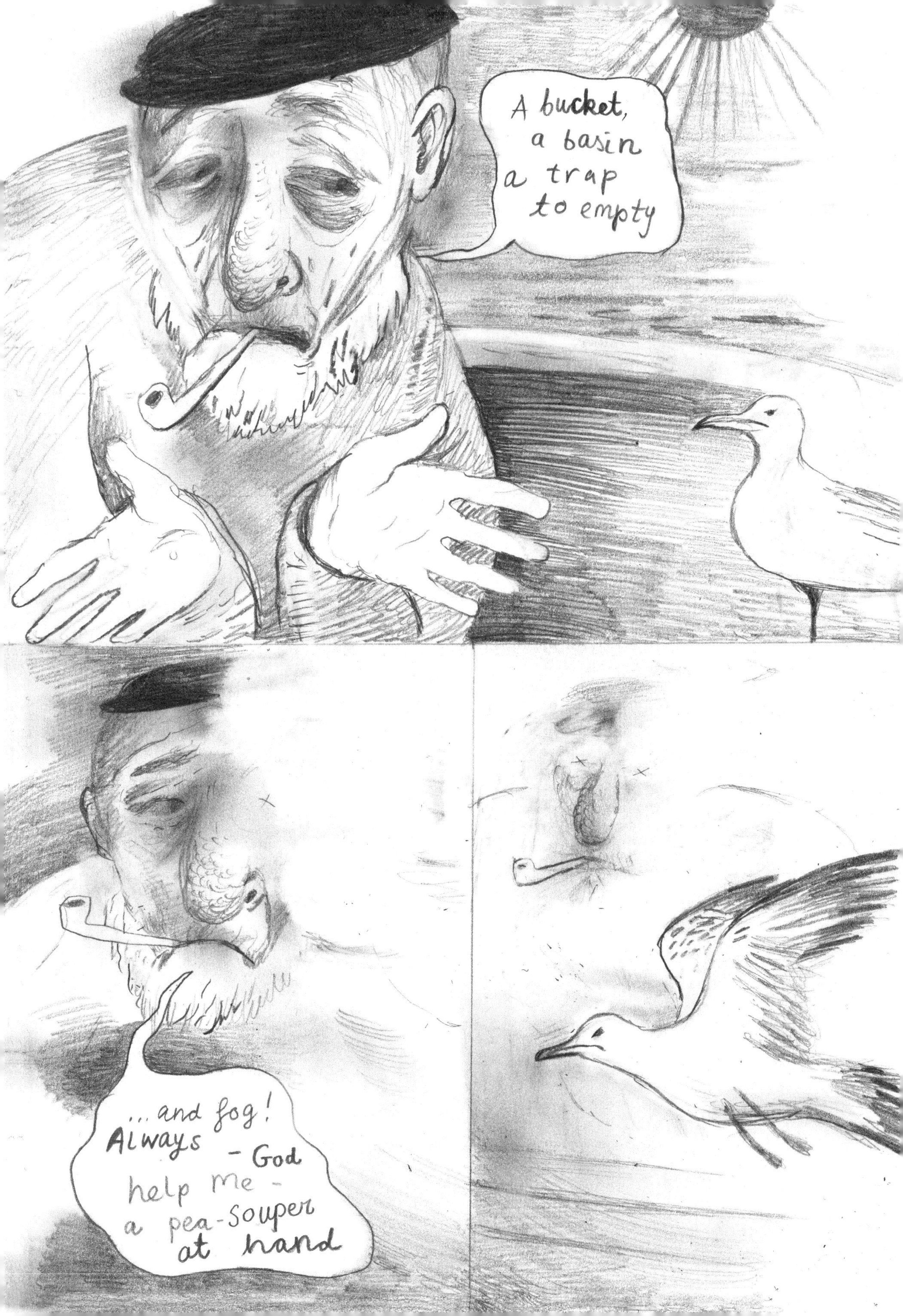
A bucket, a basin a trap to empty
...and fog! Always - God help me - a pea-souper at hand

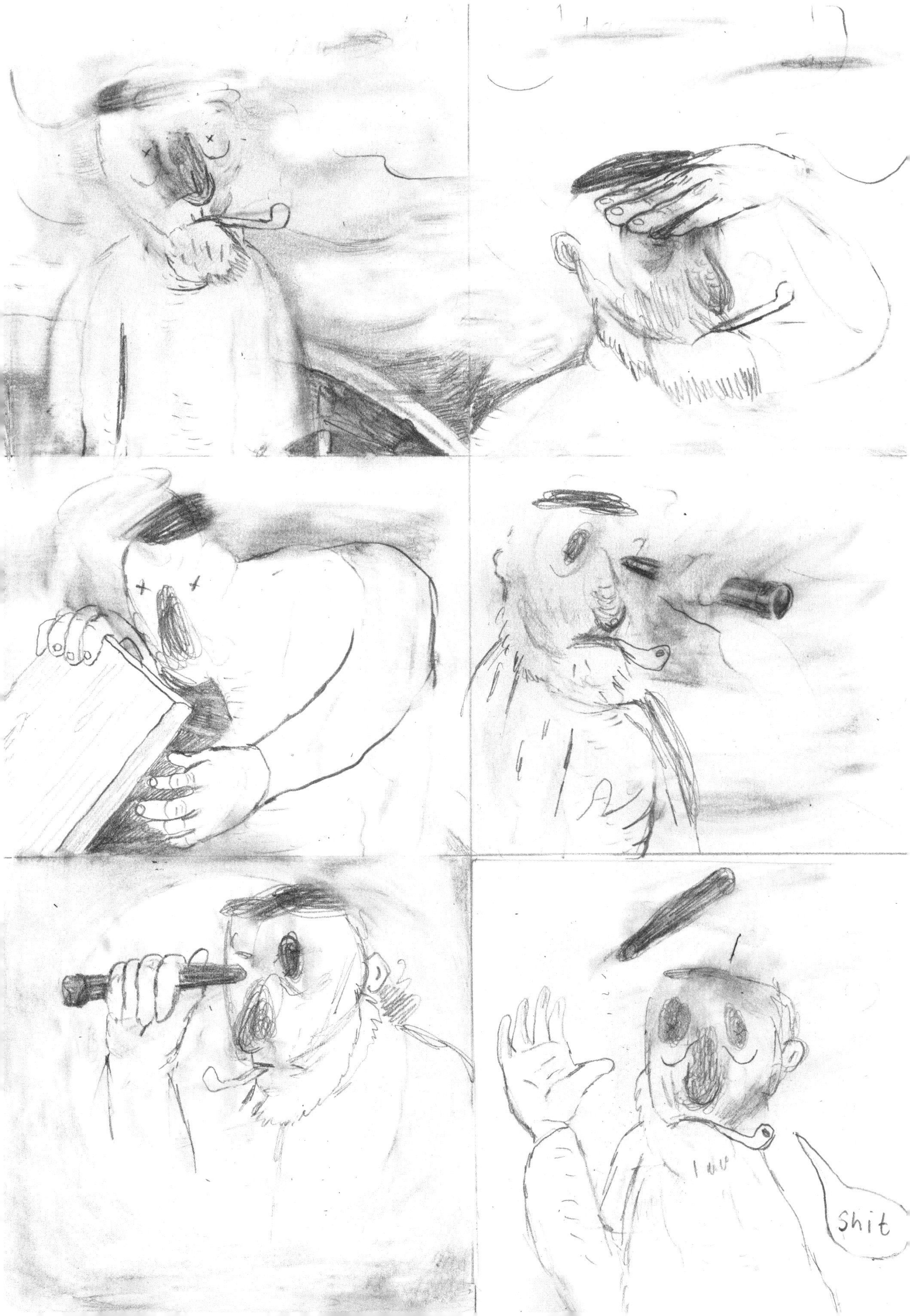
Shit

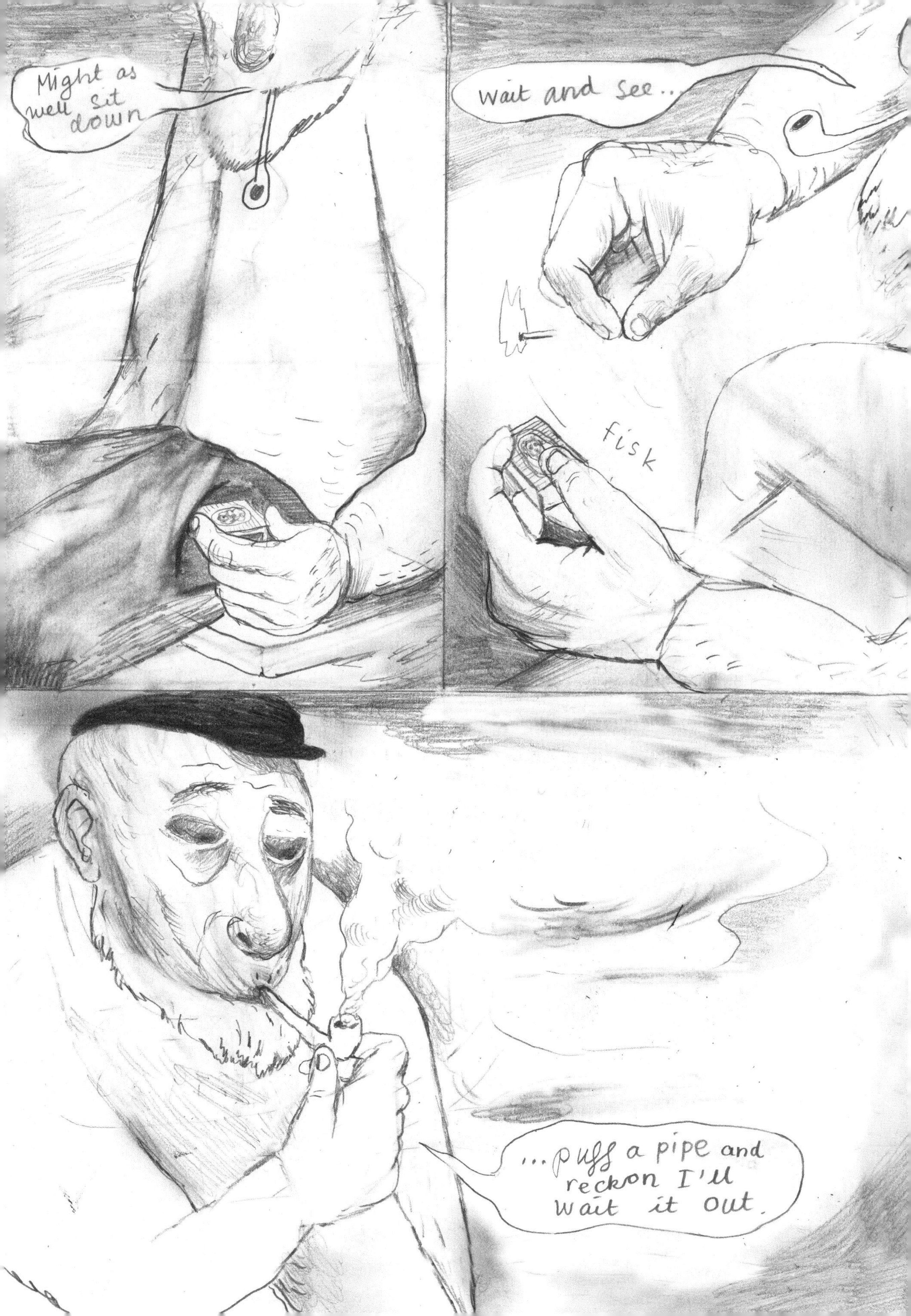
Might as well sit down
Wait and see...
fisk
...puff a pipe and reckon I'll Wait it Out.

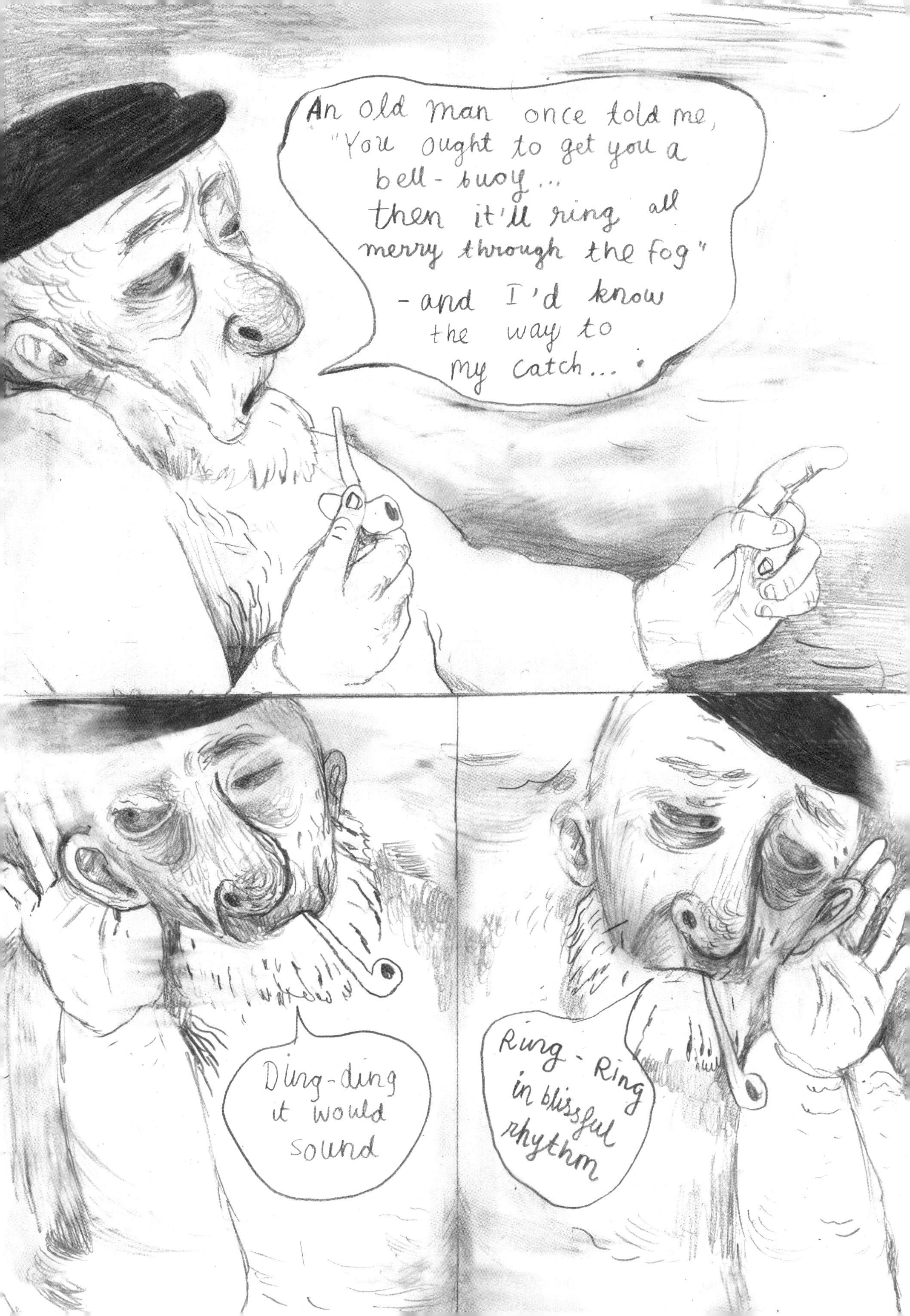
An old man once told me, "You ought to get you a bell-buoy... then it'll ring all merry through the fog" - and I'd know the way to my catch...
Ding-ding it would sound
Ring-Ring in blissful rhythm

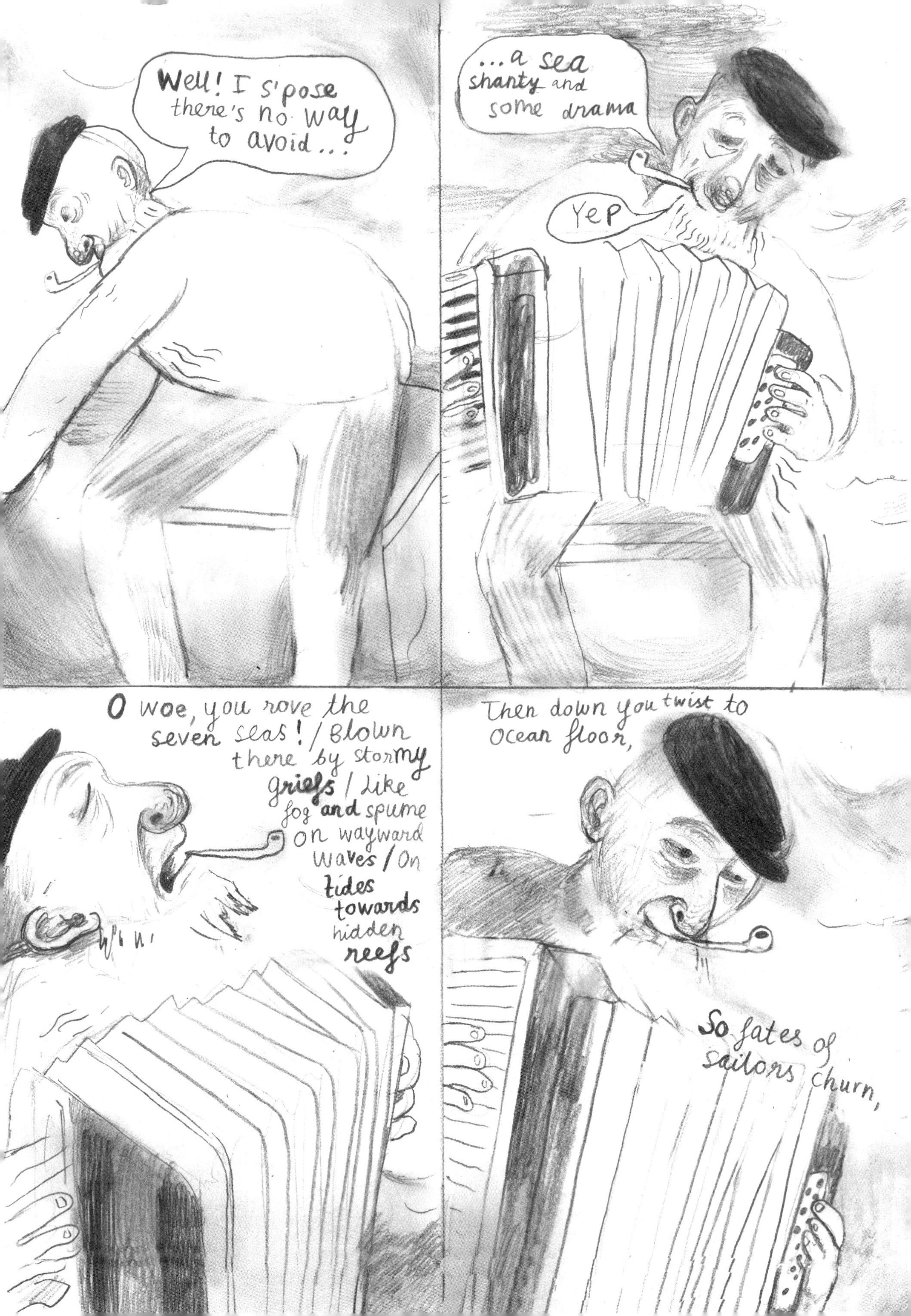
Well! I s'pose there's no way to avoid...
...a sea shanty and some drama
Yep
O woe, you rove the seven seas! / Blown there by stormy griefs / Like fog and spume on wayward waves / On tides towards hidden reefs
Then down you twist to ocean floor,
So fates of sailors churn,

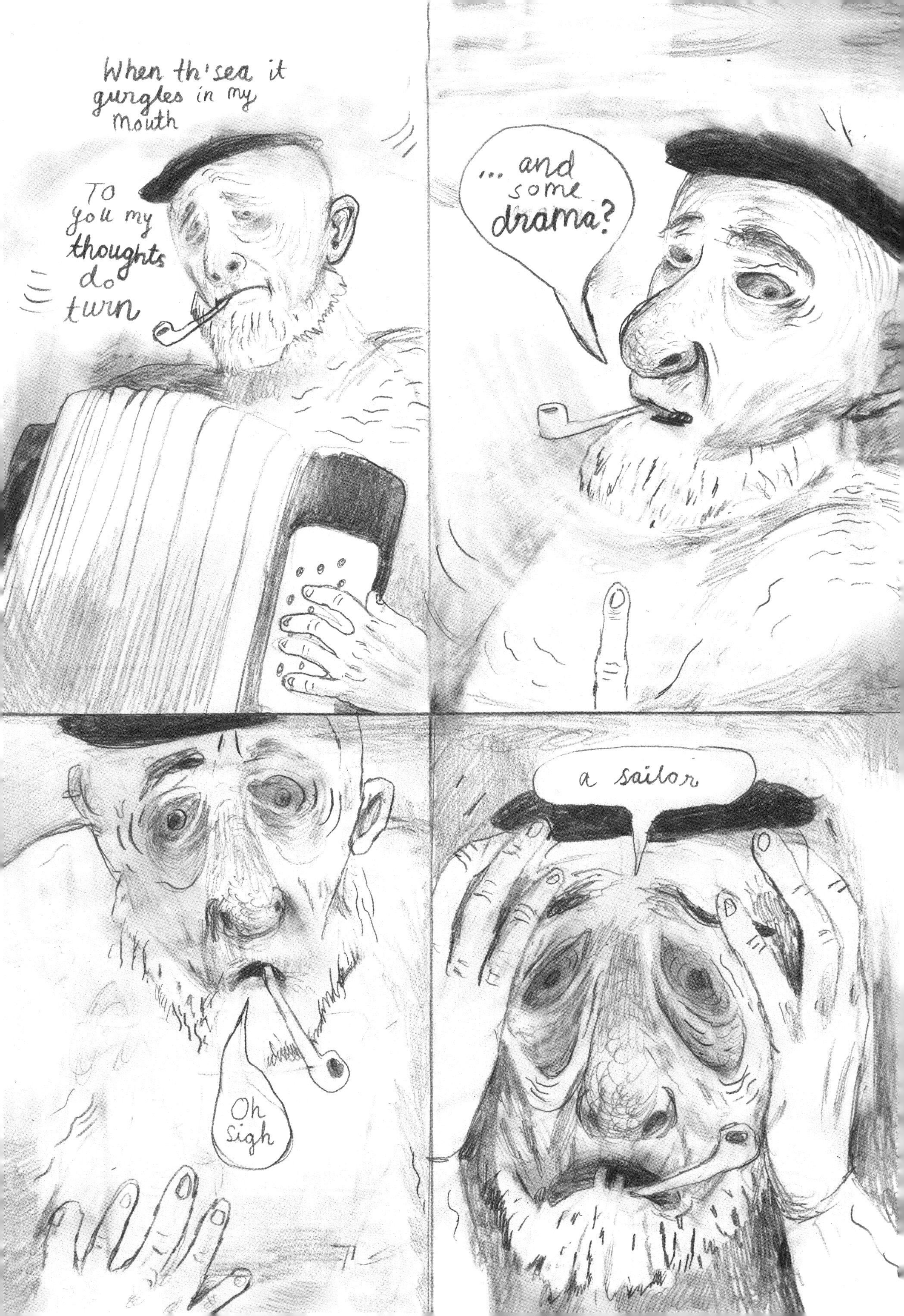
When th'sea it gurgles in my mouth
To you my thoughts do turn
... and some drama?
Oh Sigh
a sailor

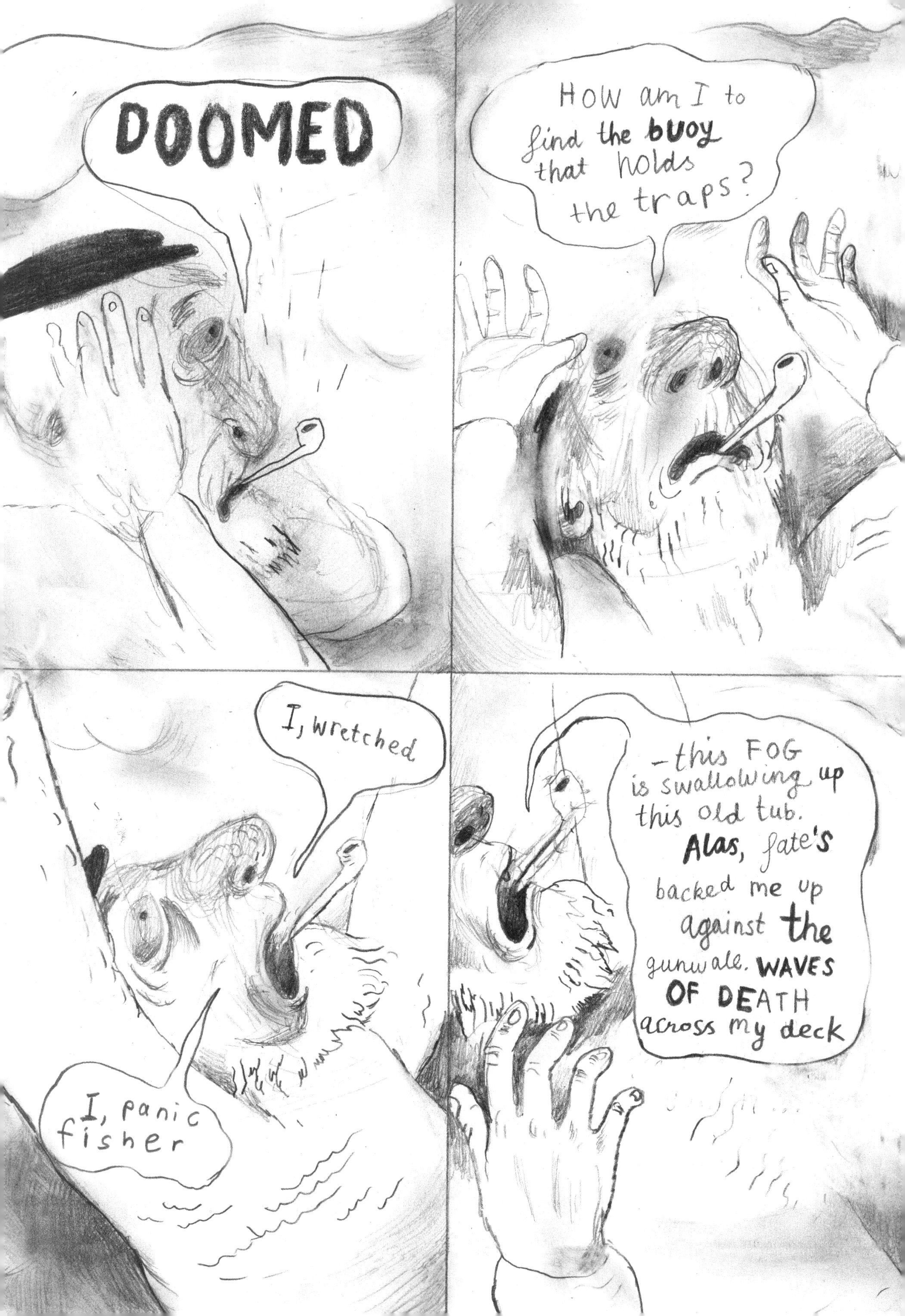
DOOMED
How am I to find the buoy that holds the traps?
I, wretched
I, panic fisher
-this FOG is swallowing up this old tub. Alas, fate's backed me up against the gunwale. WAVES OF DEATH across my deck

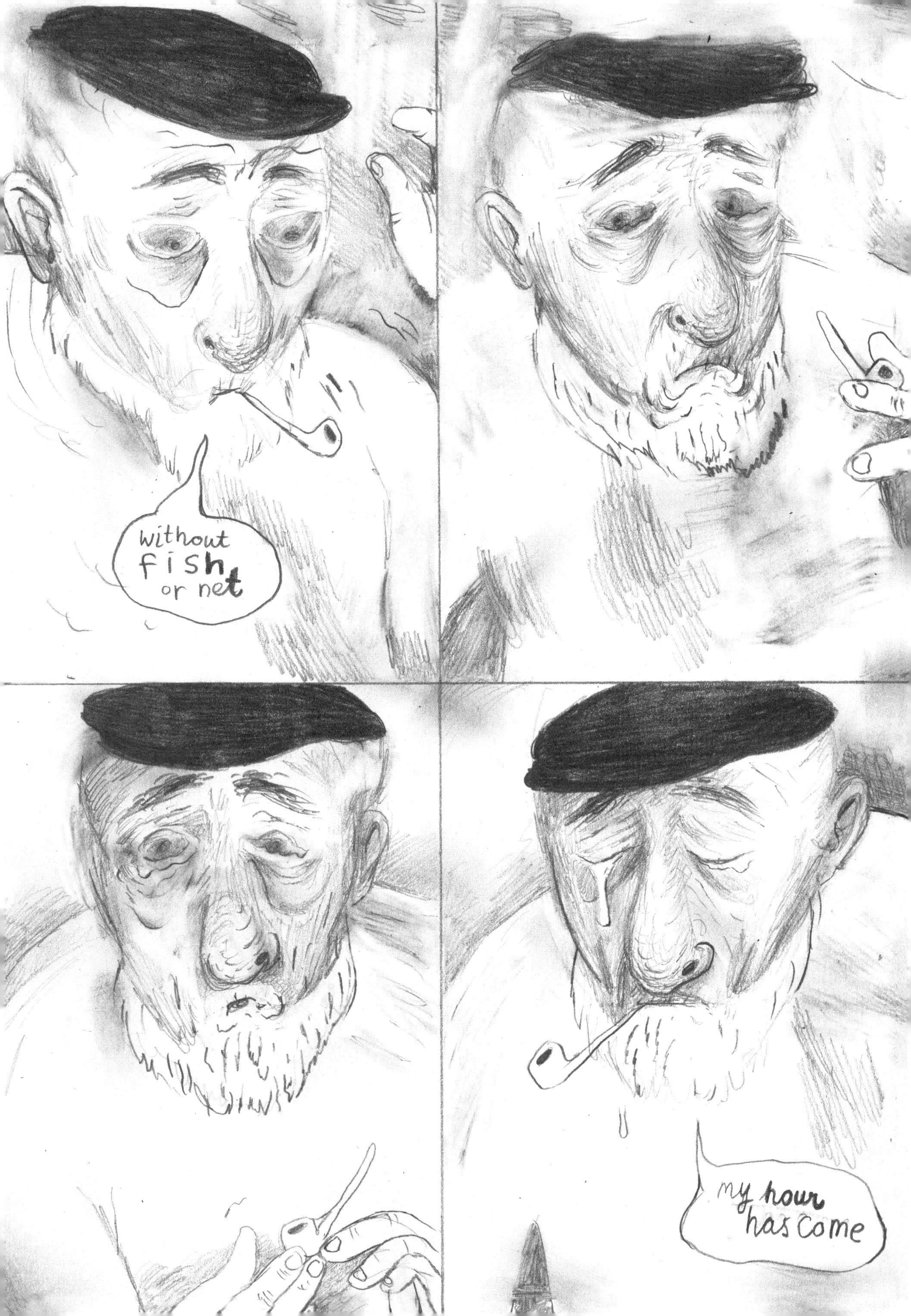
without fish or net
my hour has come

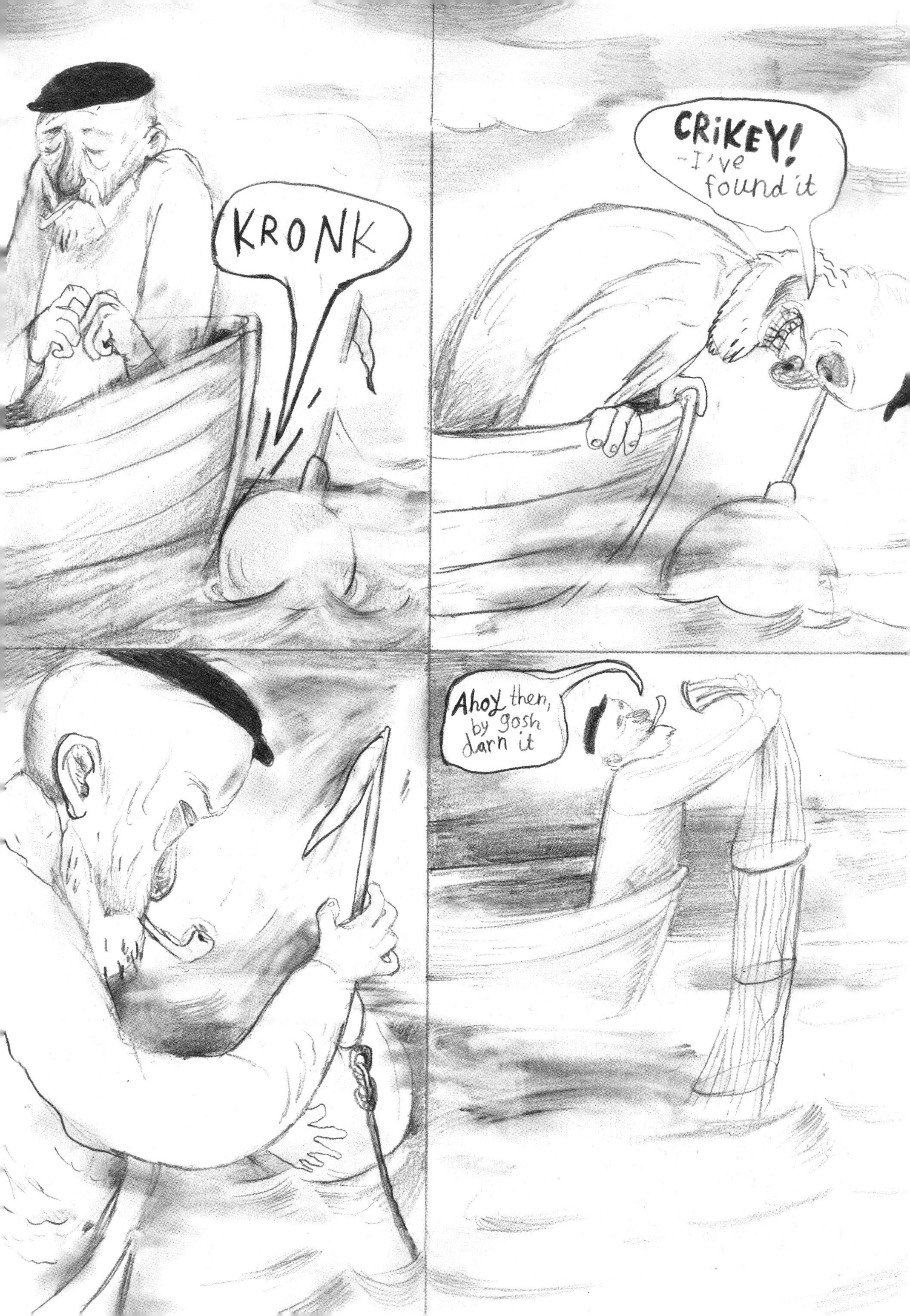
KRONK
CRiKEY! -I've found it
Ahoy then, by gosh darn it

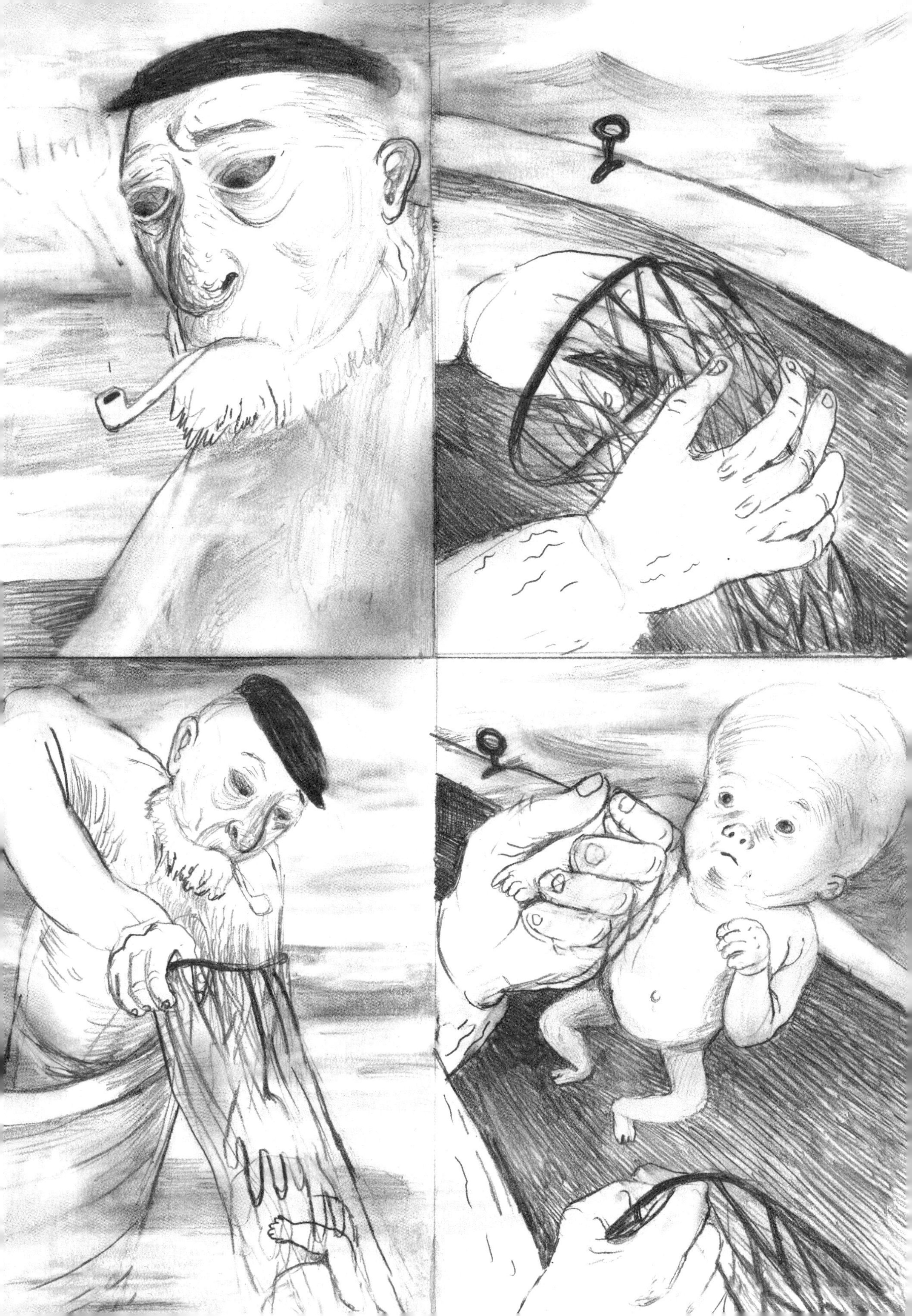
Hm!

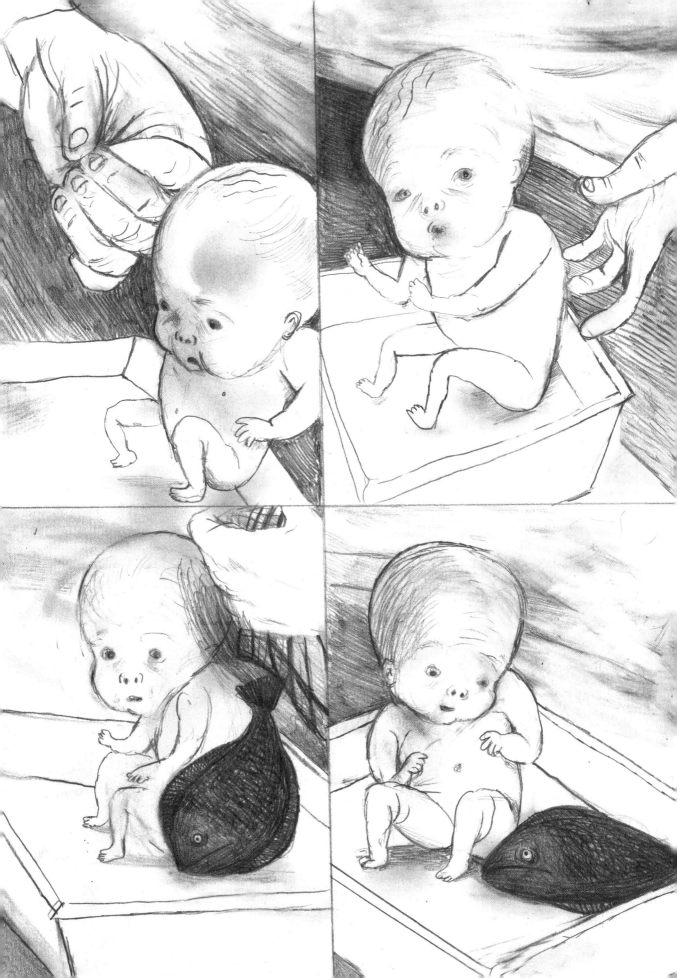

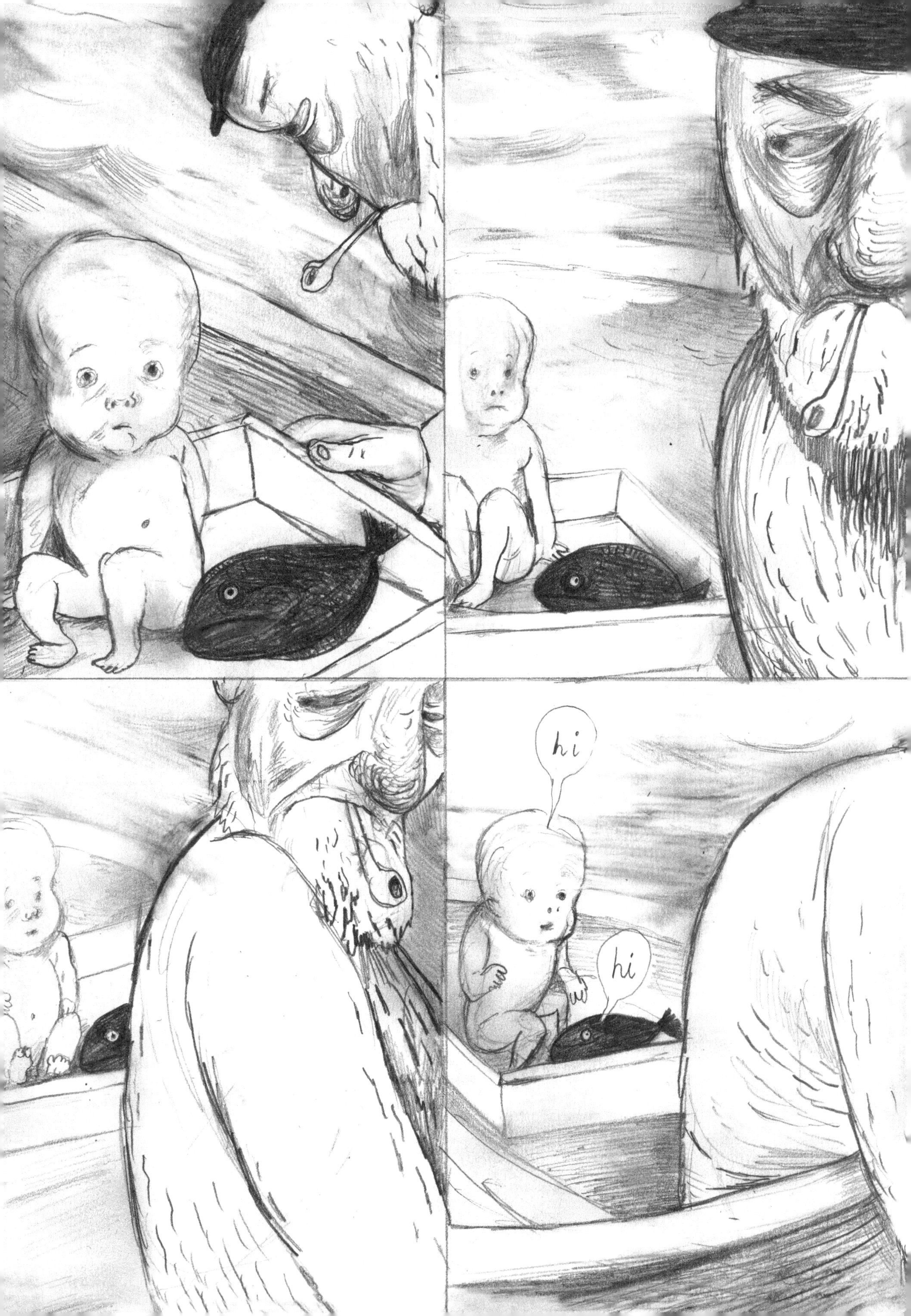
hi
hi

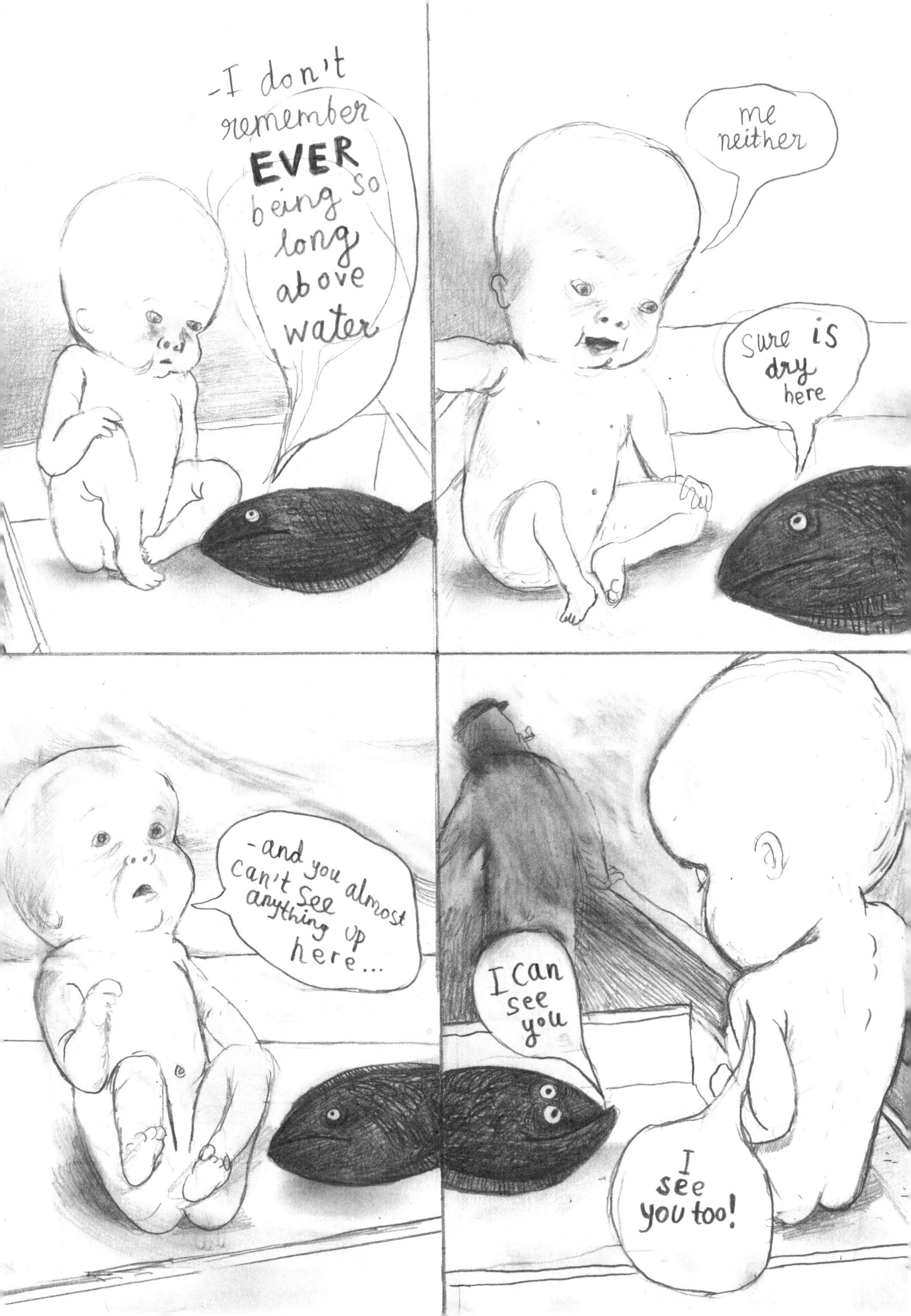
-I don't remember EVER being so long above water
me neither
Sure is dry here
-and you almost can't see anything up here...
I can see you
I see you too!

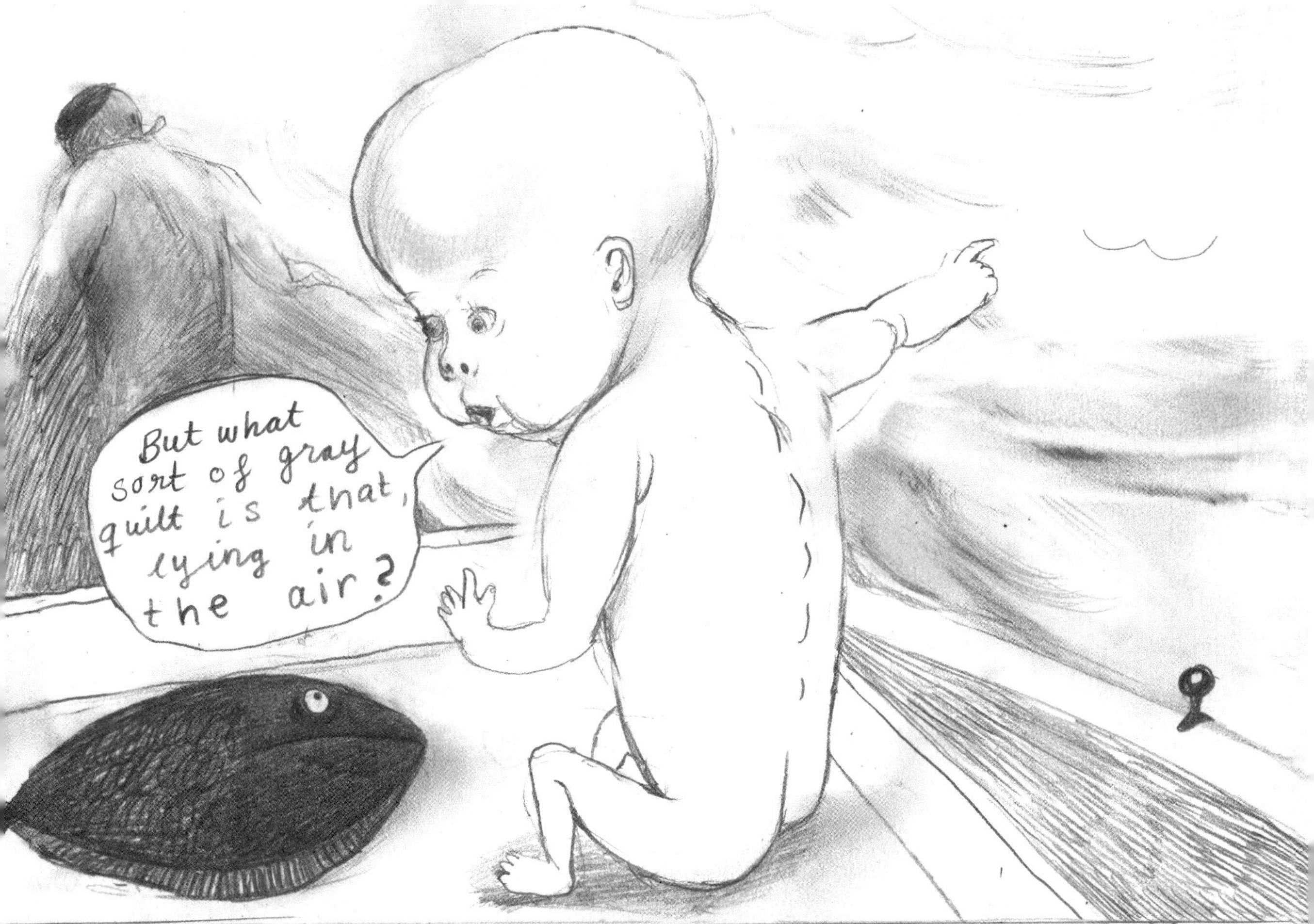
But what sort of gray quilt is that, lying in the air?

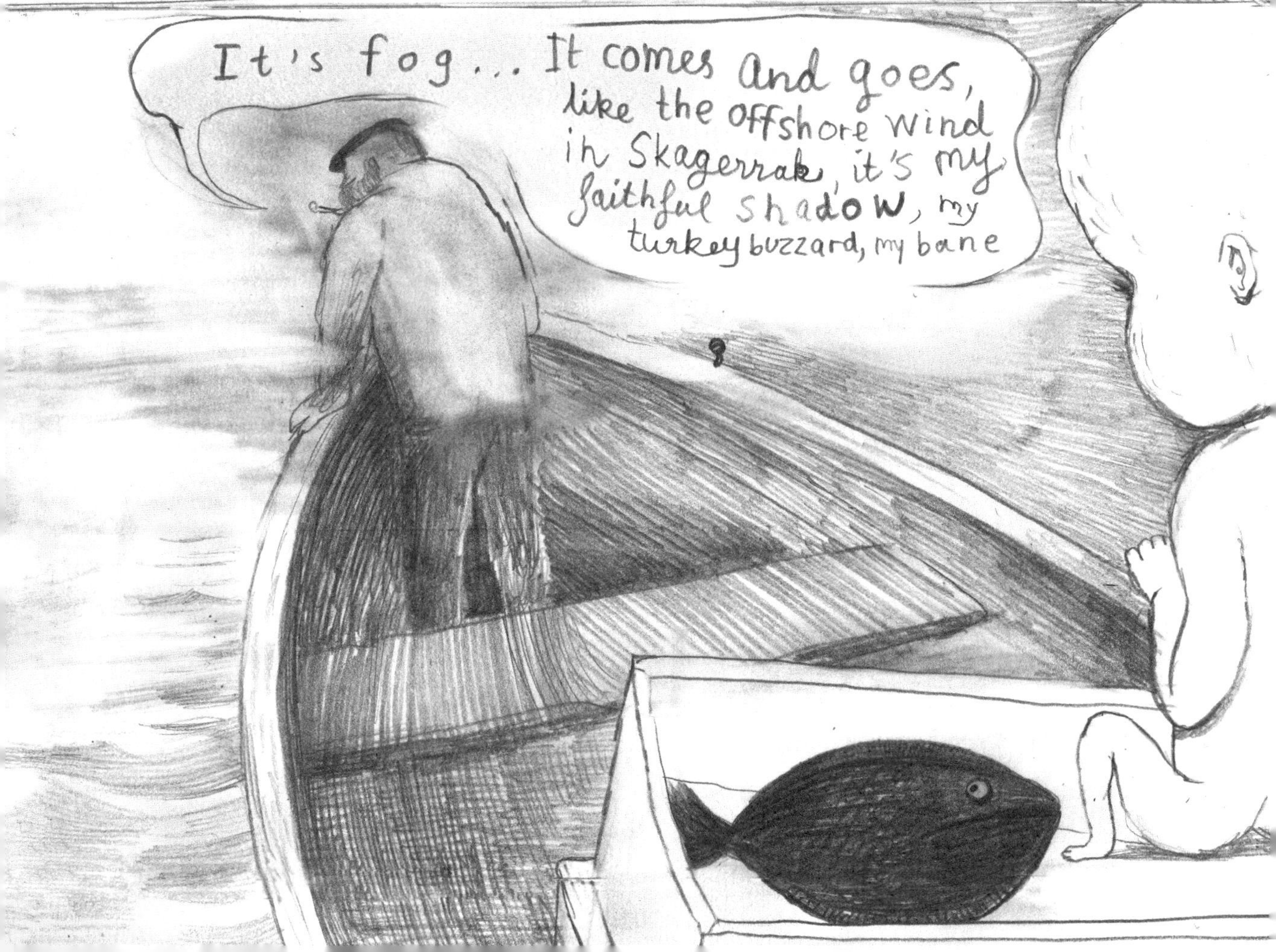
It's fog... It comes and goes, like the offshore wind in Skagerrak, it's my faithful shadow, my turkey buzzard, my bane

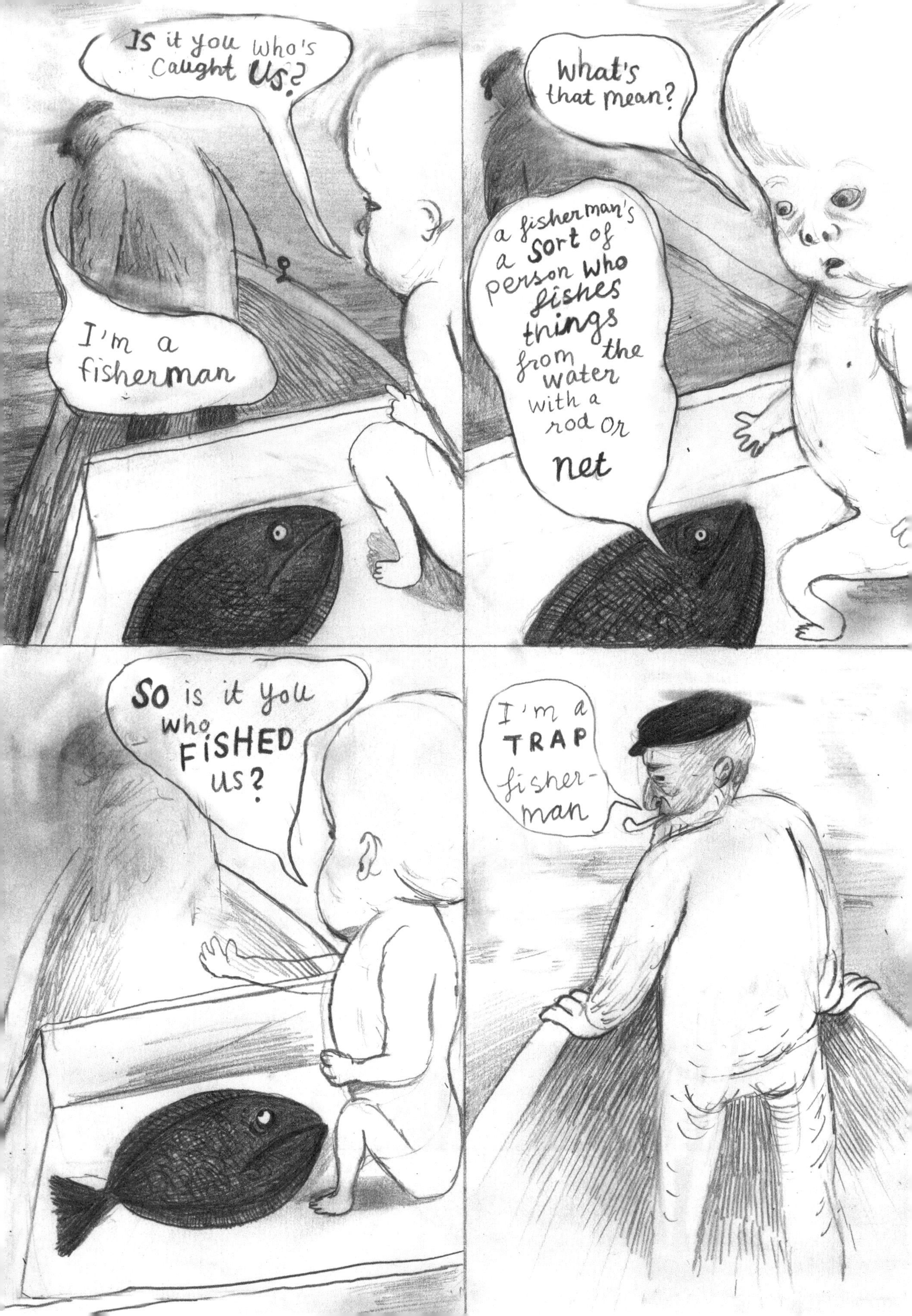
Is it you who's Caught Us?
I'm a fisherman
What's that mean?
a fisherman's a sort of person who fishes things from the water with a rod or net
So is it you who FISHED us?
I'm a TRAP fisher-man

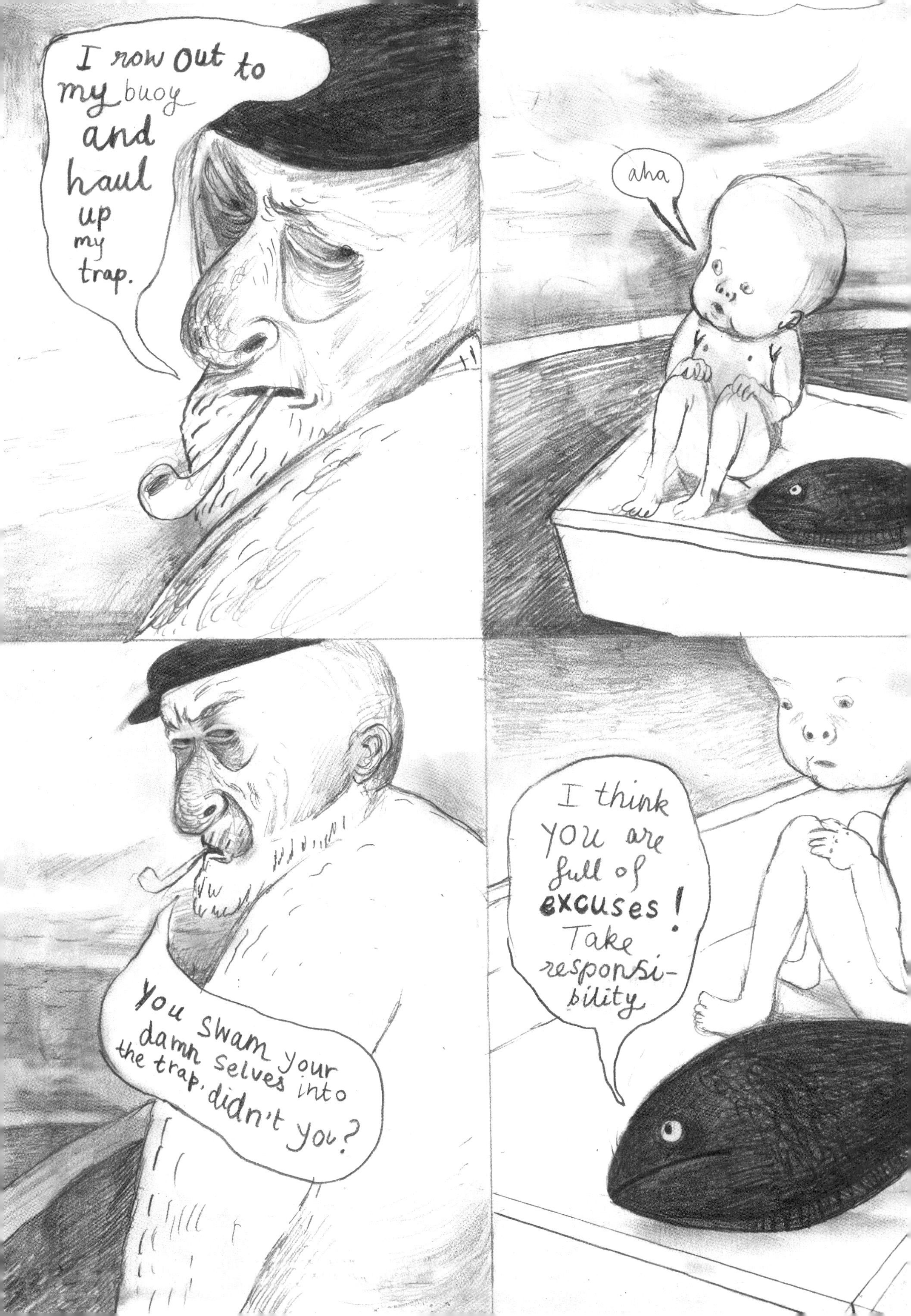
I row out to my buoy and haul up my trap.
aha
You swam your damn selves into the trap, didn't you?
I think you are full of excuses! Take responsibility

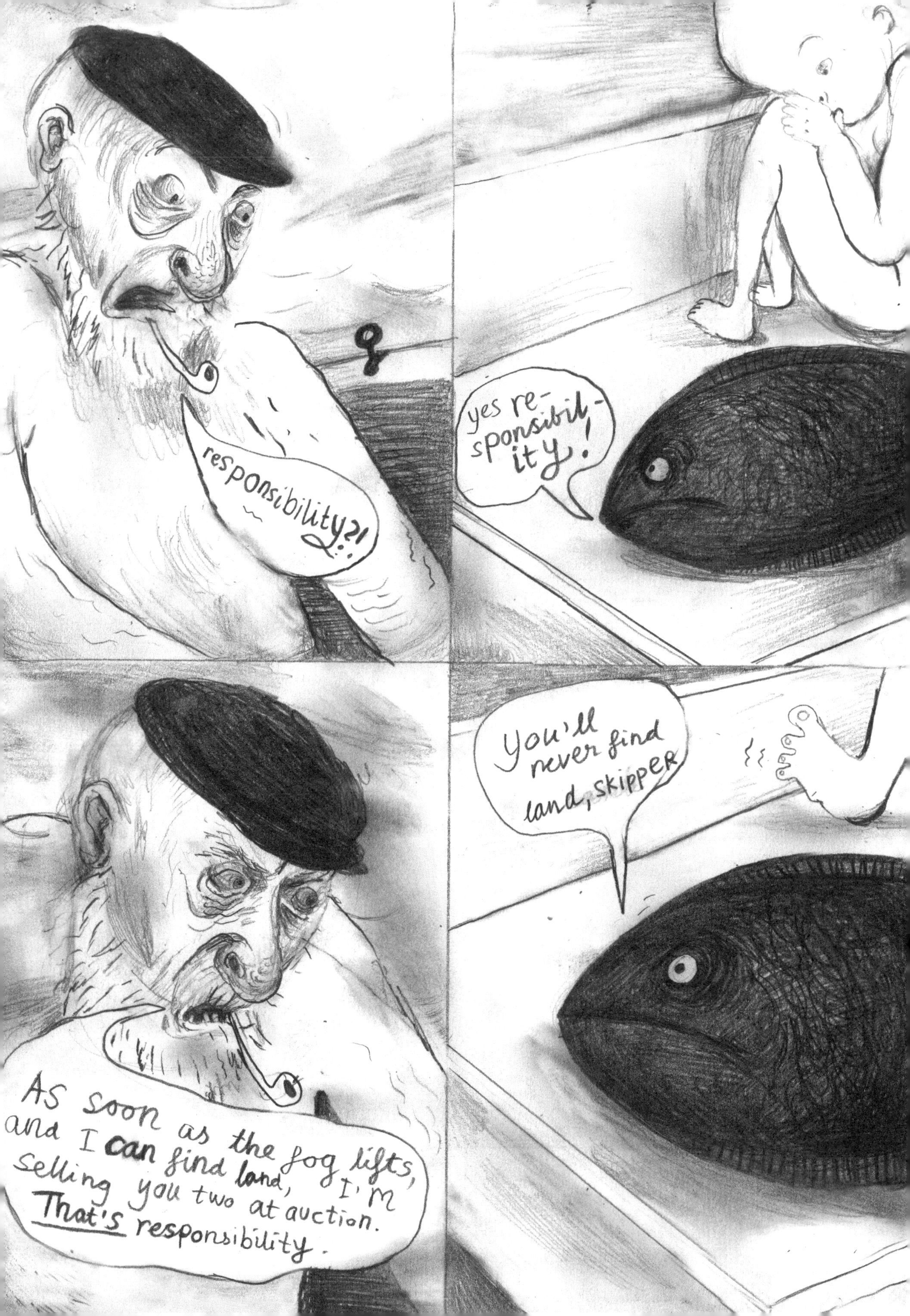
responsibility?!
yes re-sponsibil-ity!
As soon as the fog lifts, and I **can** find land, I'm selling you two at auction. That's responsibility.
You'll never find land, skipper

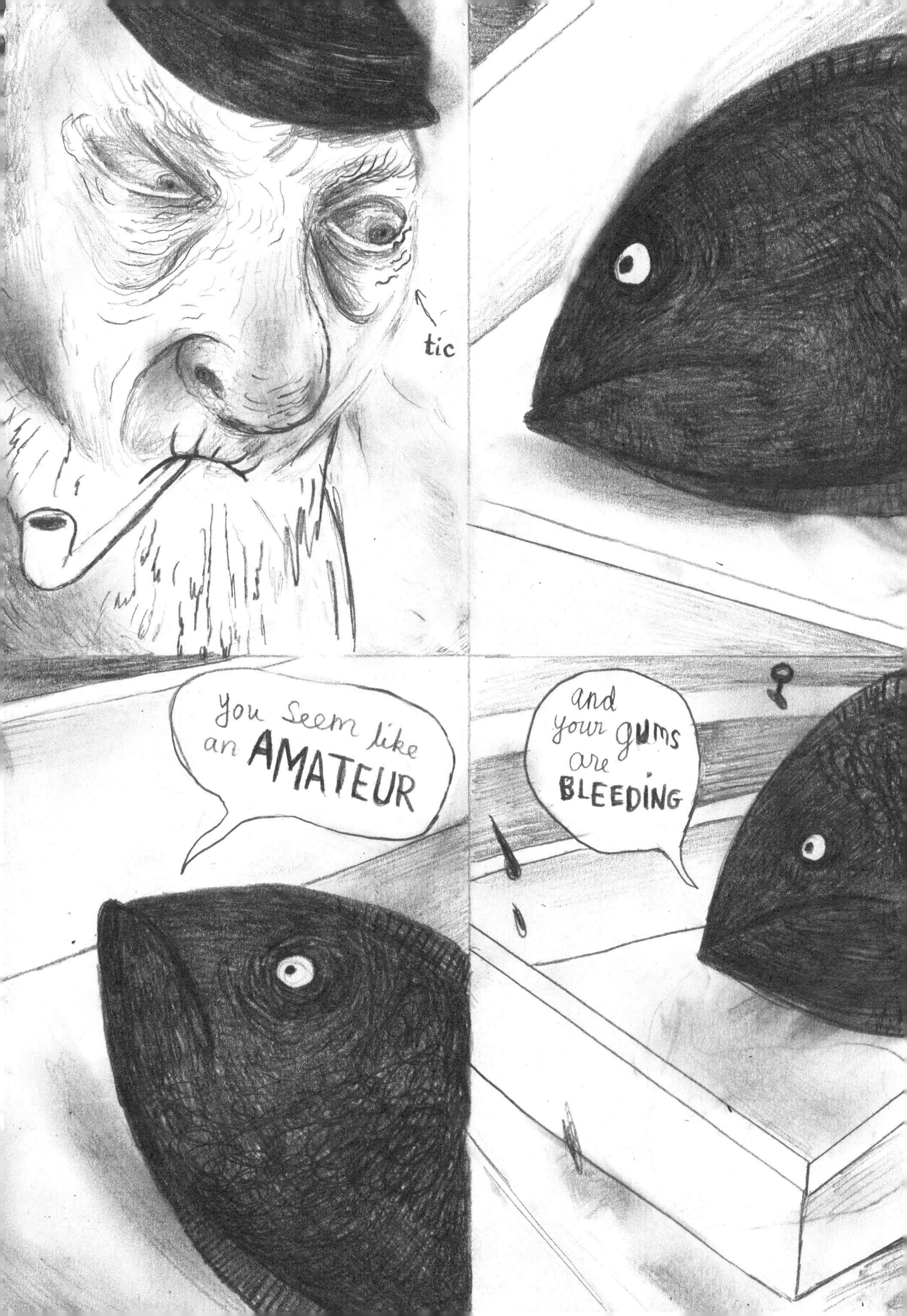
tic
You seem like an AMATEUR
and your gums are BLEEDING

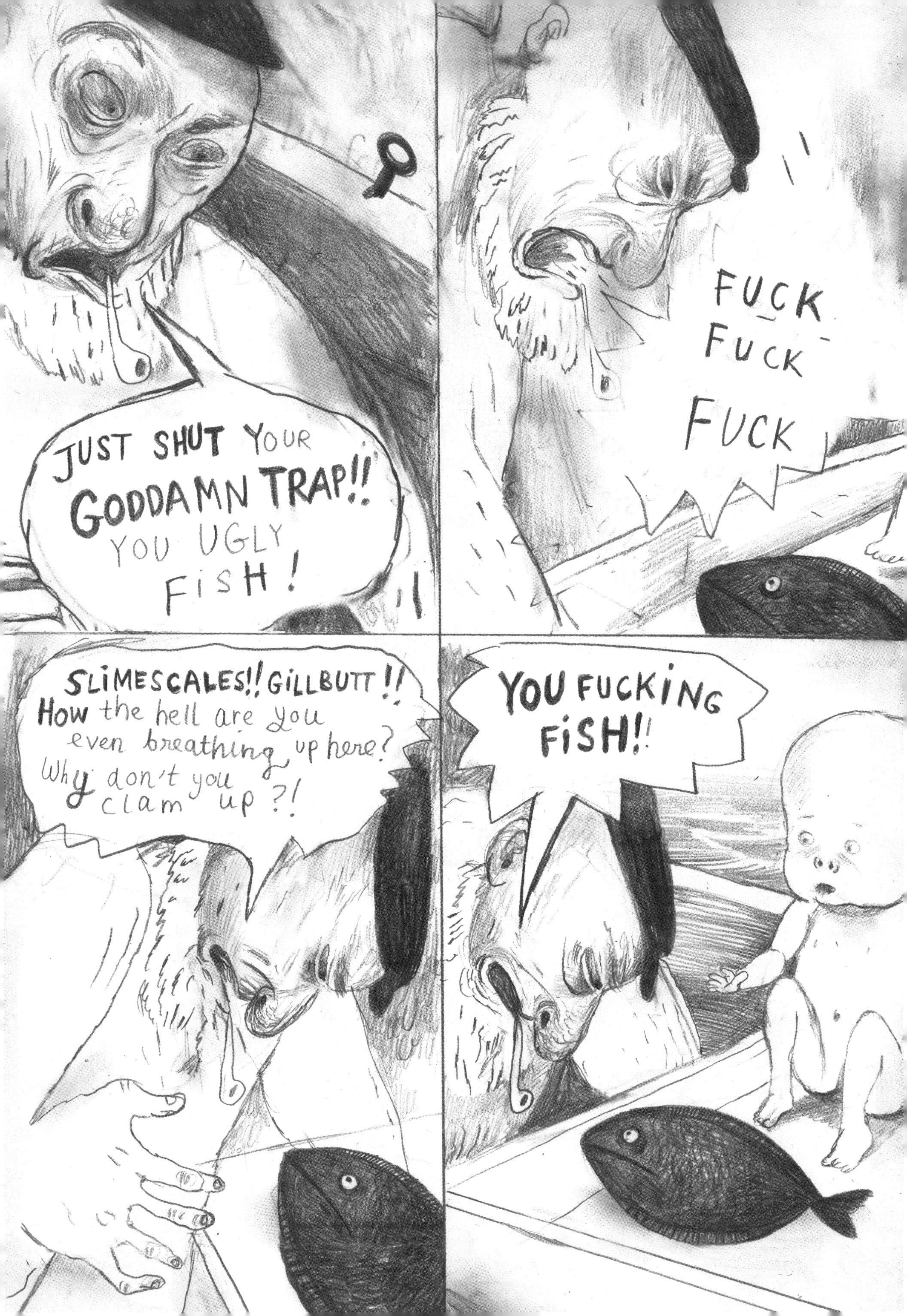
JUST SHUT YOUR GODDAMN TRAP!! YOU UGLY FISH!
FUCK FUCK FUCK
SLIMESCALES!! GILLBUTT!! How the hell are you even breathing up here? Why don't you clam up?!
YOU FUCKING FISH!!

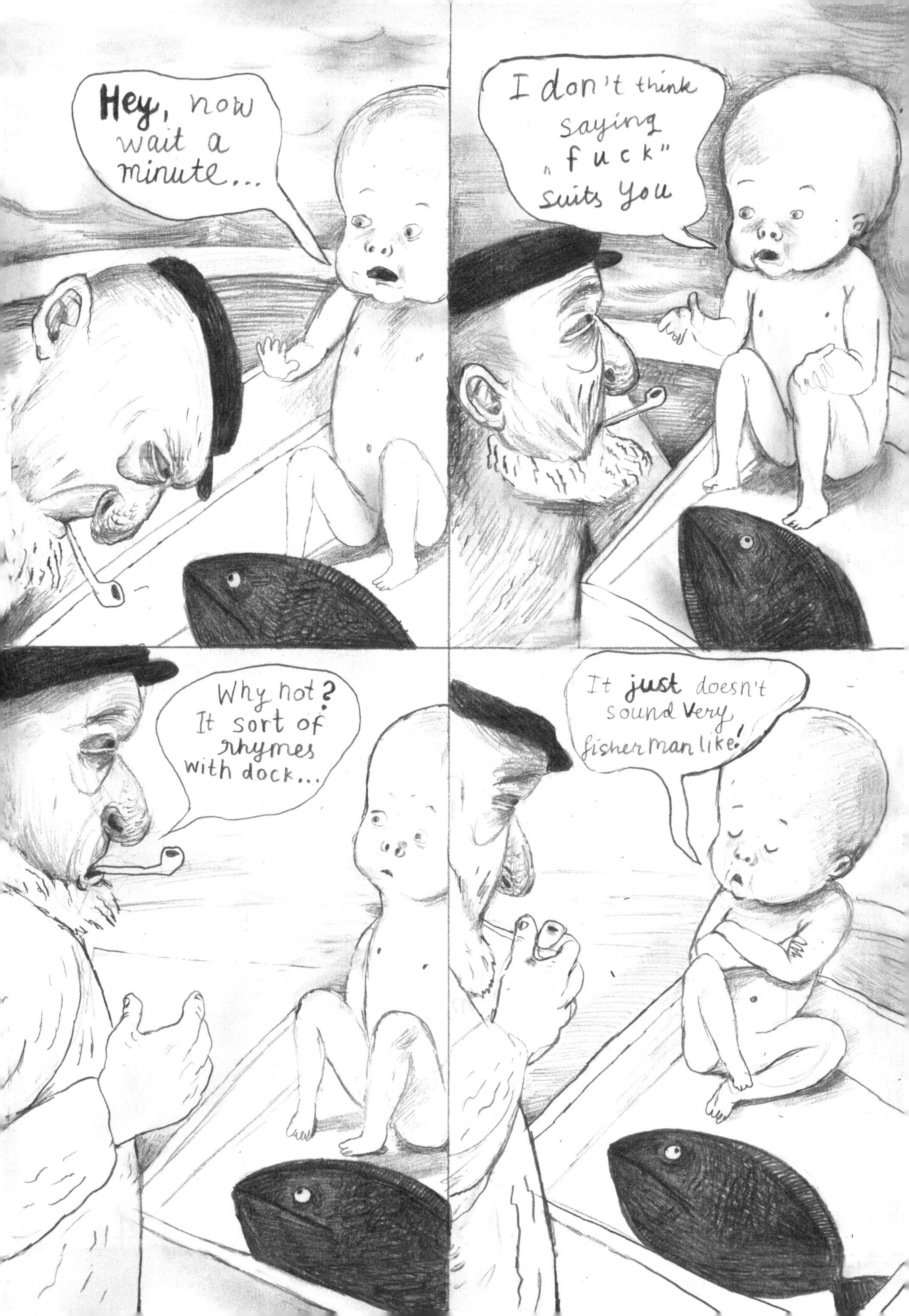
Hey, now wait a minute...
I don't think saying „fuck" suits you
Why not? It sort of rhymes with dock...
It **just** doesn't sound Very fisherman like!

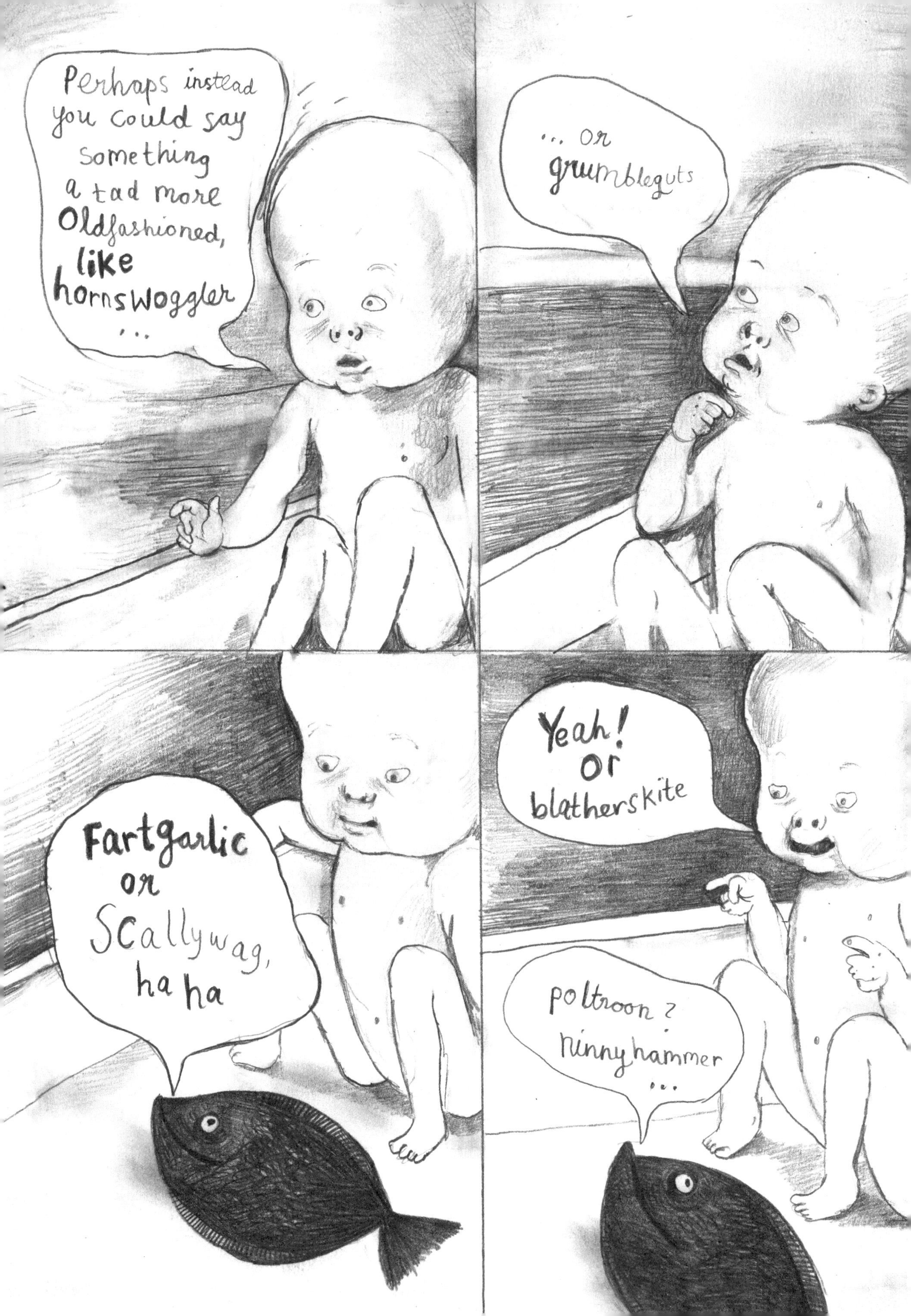
Perhaps instead you could say something a tad more Oldfashioned, like hornswoggler ...
... or grumbleguts
Fartgarlic or Scallywag, ha ha
Yeah! or blatherskite
poltroon? ninnyhammer ...

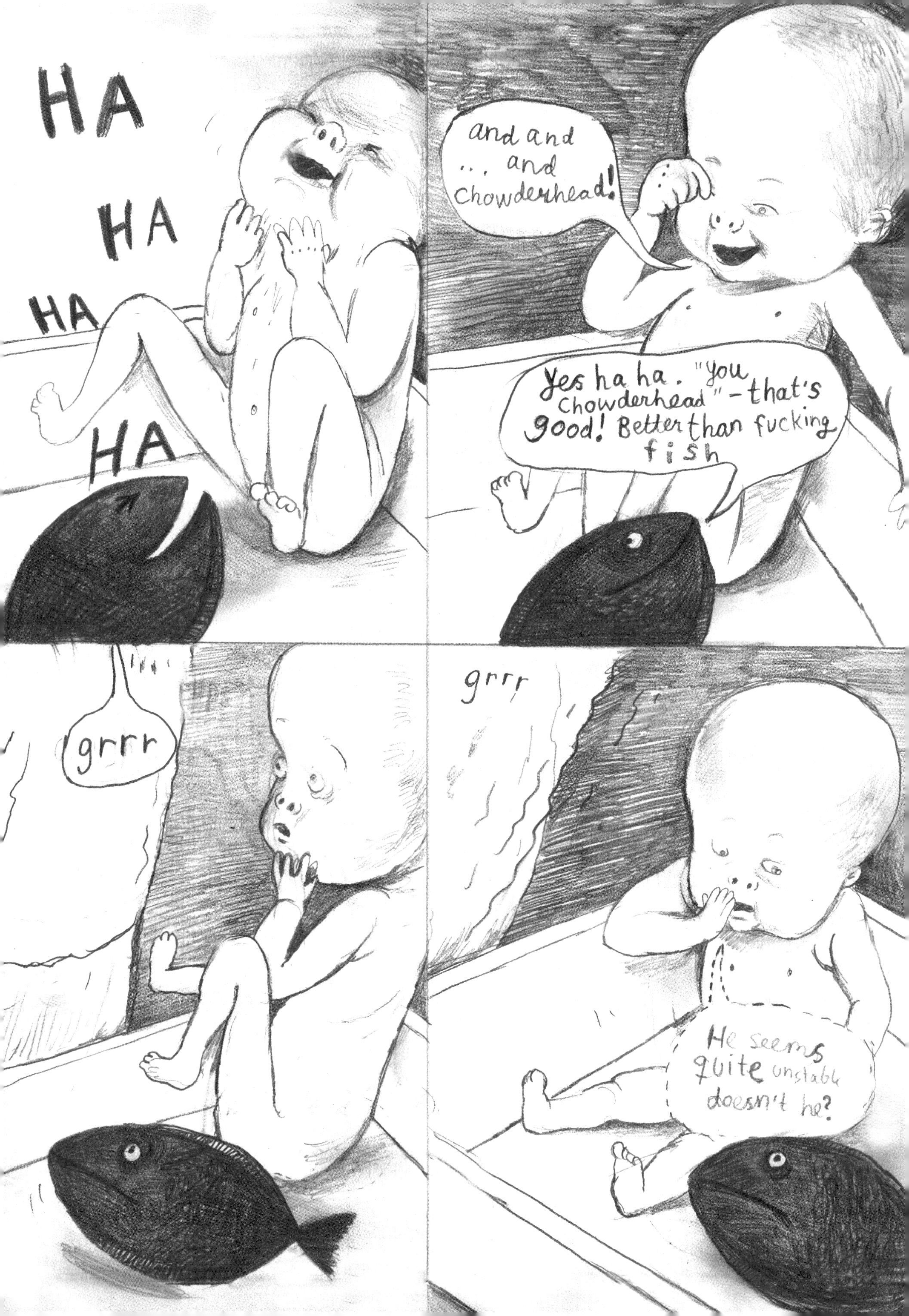
HA
HA
HA
HA
and and ... and Chowderhead!
Yes ha ha. "You Chowderhead" - that's good! Better than fucking fish
grrr
grrr
He seems quite unstable doesn't he?

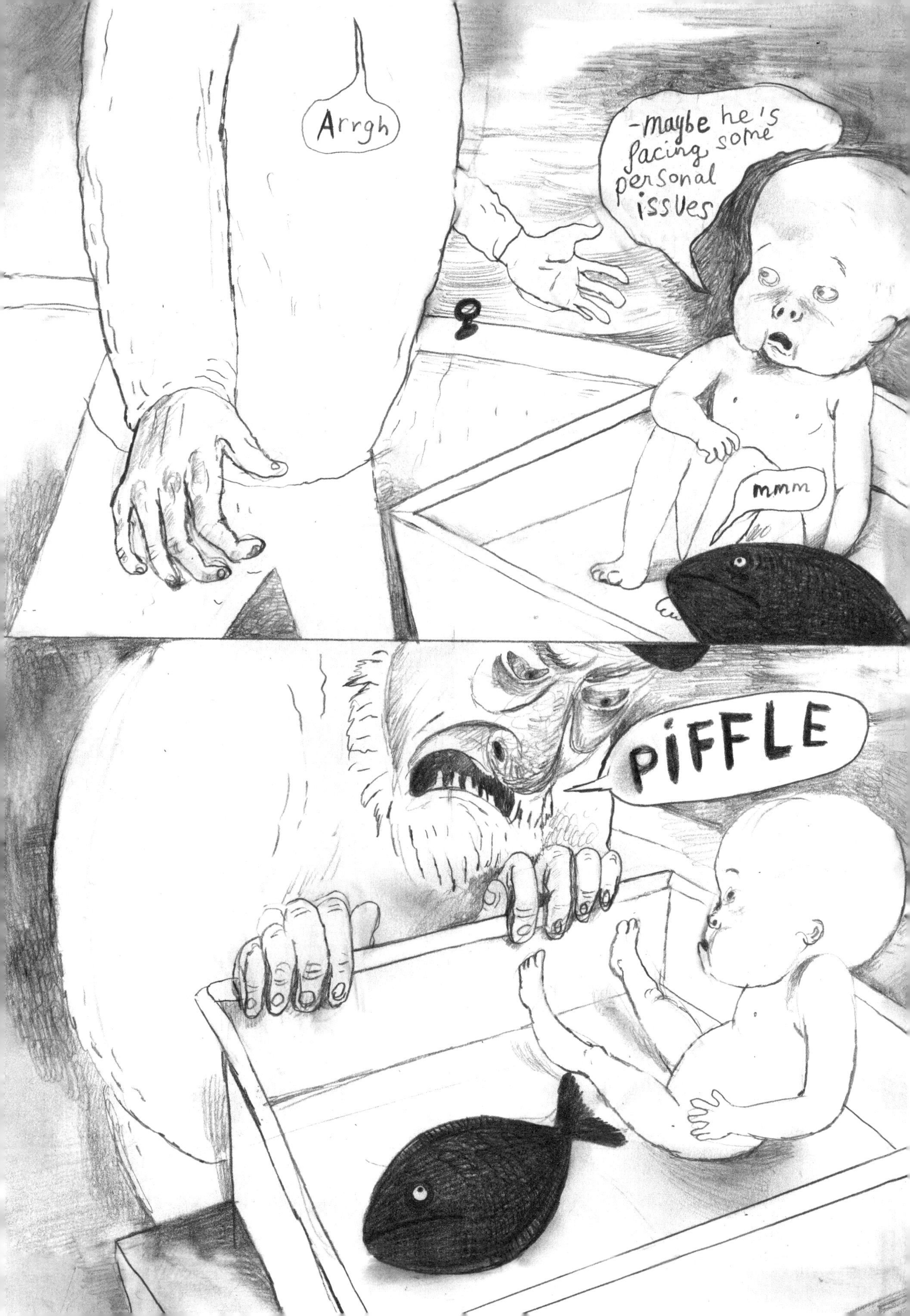
Arrgh
-maybe he's facing some personal issues
mmm
PIFFLE

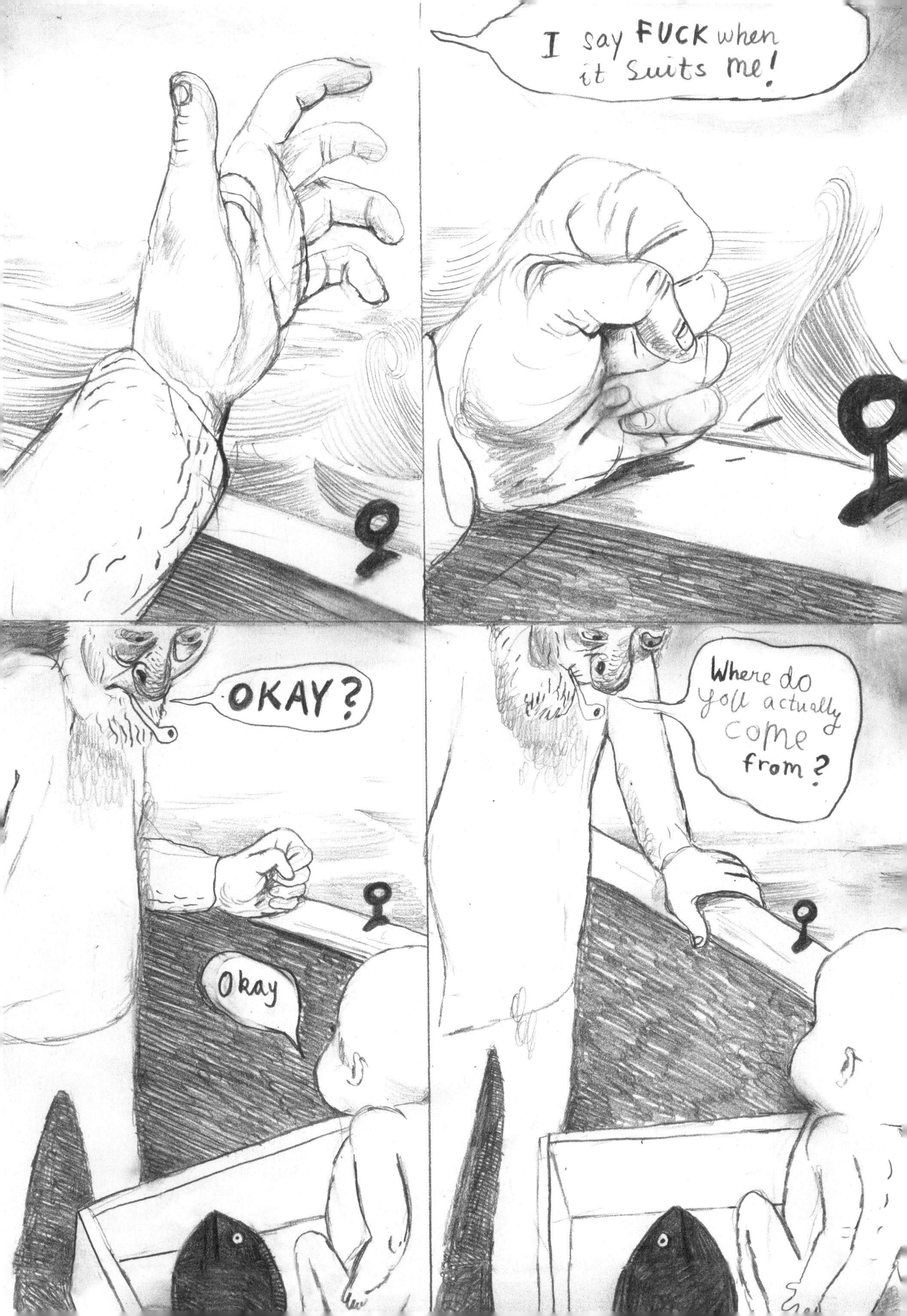

I say FUCK when it suits me!
OKAY?
Okay
Where do you actually come from?

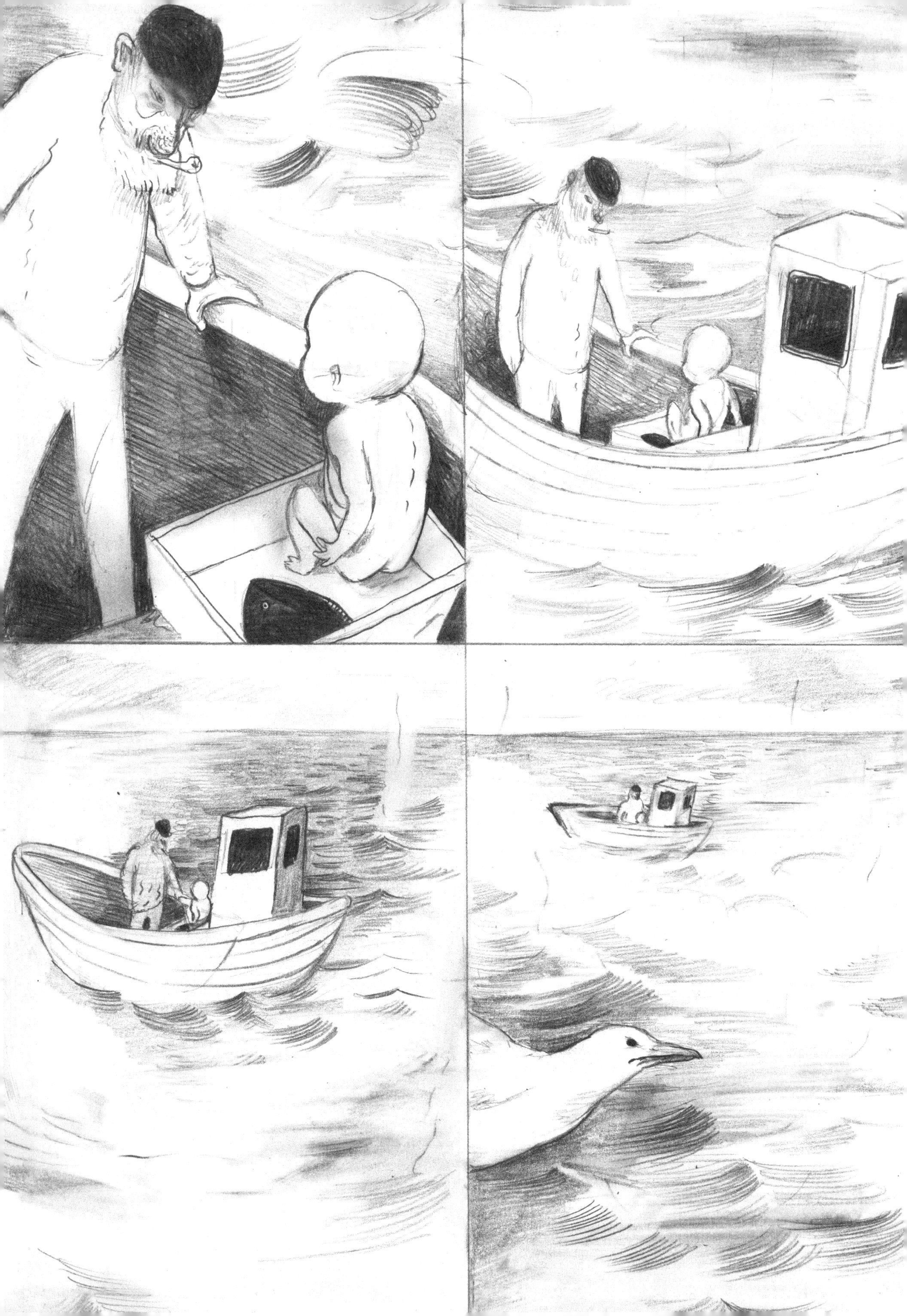

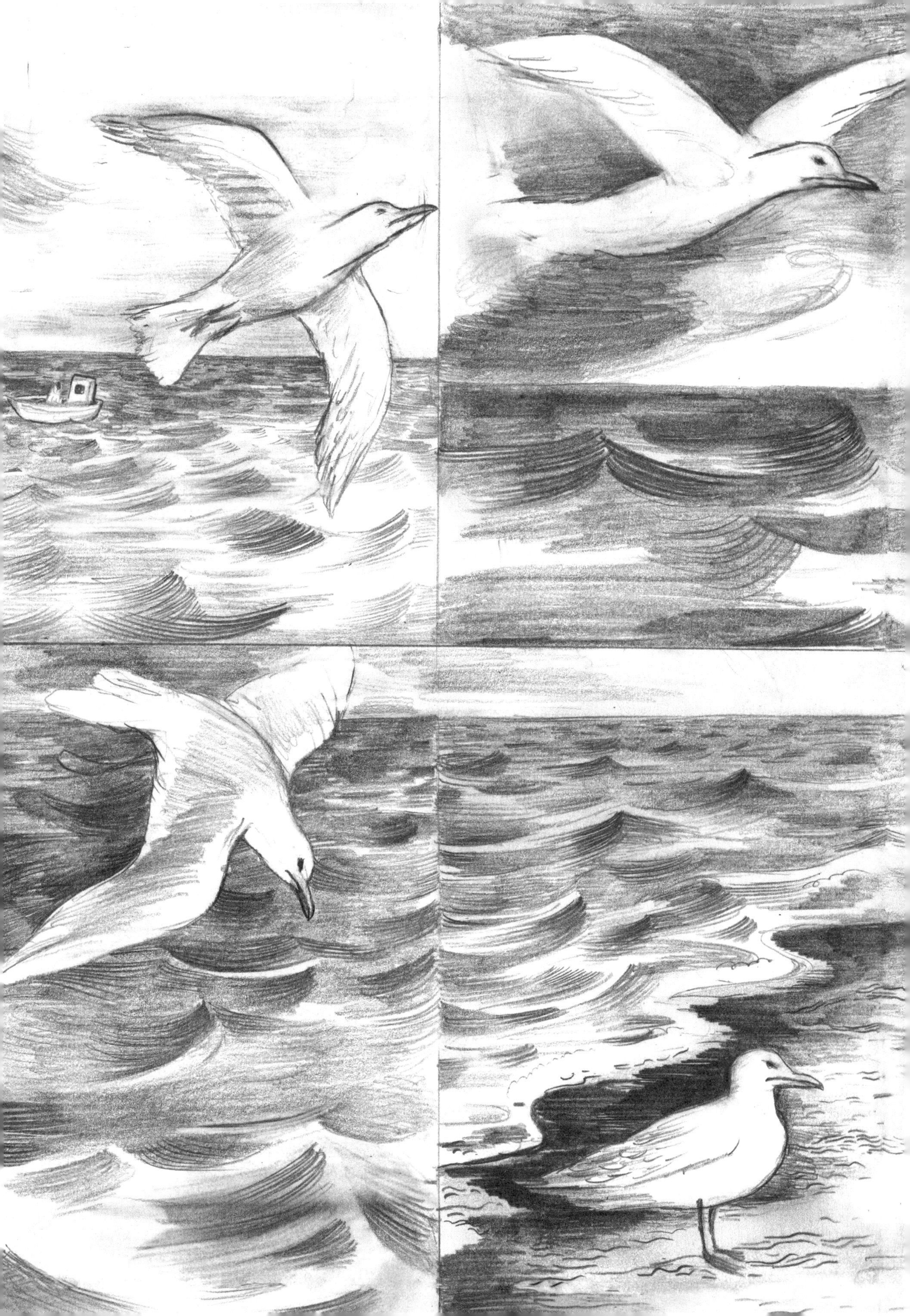

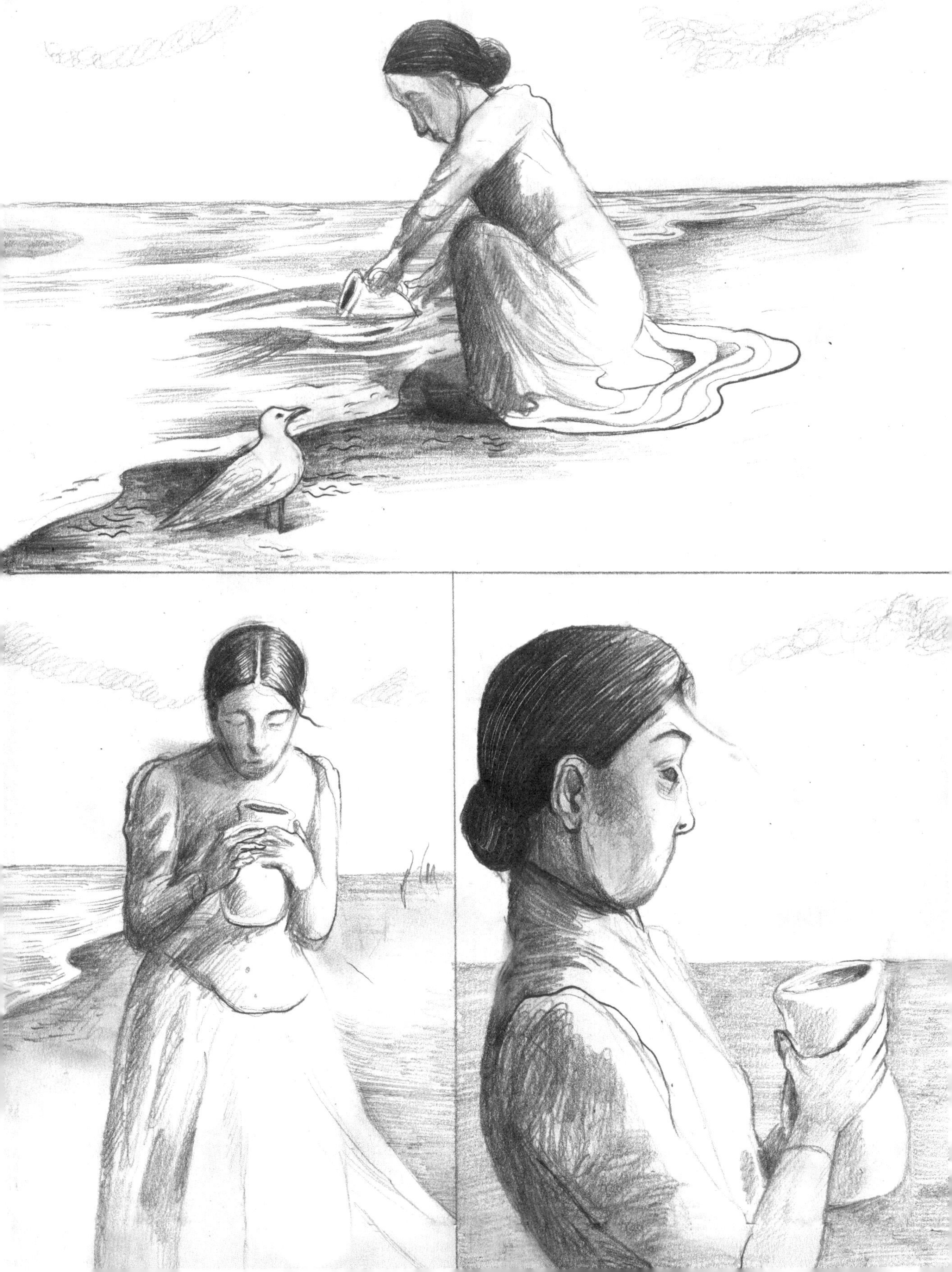

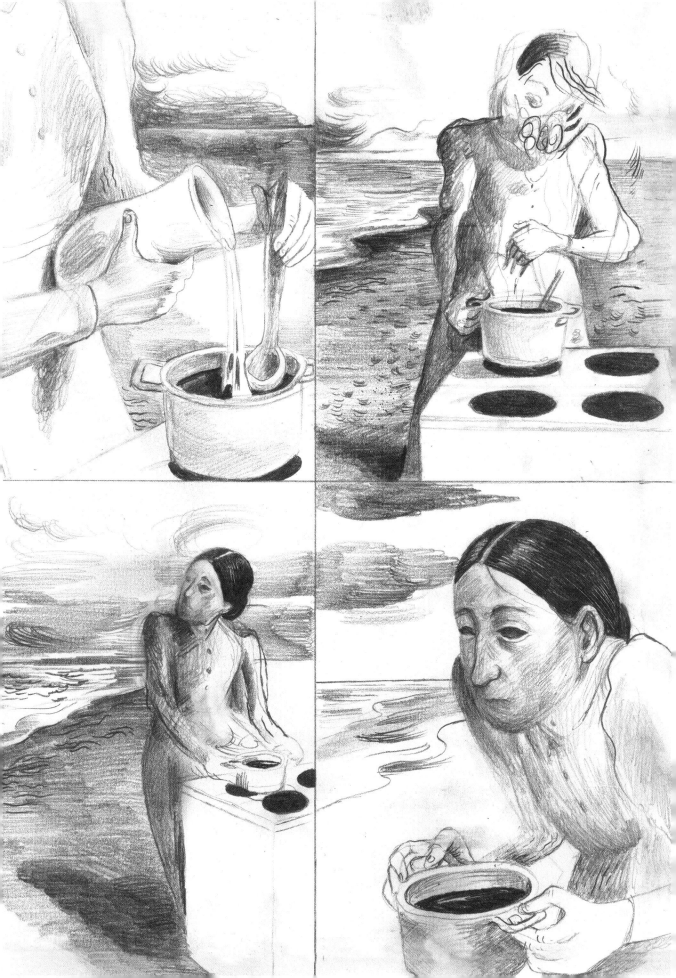

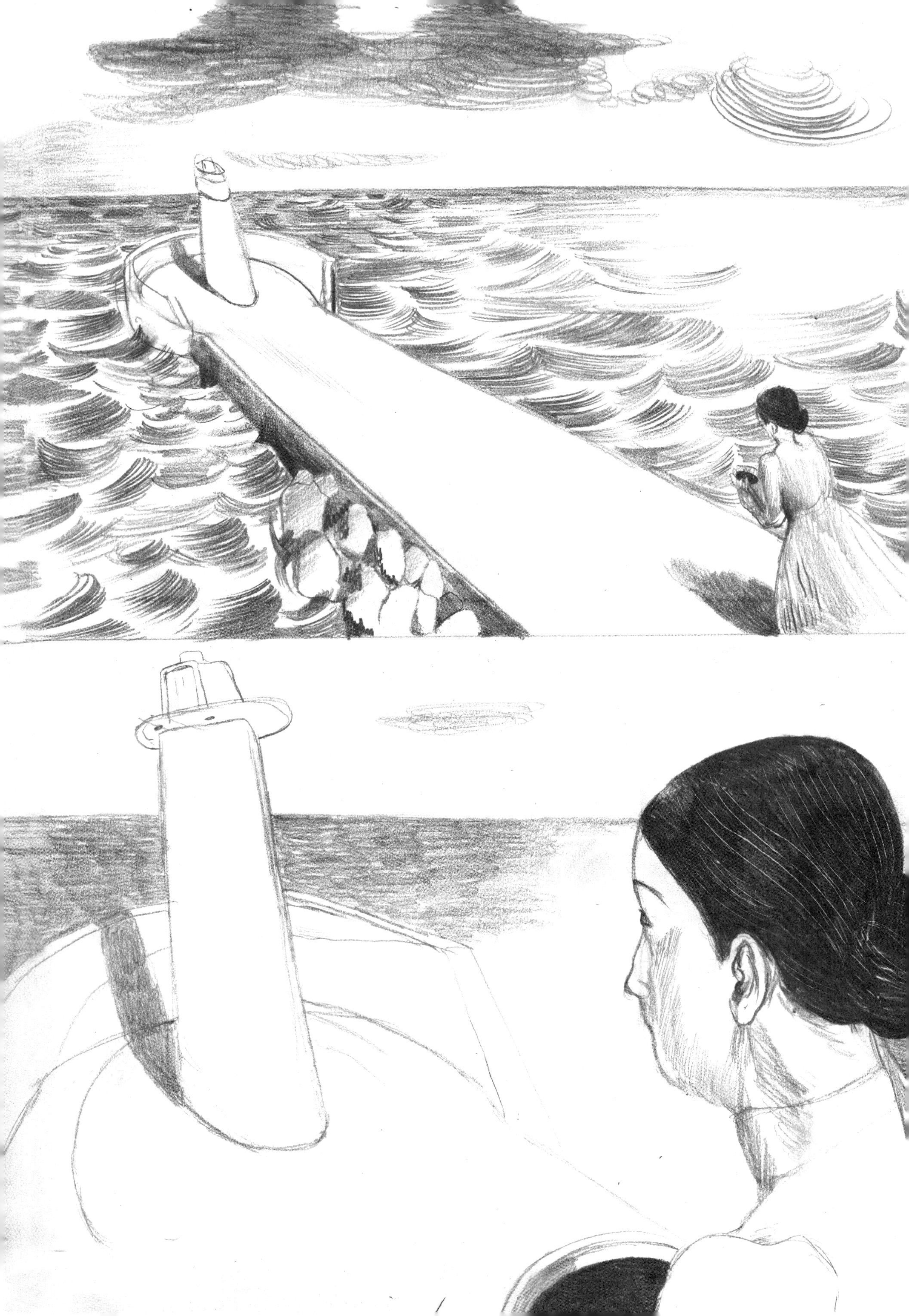

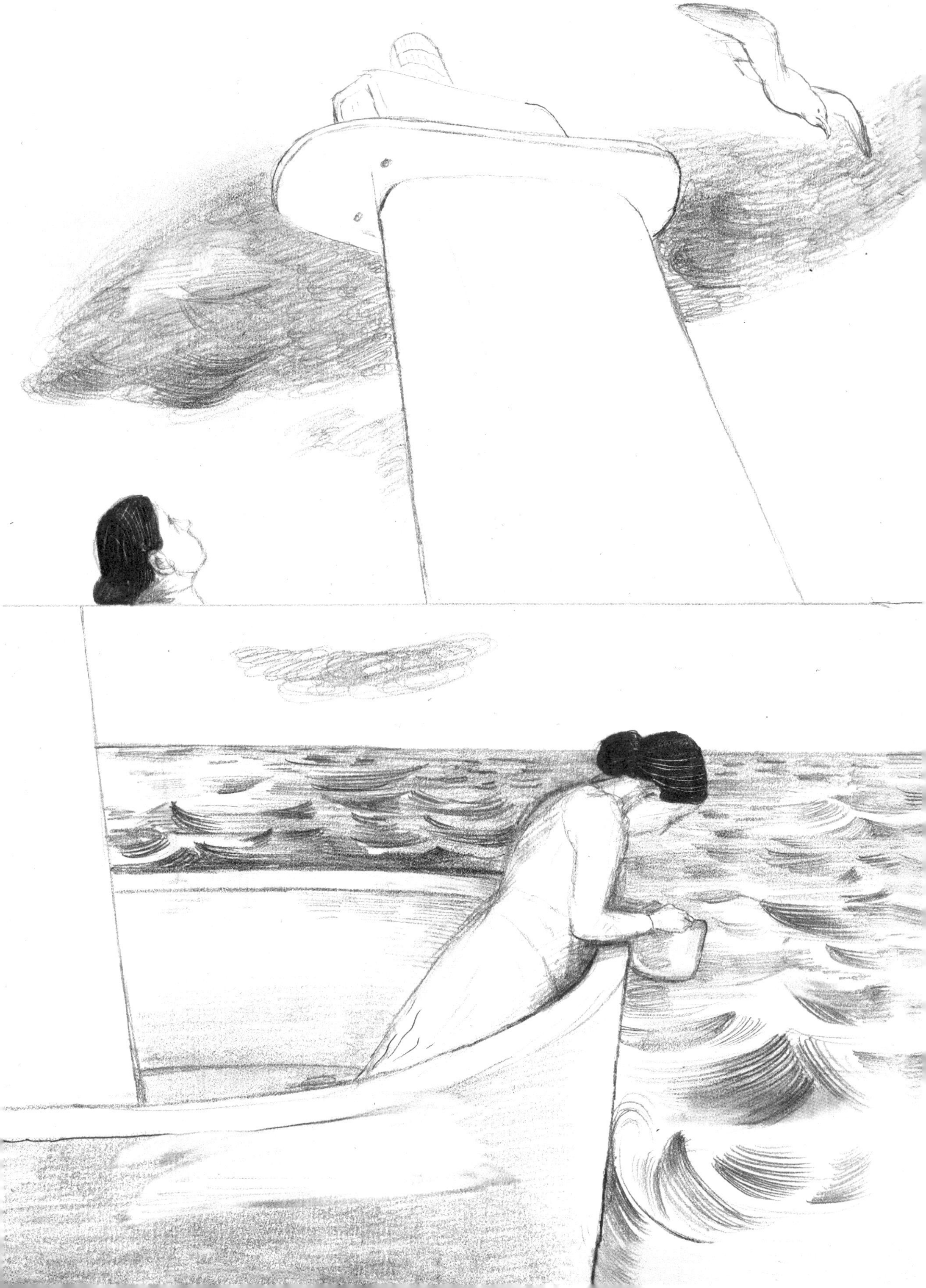

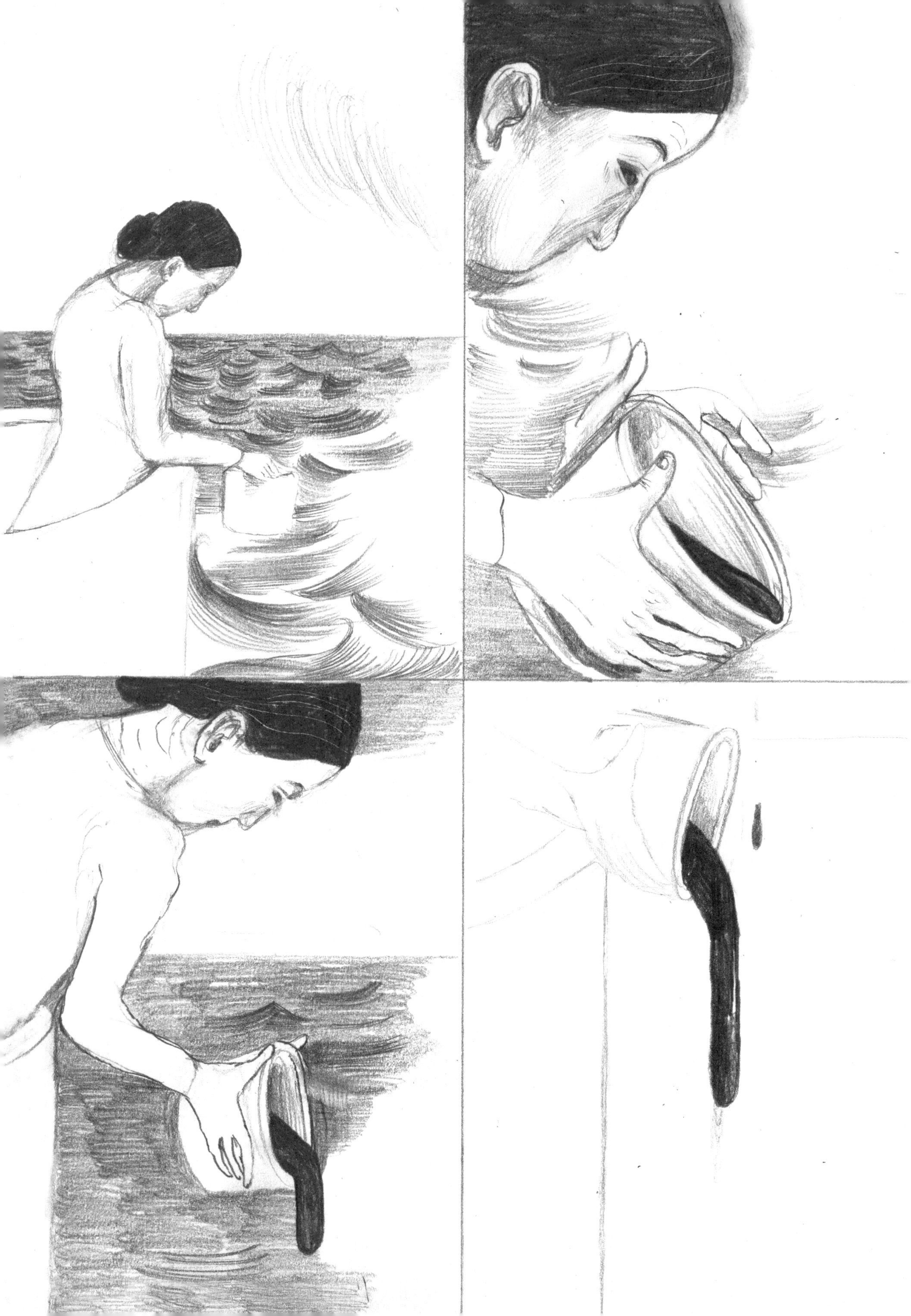

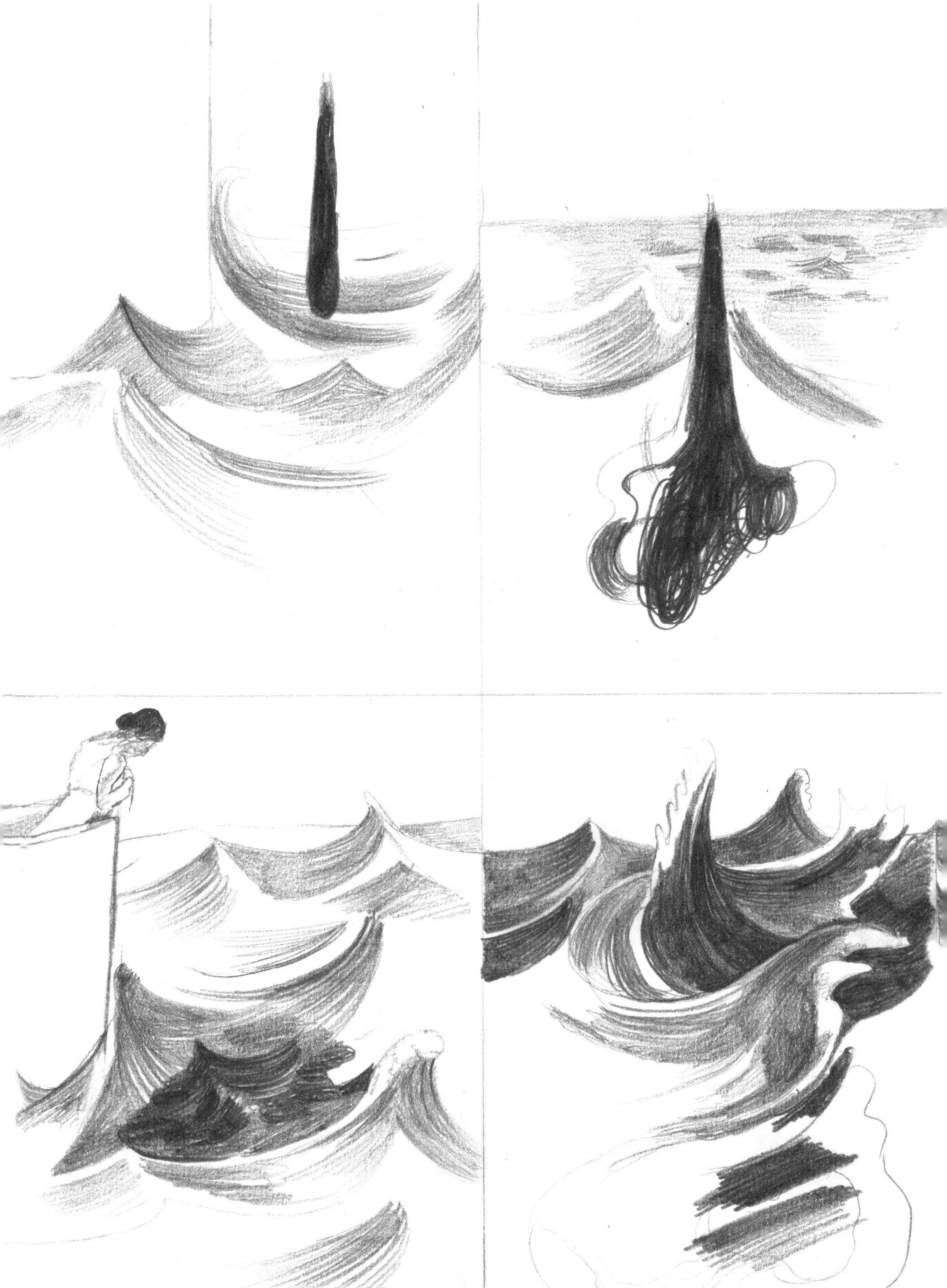

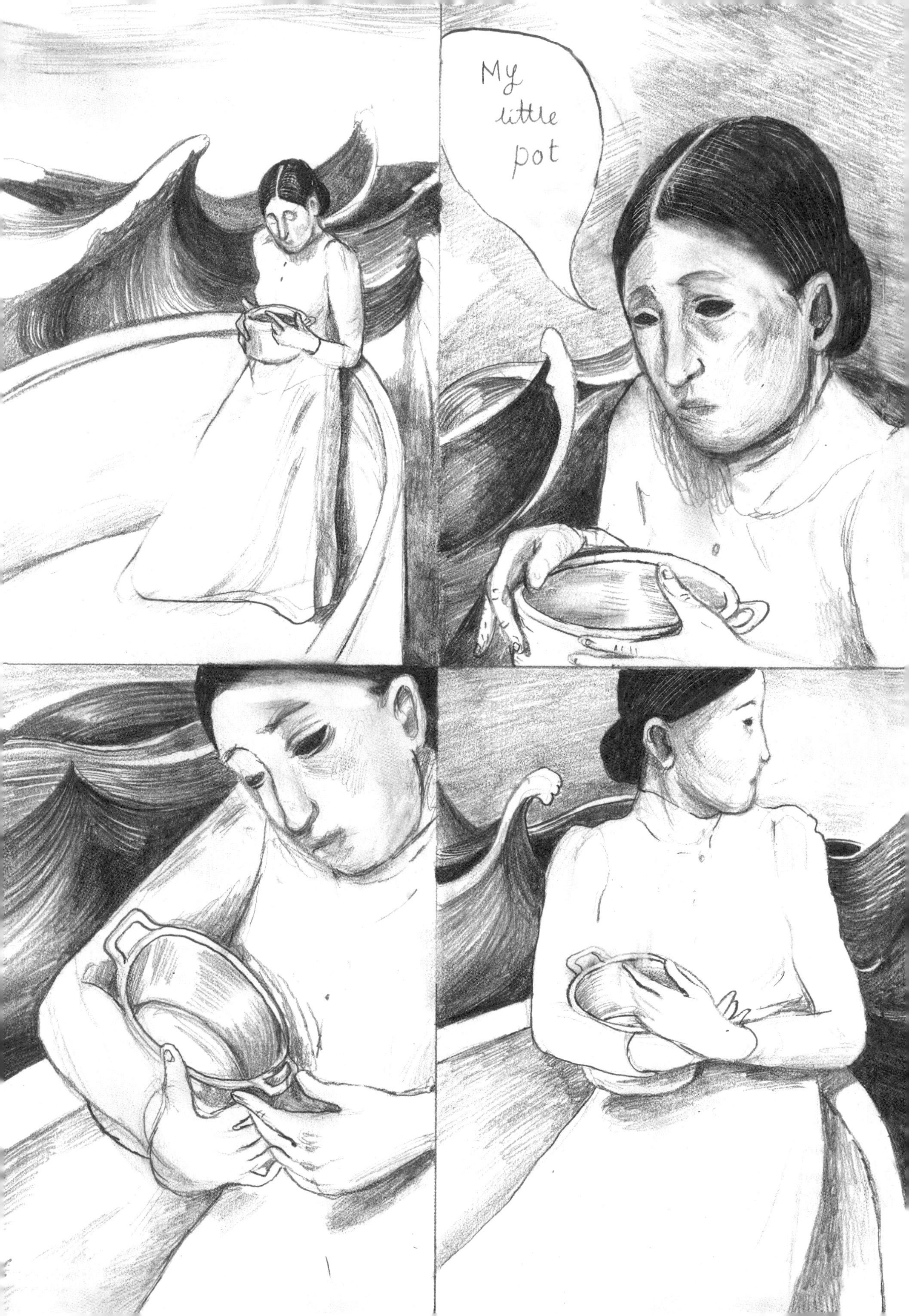
My little pot

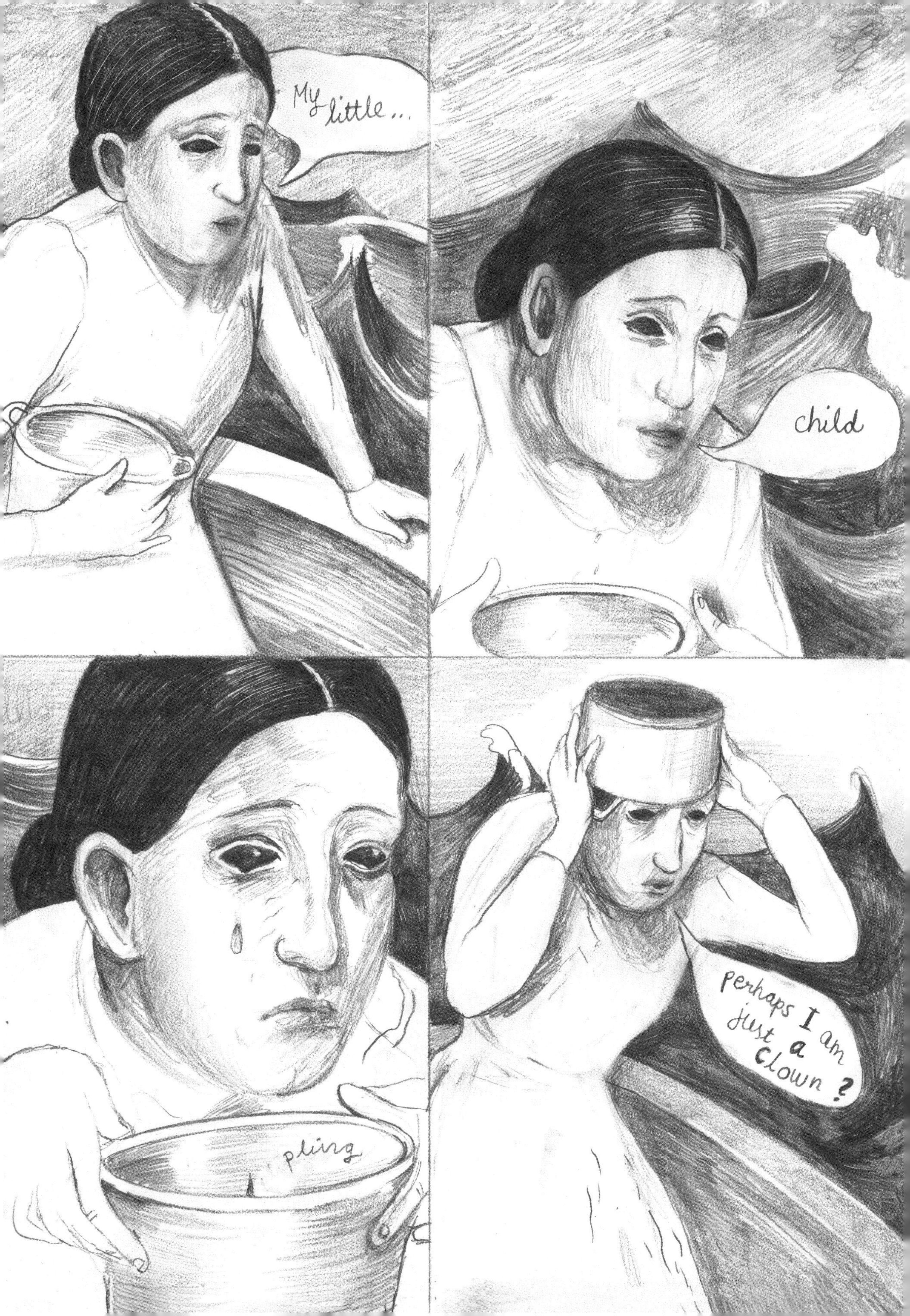
My little...
child
pling
perhaps I am just a clown?

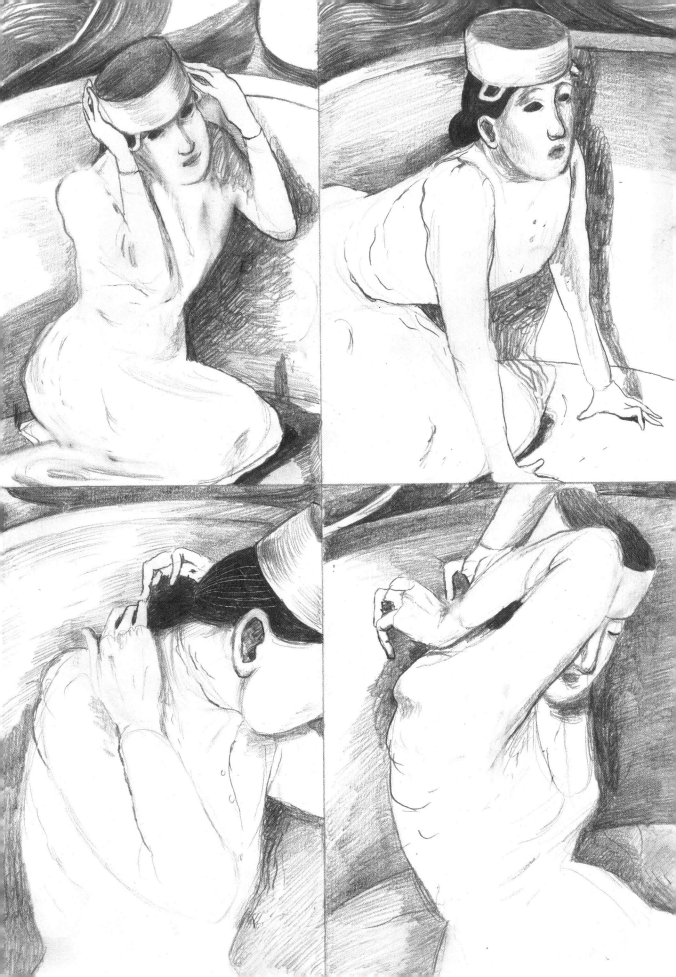

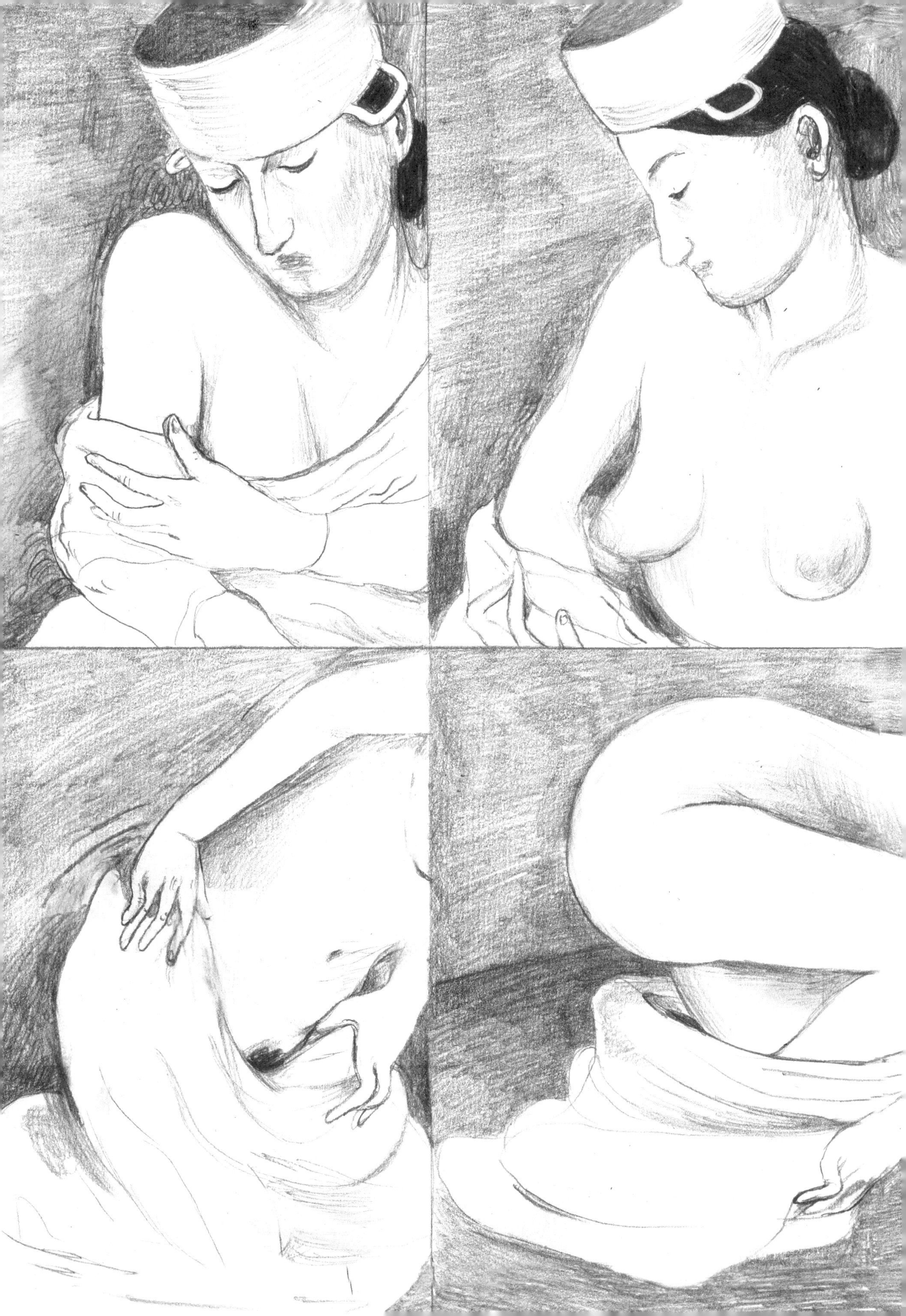

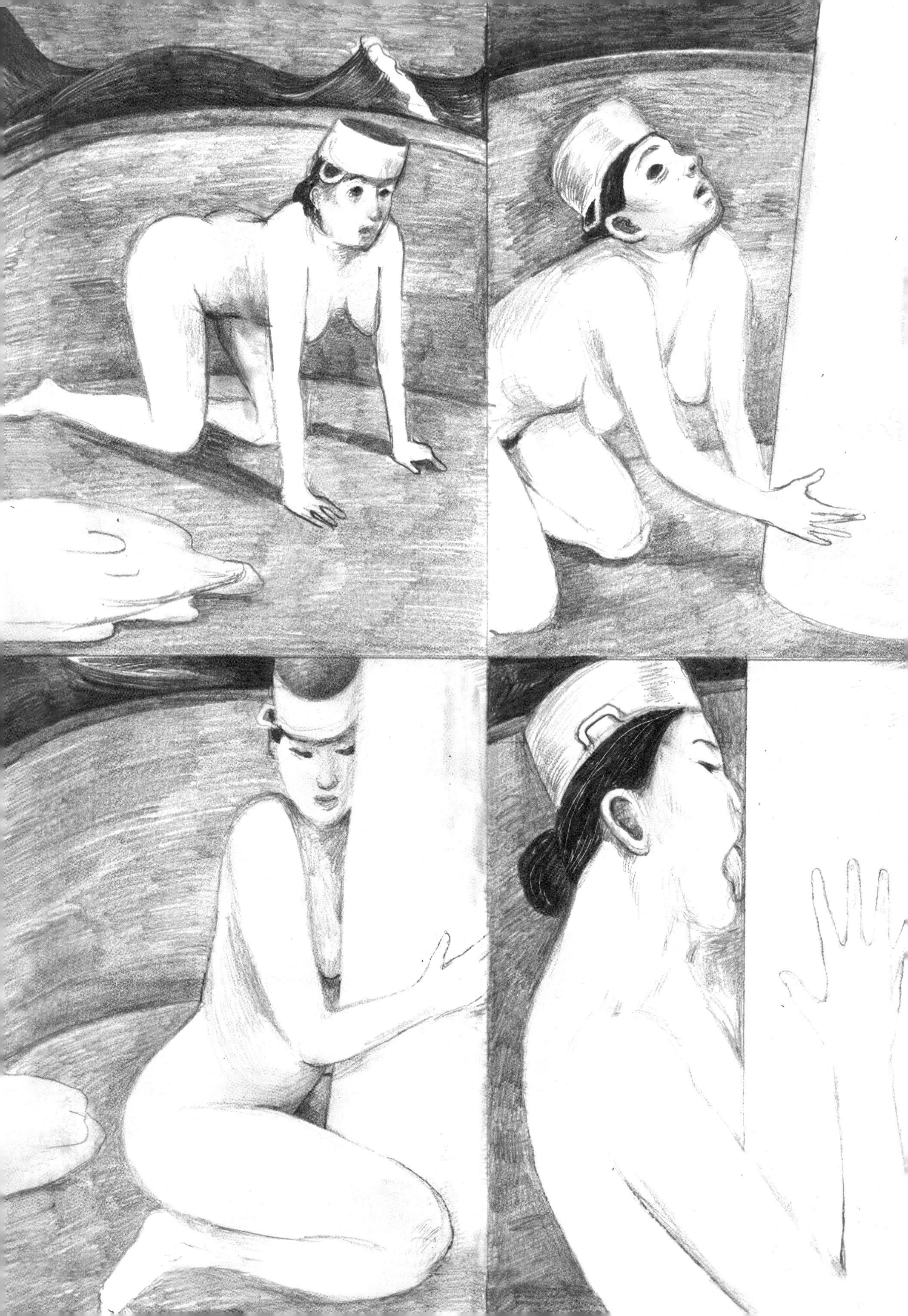

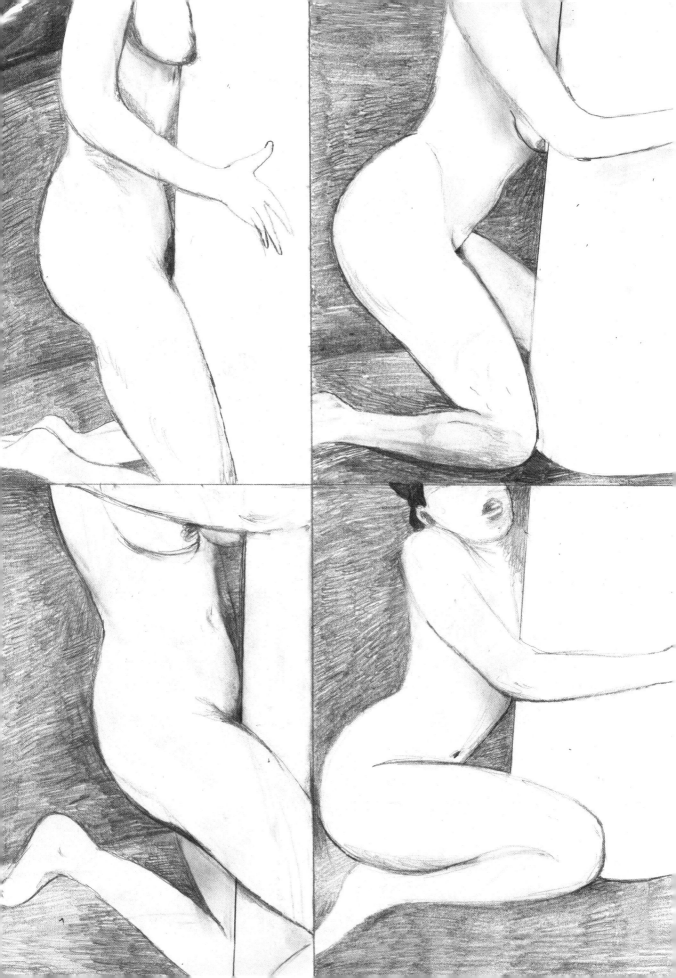

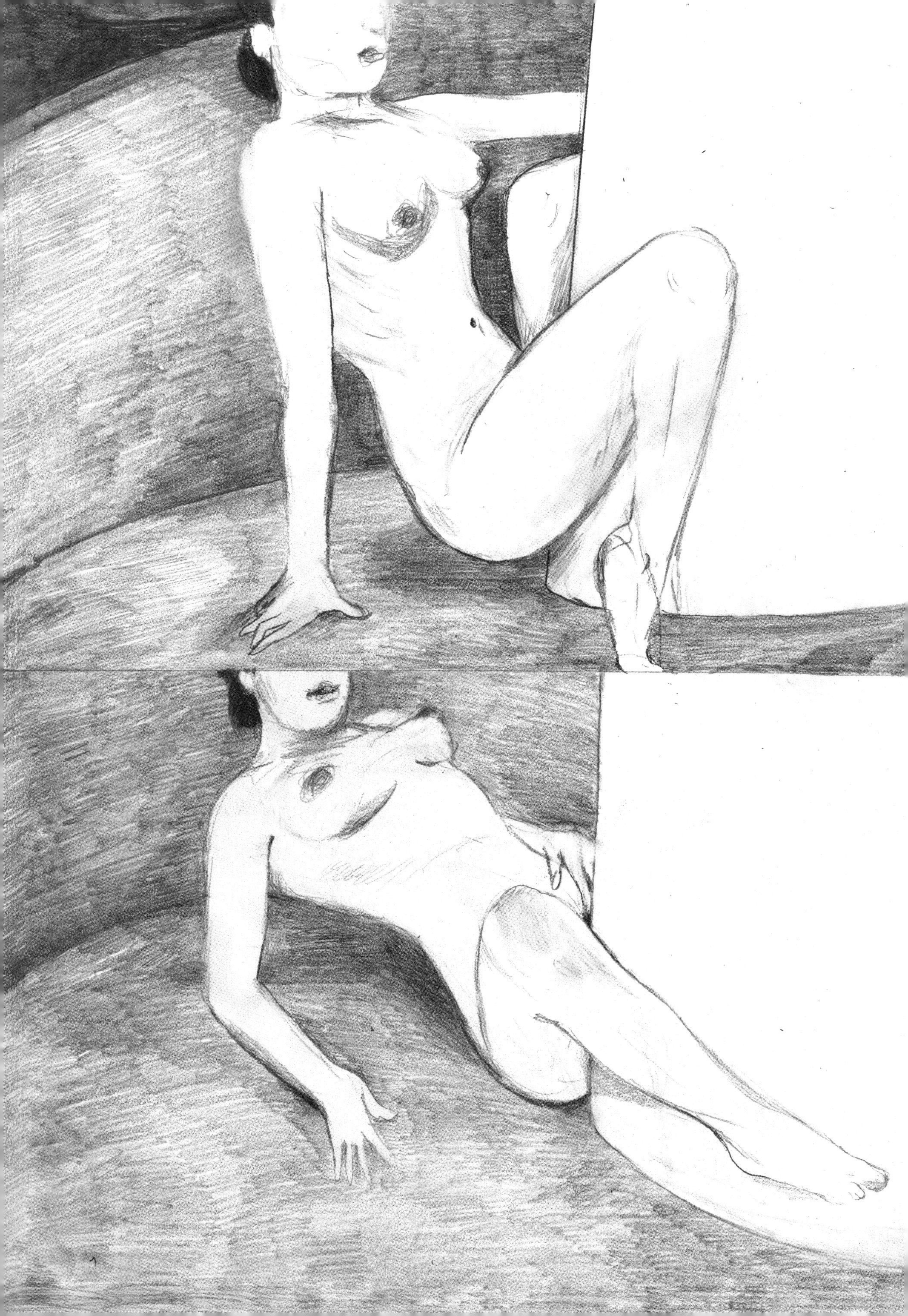

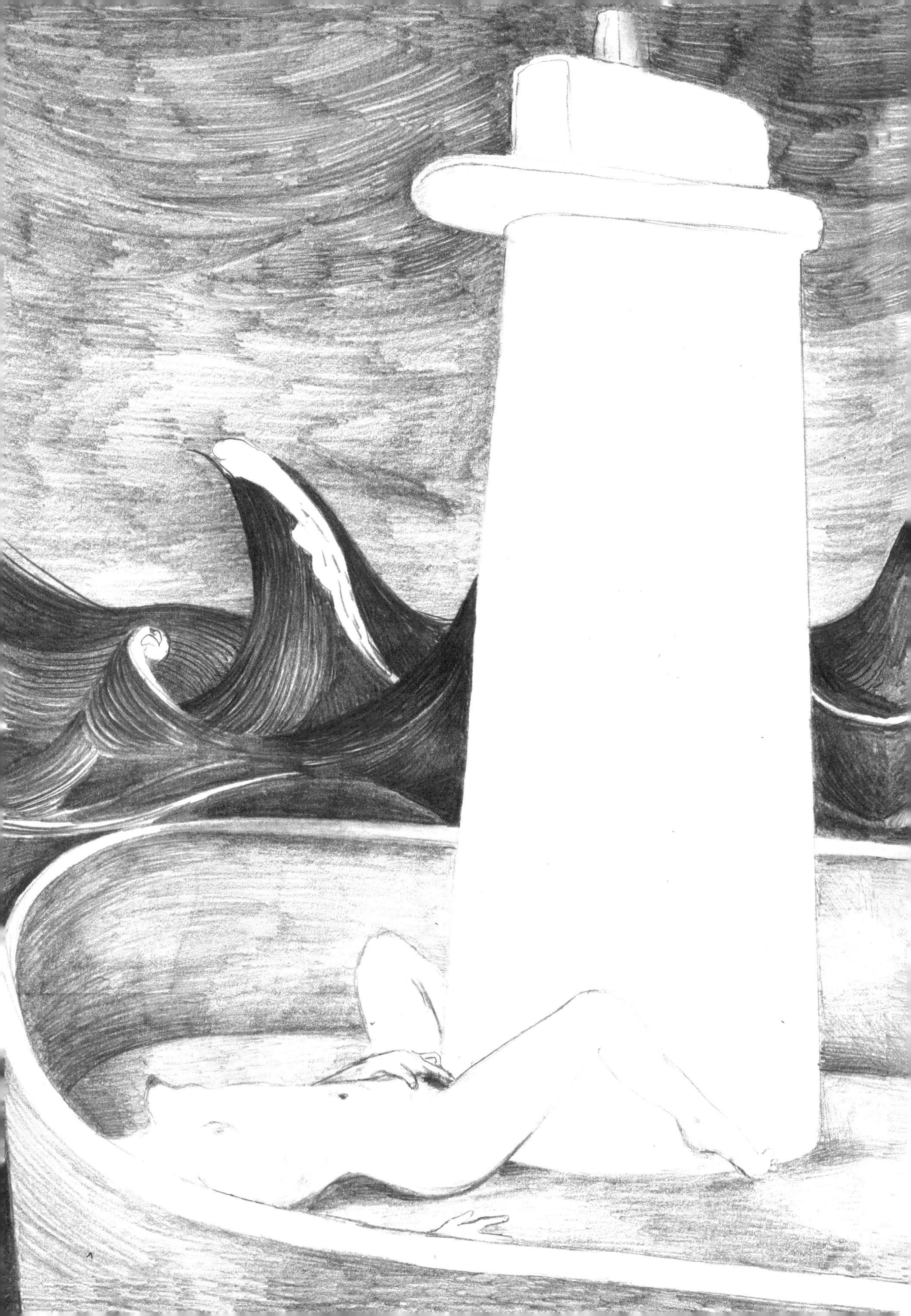

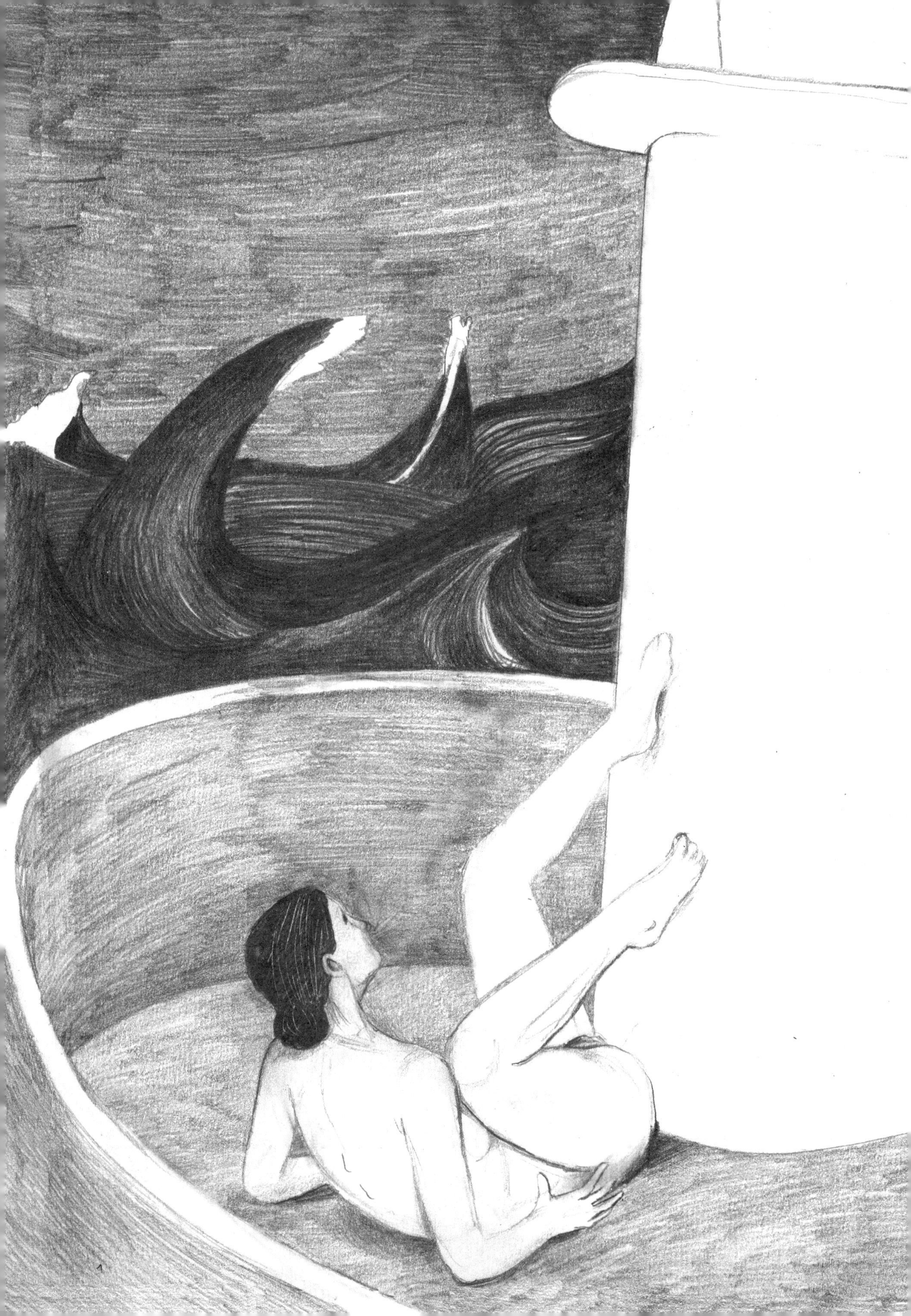

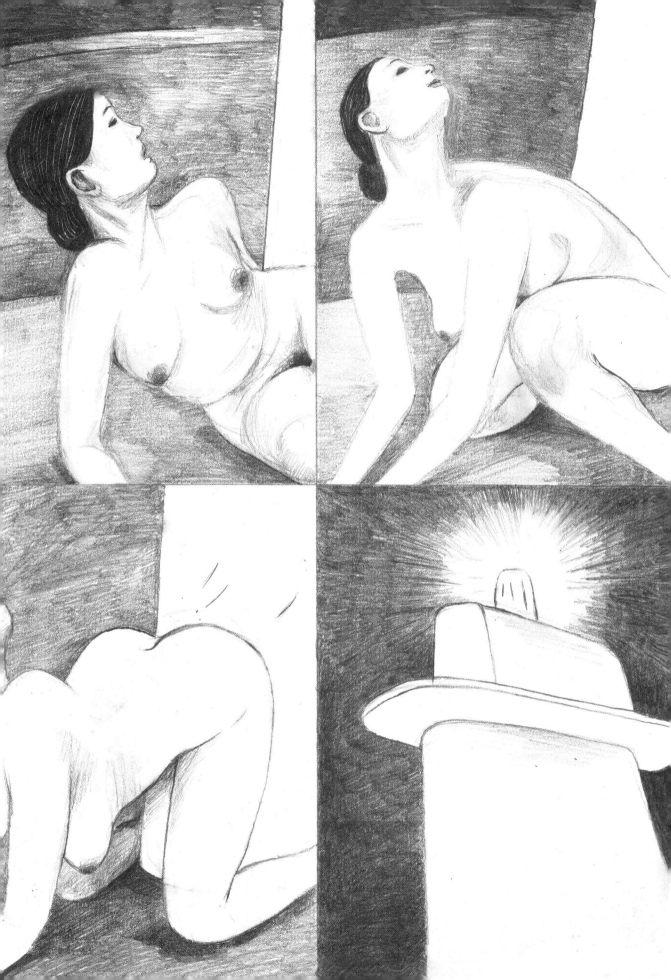

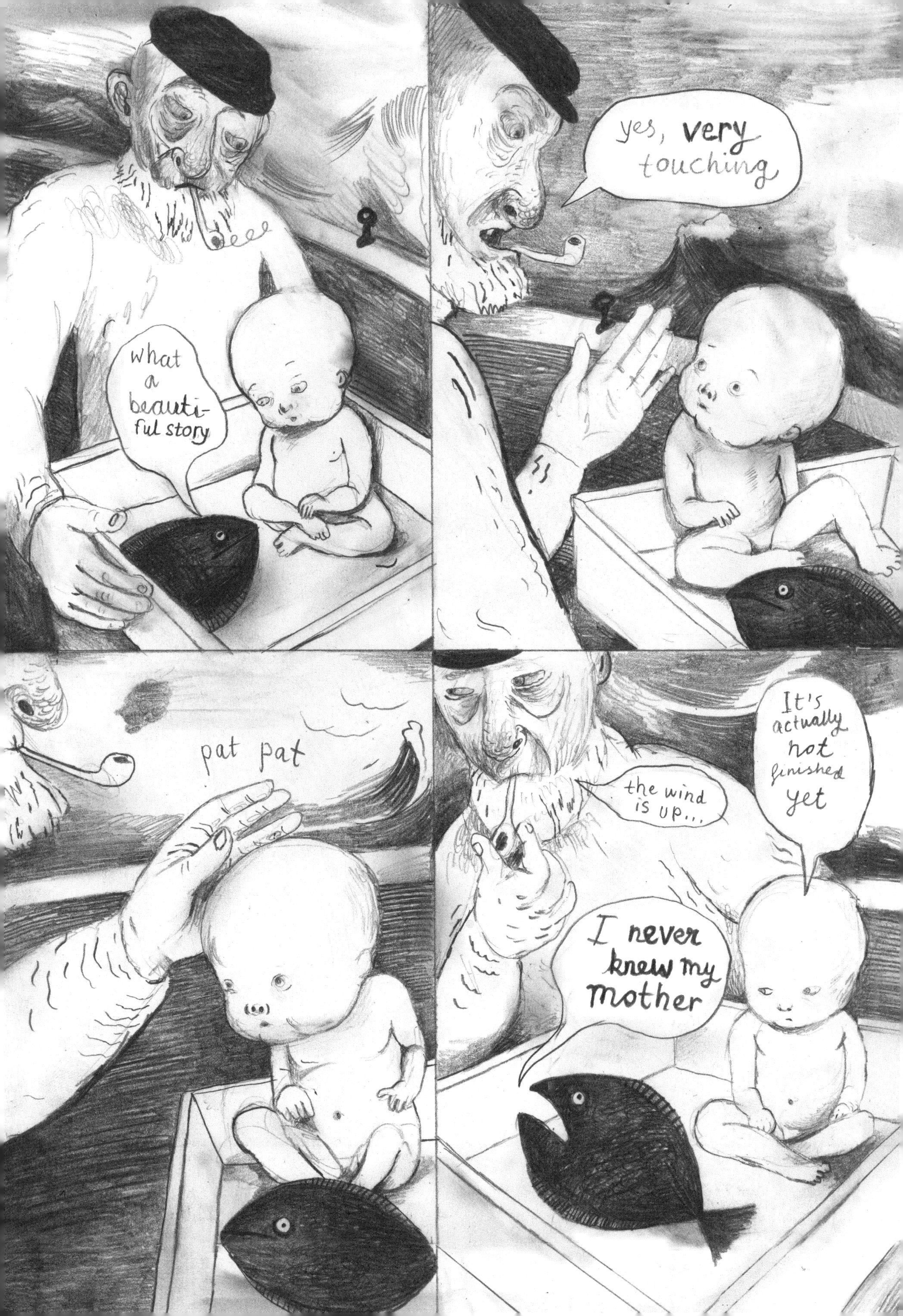
what a beauti-ful story
yes, very touching
pat pat
the wind is up...
It's actually not finished yet
I never knew my mother

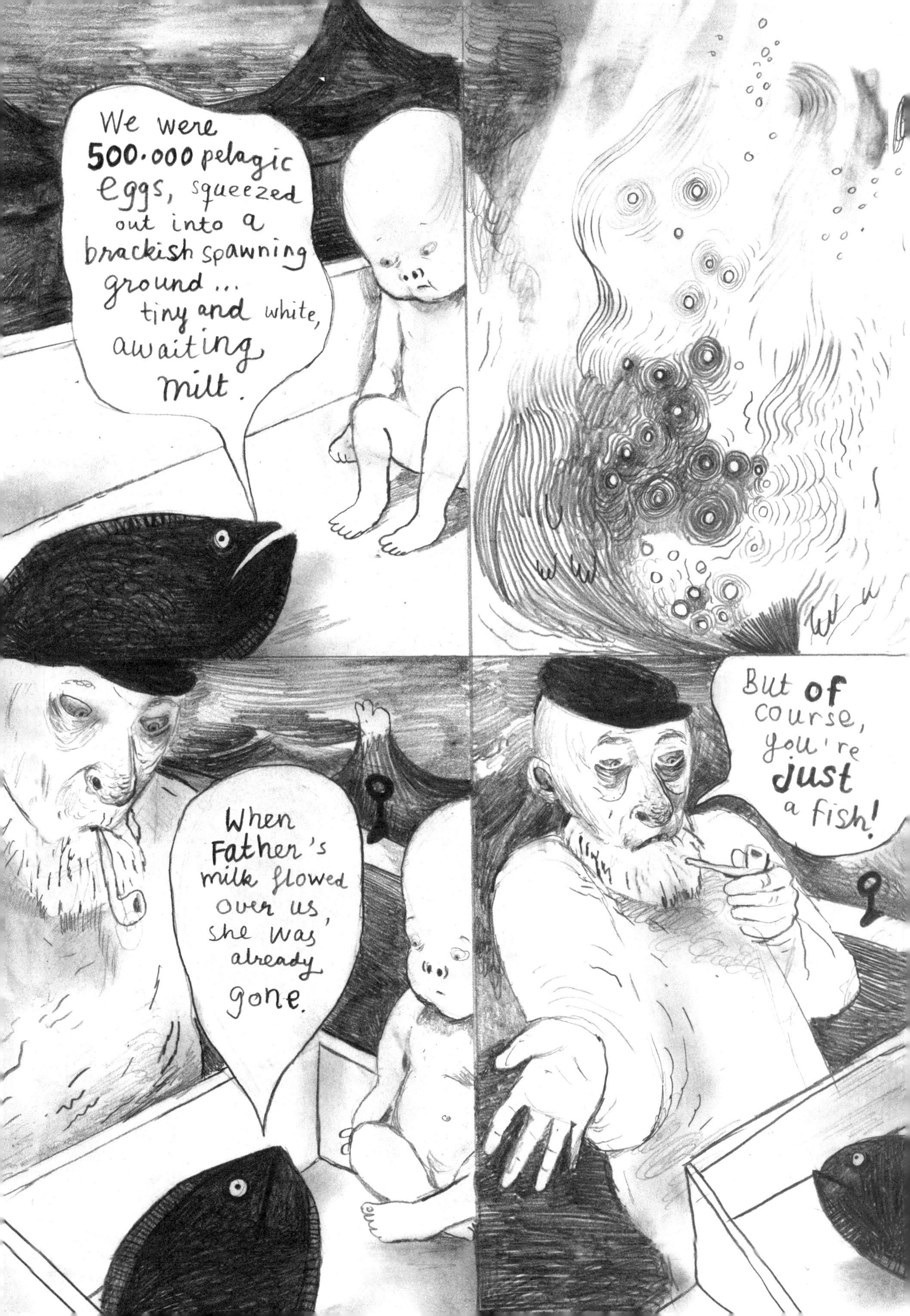
We were 500.000 pelagic eggs, squeezed out into a brackish spawning ground... tiny and white, awaiting milt.
When Father's milk flowed over us, she was already gone.
But of course, you're just a fish!

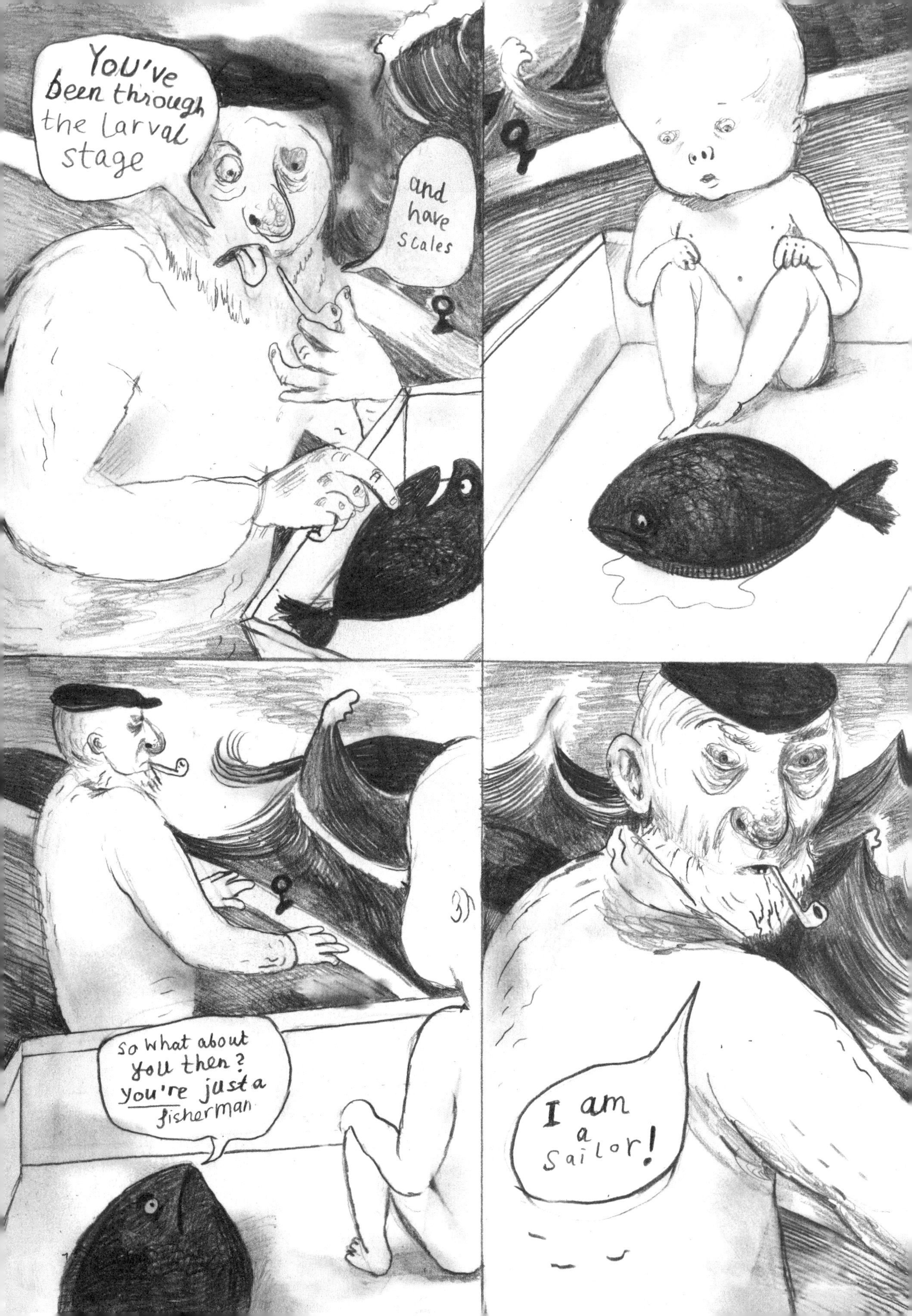
You've been through the larval stage
and have scales
So what about you then? you're just a fisherman
I am a sailor!

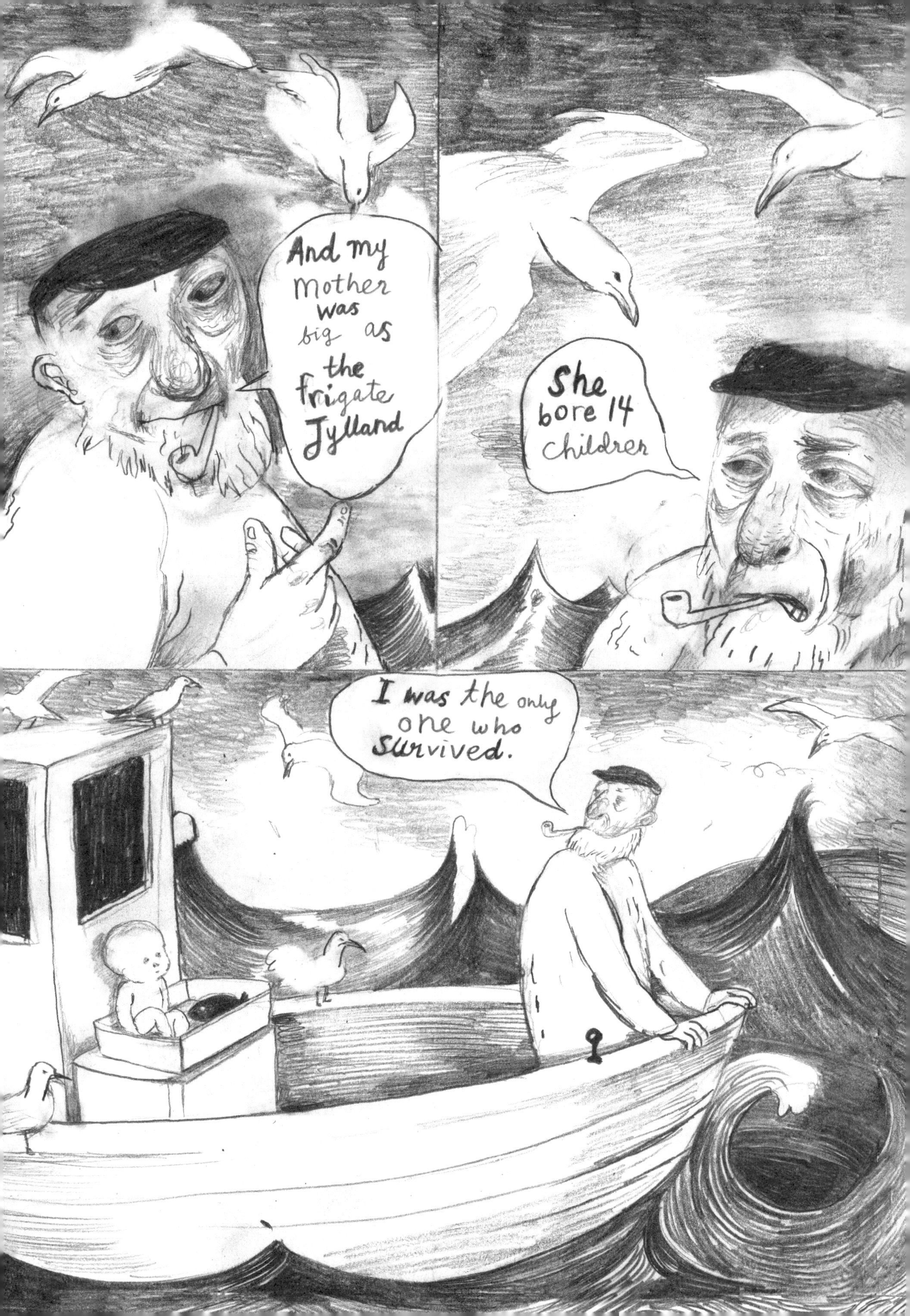
And my mother was big as the frigate Jylland
She bore 14 children
I was the only one who survived.

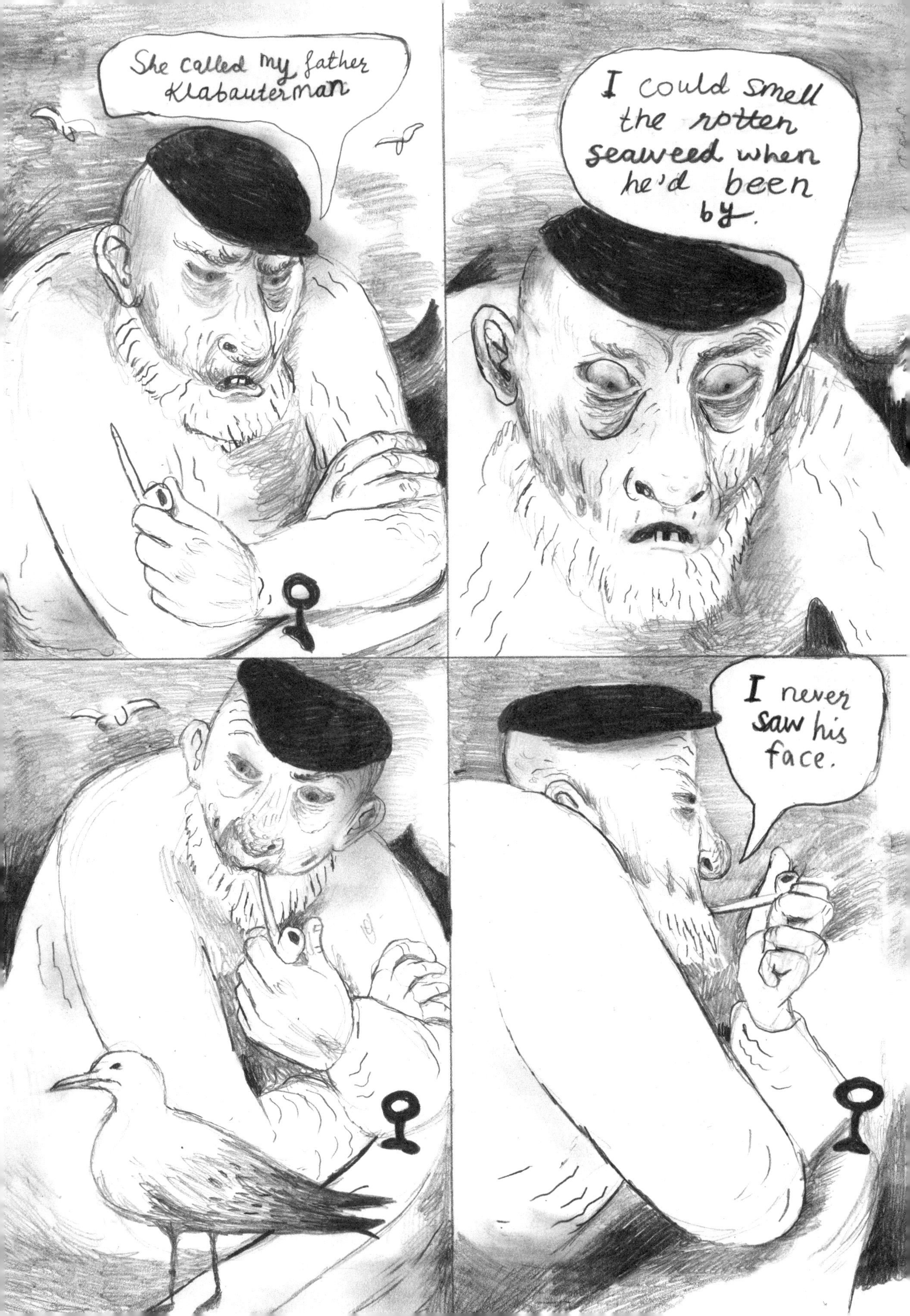
She called my father Klabauterman
I could smell the rotten seaweed when he'd been by.
I never saw his face.

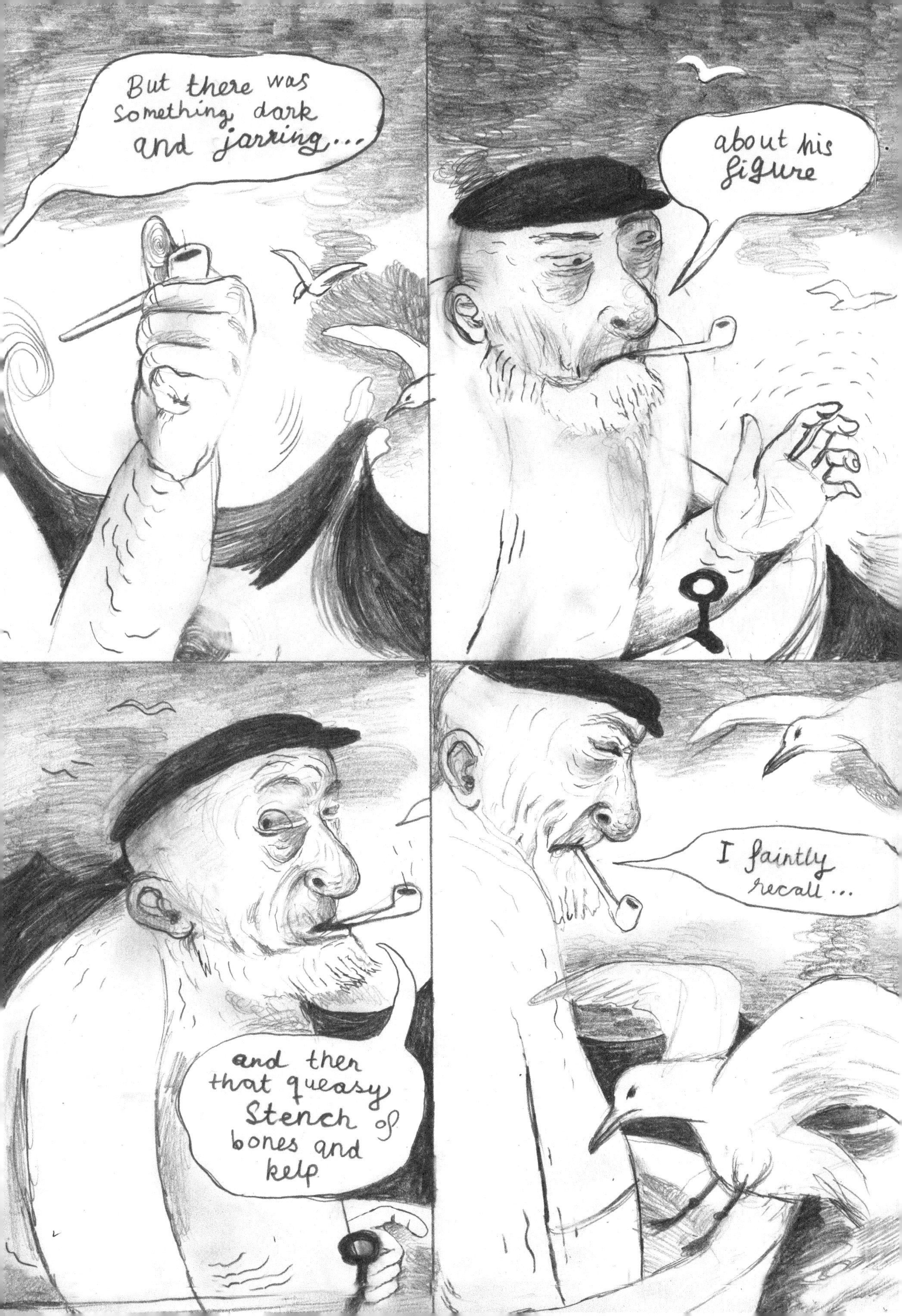
But there was something dark and jarring...
about his figure
and then that queasy Stench of bones and kelp
I faintly recall...

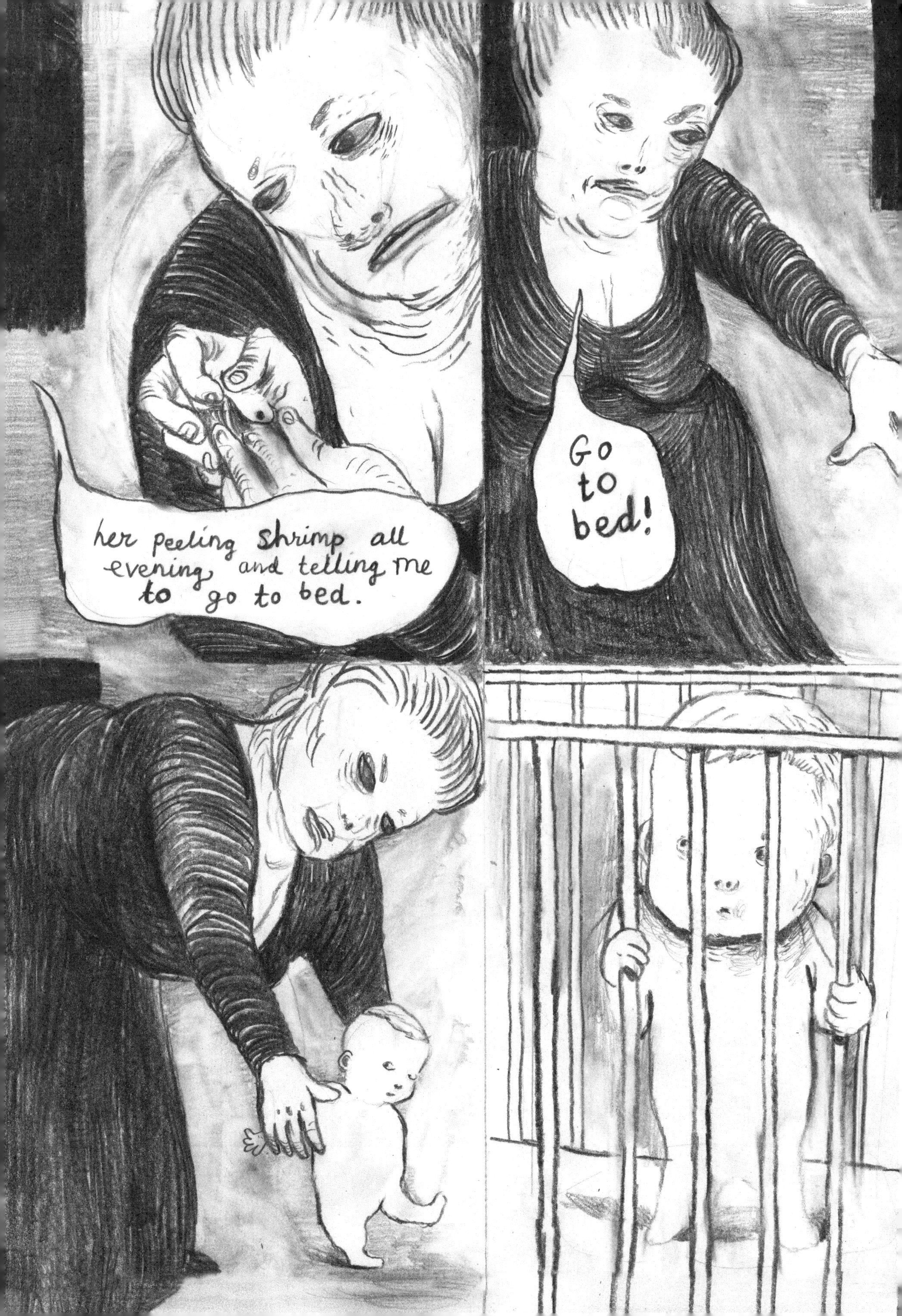
her peeling shrimp all evening and telling me to go to bed.
Go to bed!

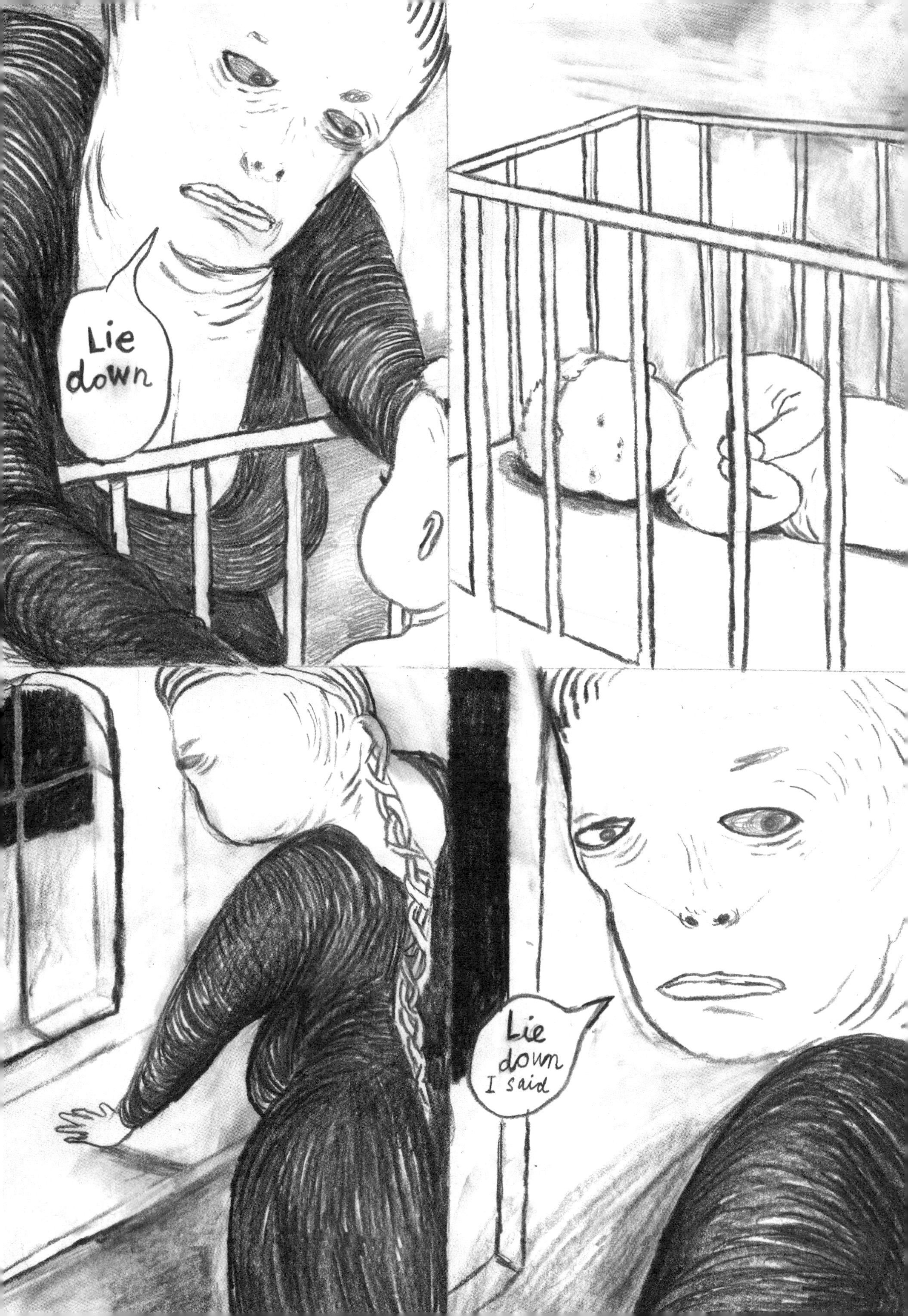
Lie down
Lie down I said

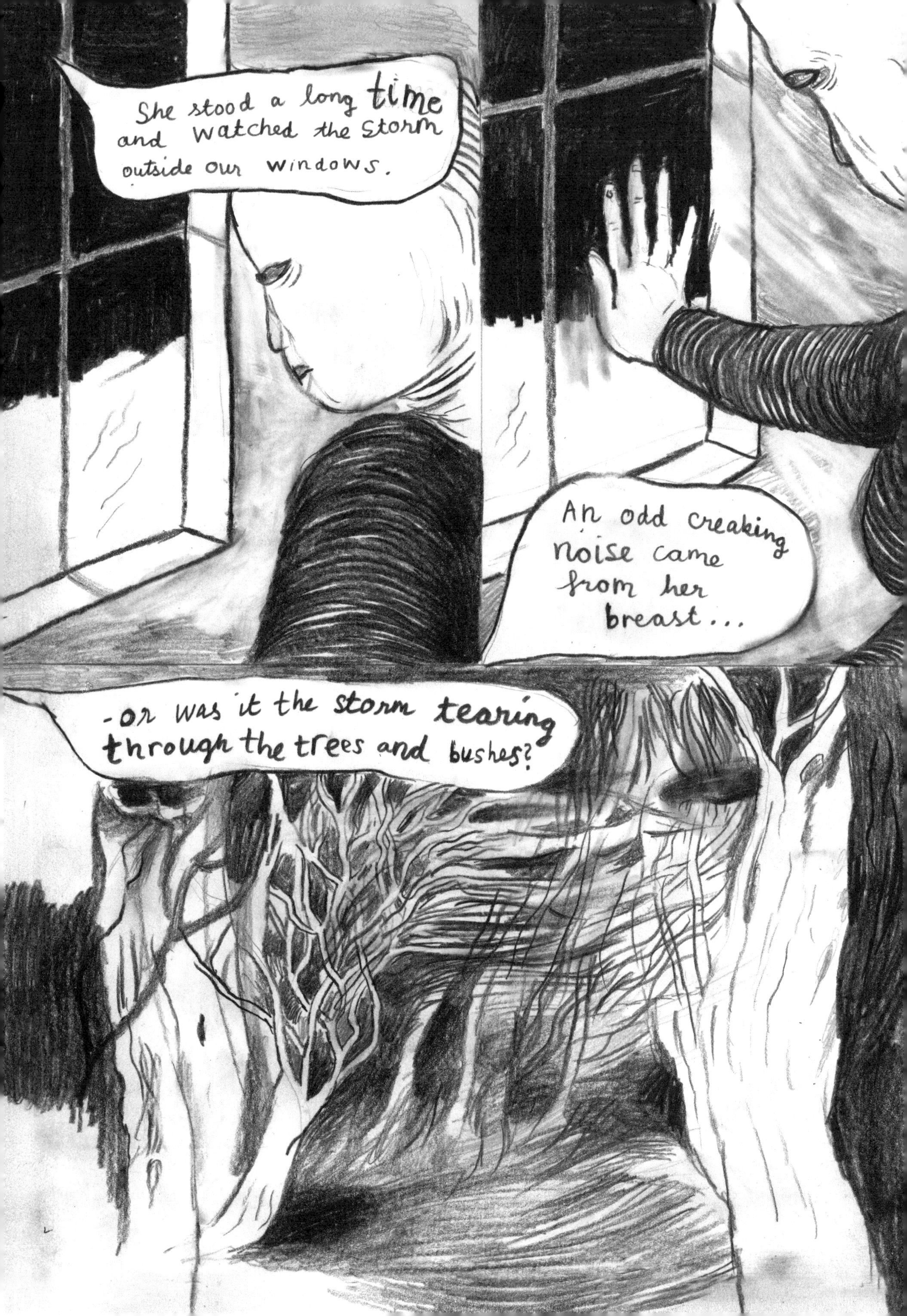
She stood a long time and watched the storm outside our windows.
An odd creaking noise came from her breast...
-or was it the storm tearing through the trees and bushes?

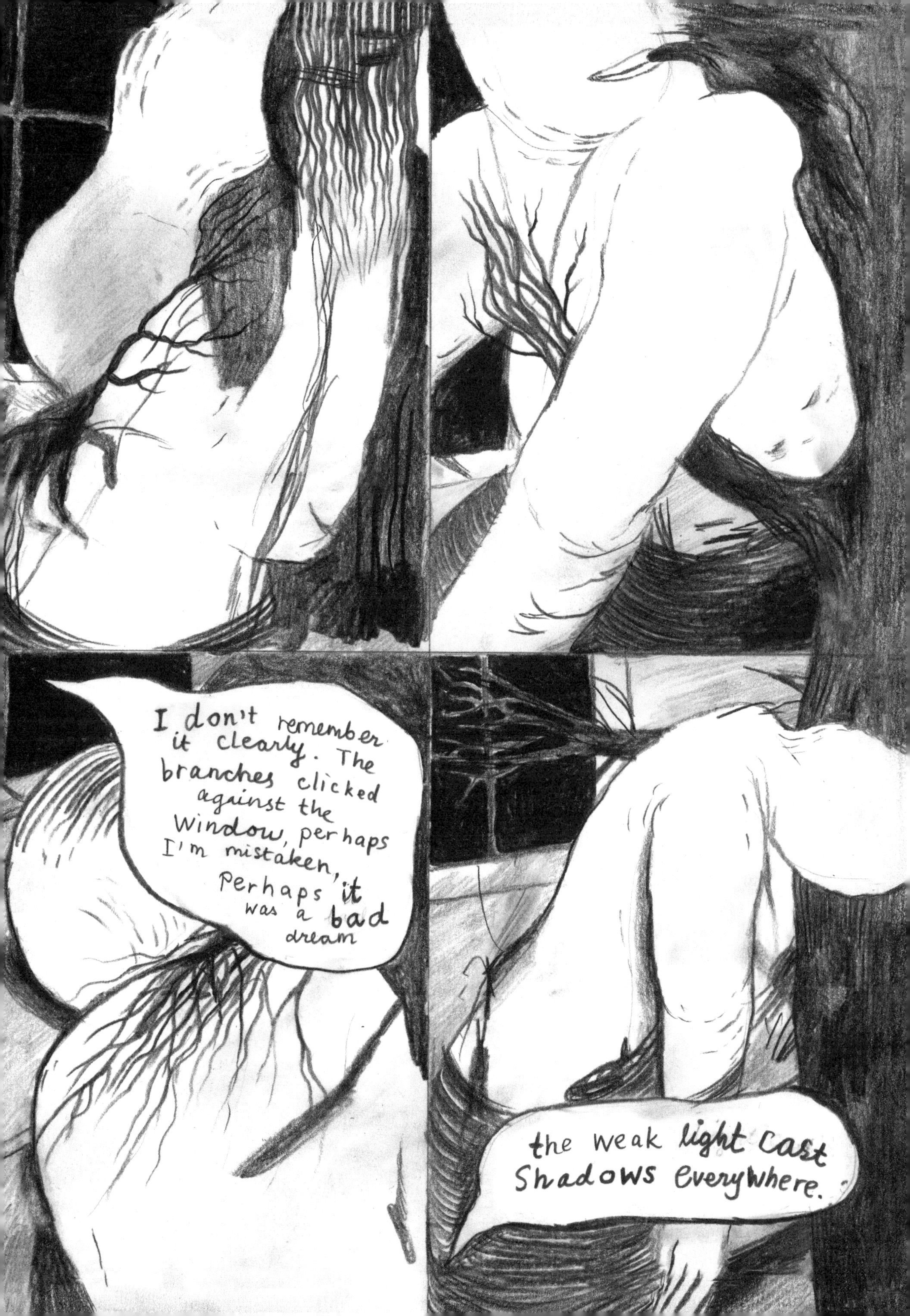
I don't remember it clearly. The branches clicked against the window, perhaps I'm mistaken, perhaps it was a bad dream
the weak light cast shadows everywhere.

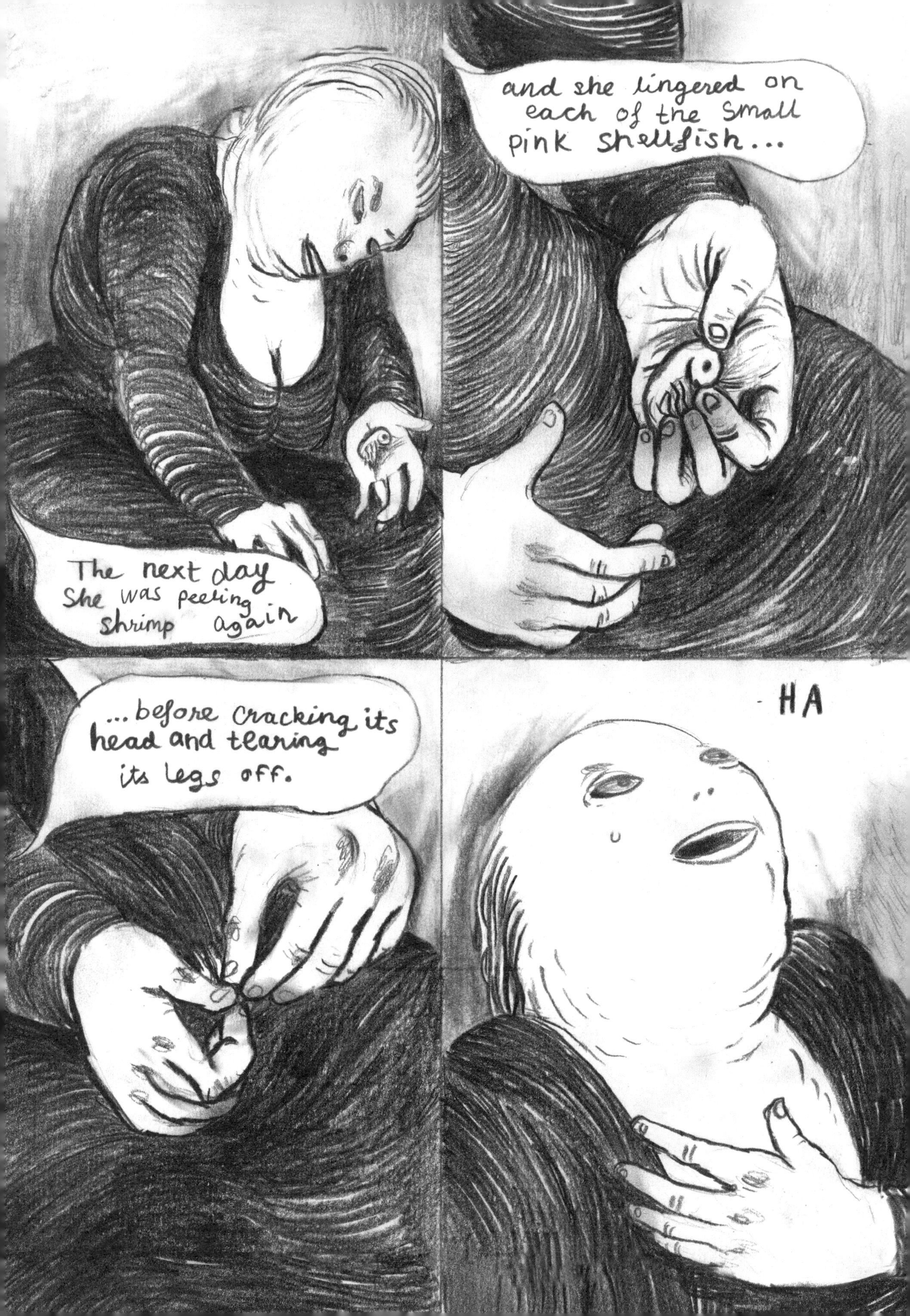
The next day She was peeling shrimp again
and she lingered on each of the small pink shellfish...
...before cracking its head and tearing its legs off.
HA

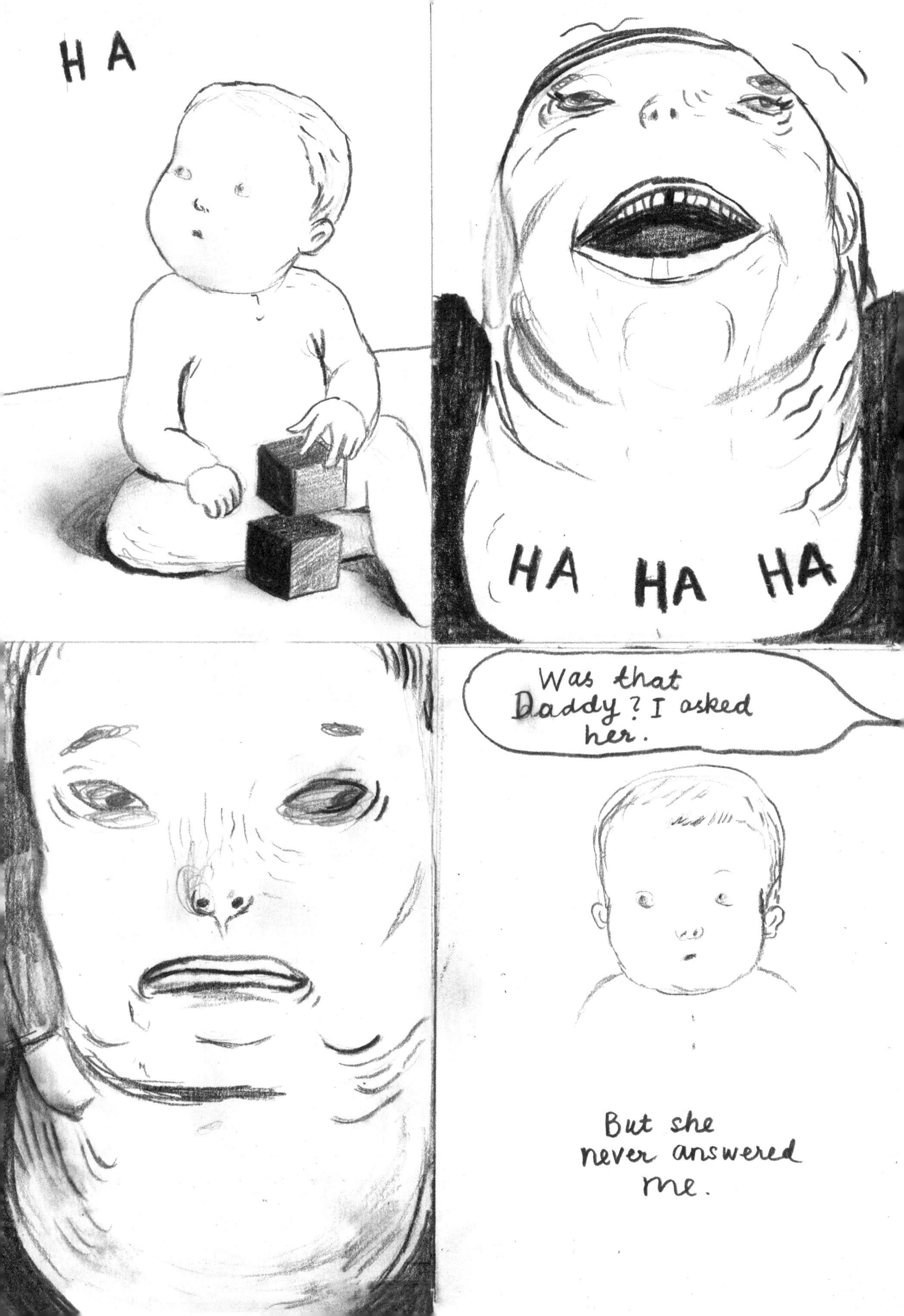
H A
HA HA HA
Was that Daddy? I asked her.
But she never answered me.

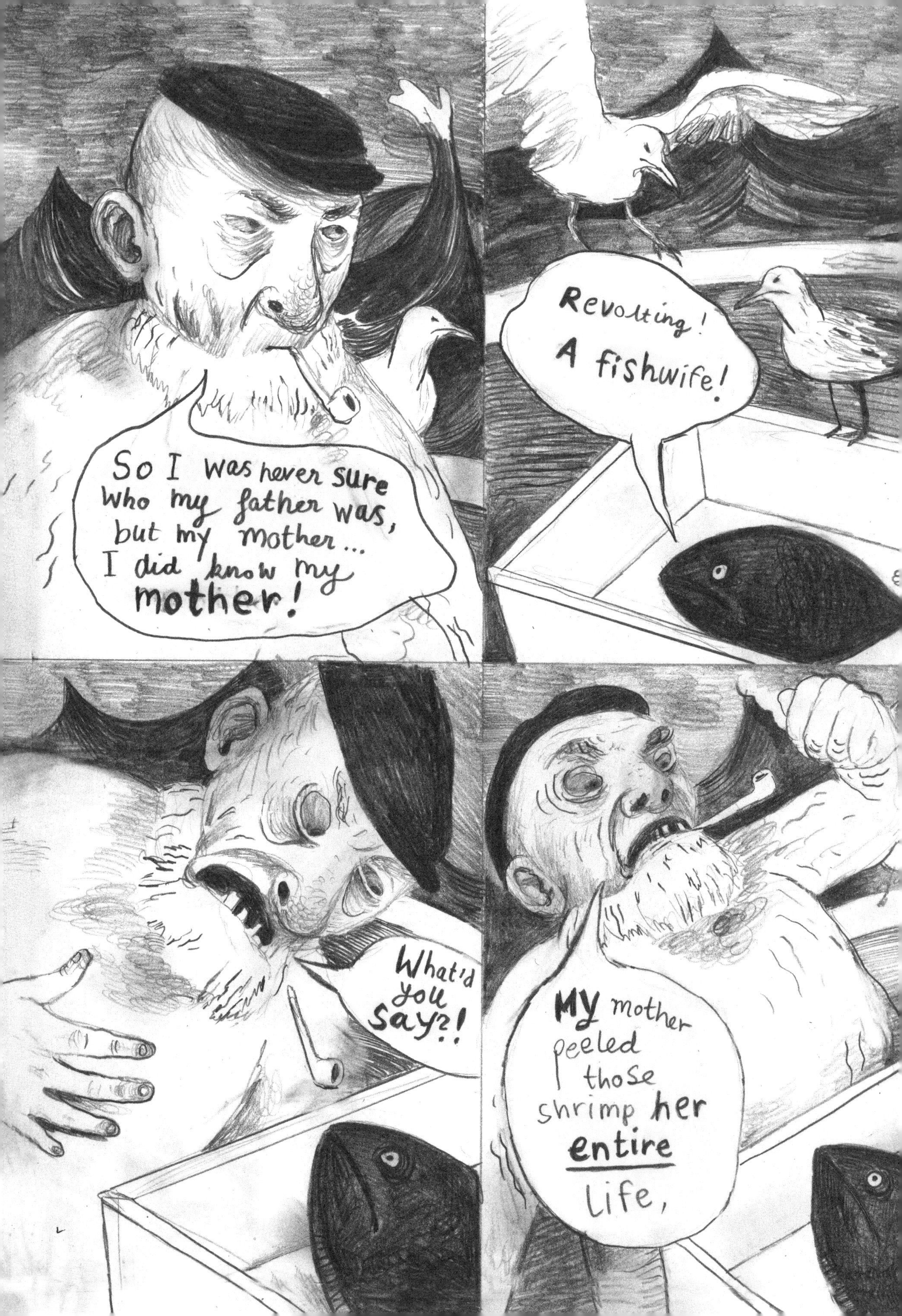
So I was never sure who my father was, but my mother... I did know my mother!
Revolting! A fishwife!
What'd you say?!
My mother peeled those shrimp her entire life,

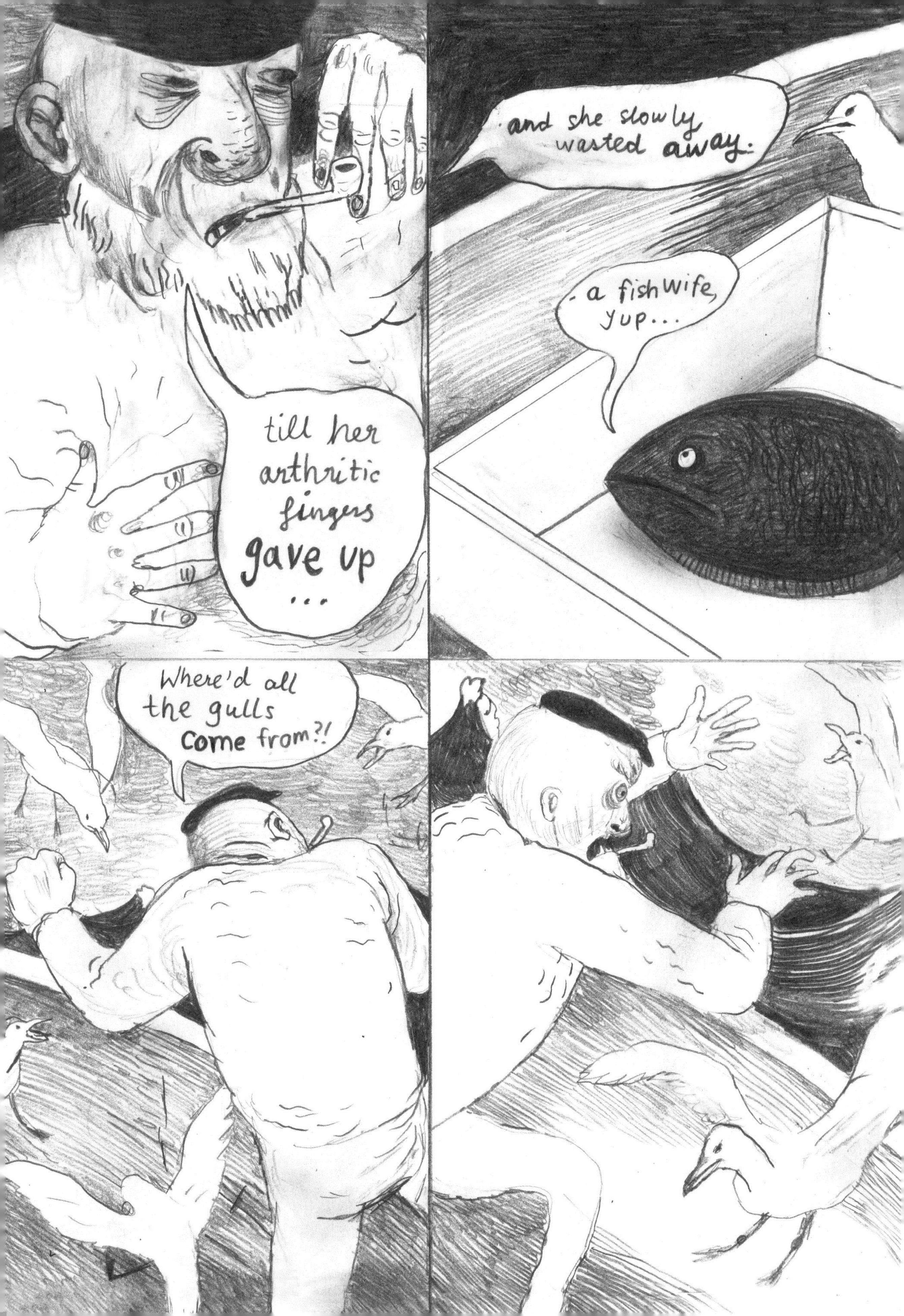
till her arthritic fingers gave up ...
and she slowly wasted away.
- a fishwife, yup...
Where'd all the gulls come from?!

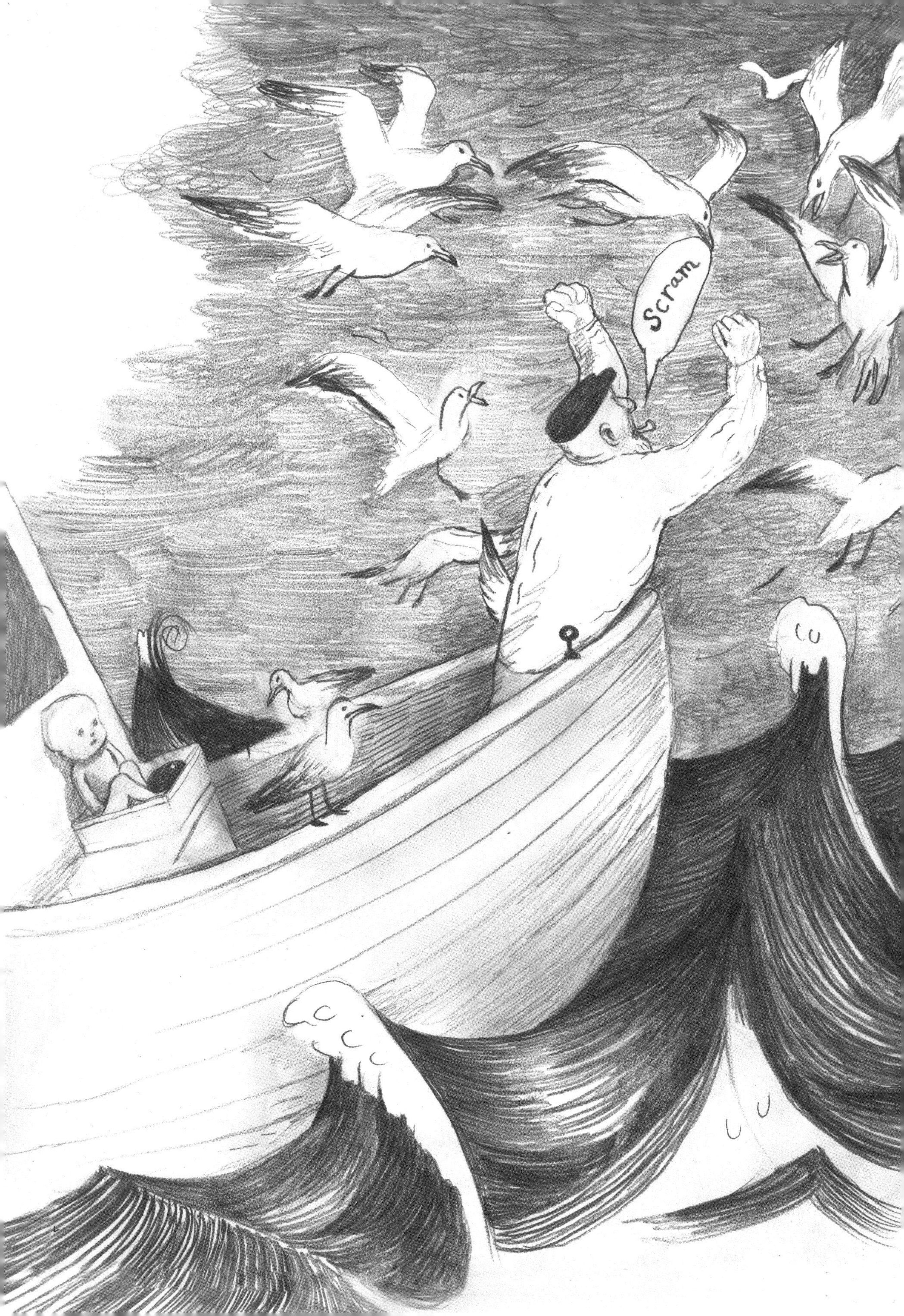
Scram

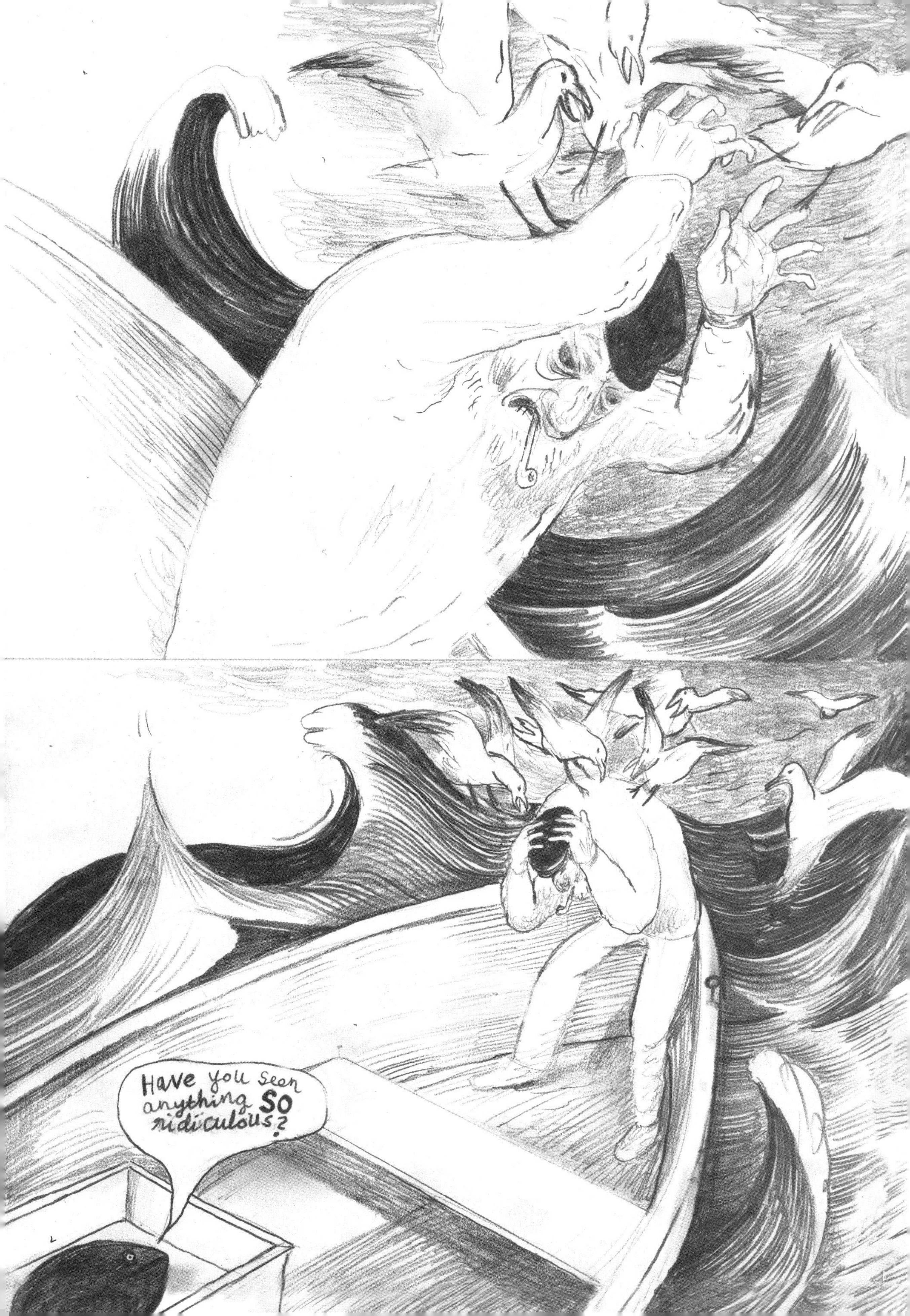
Have you seen anything SO ridiculous?

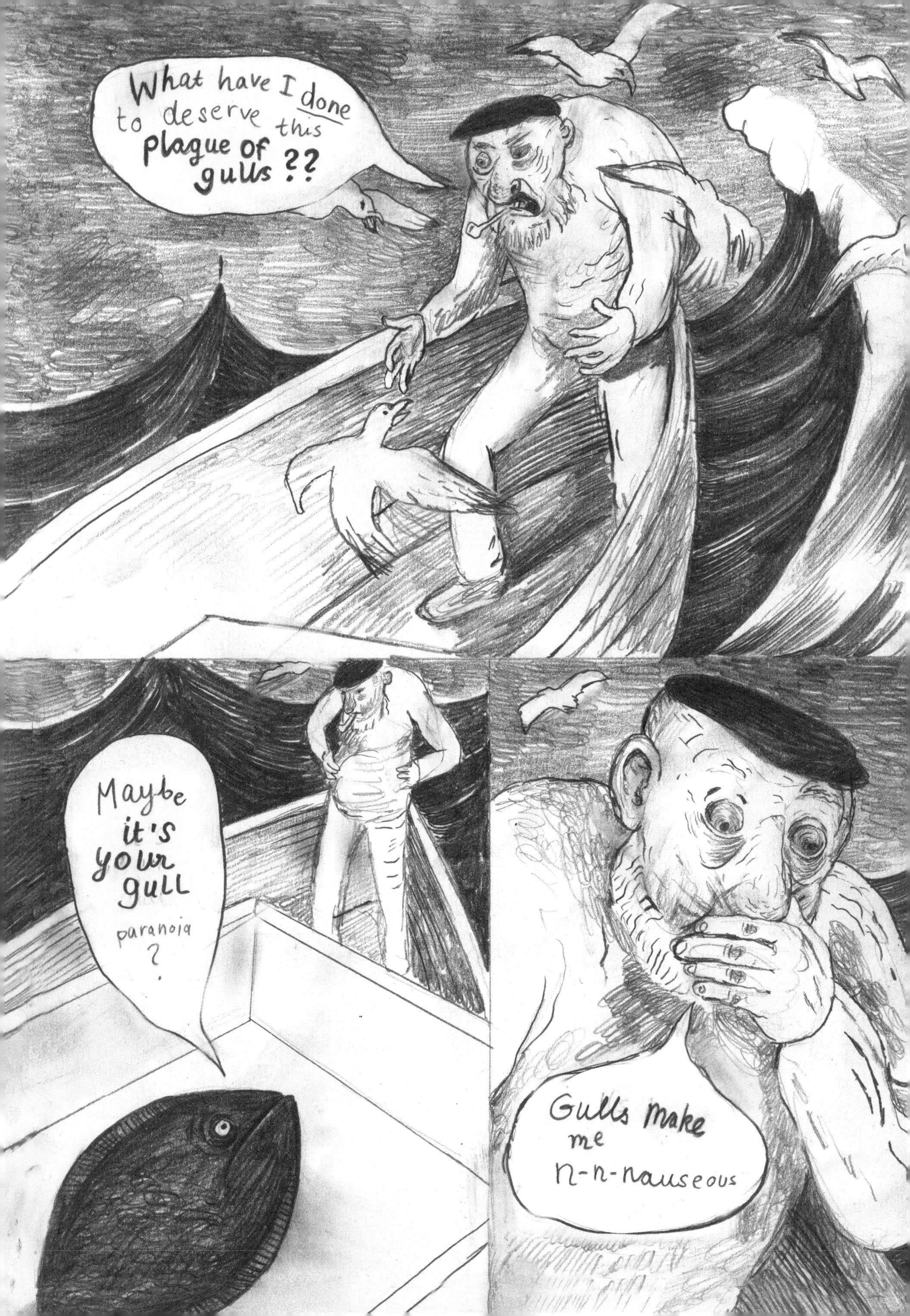
What have I done to deserve this plague of gulls??
Maybe it's your gull paranoia?
Gulls make me n-n-nauseous

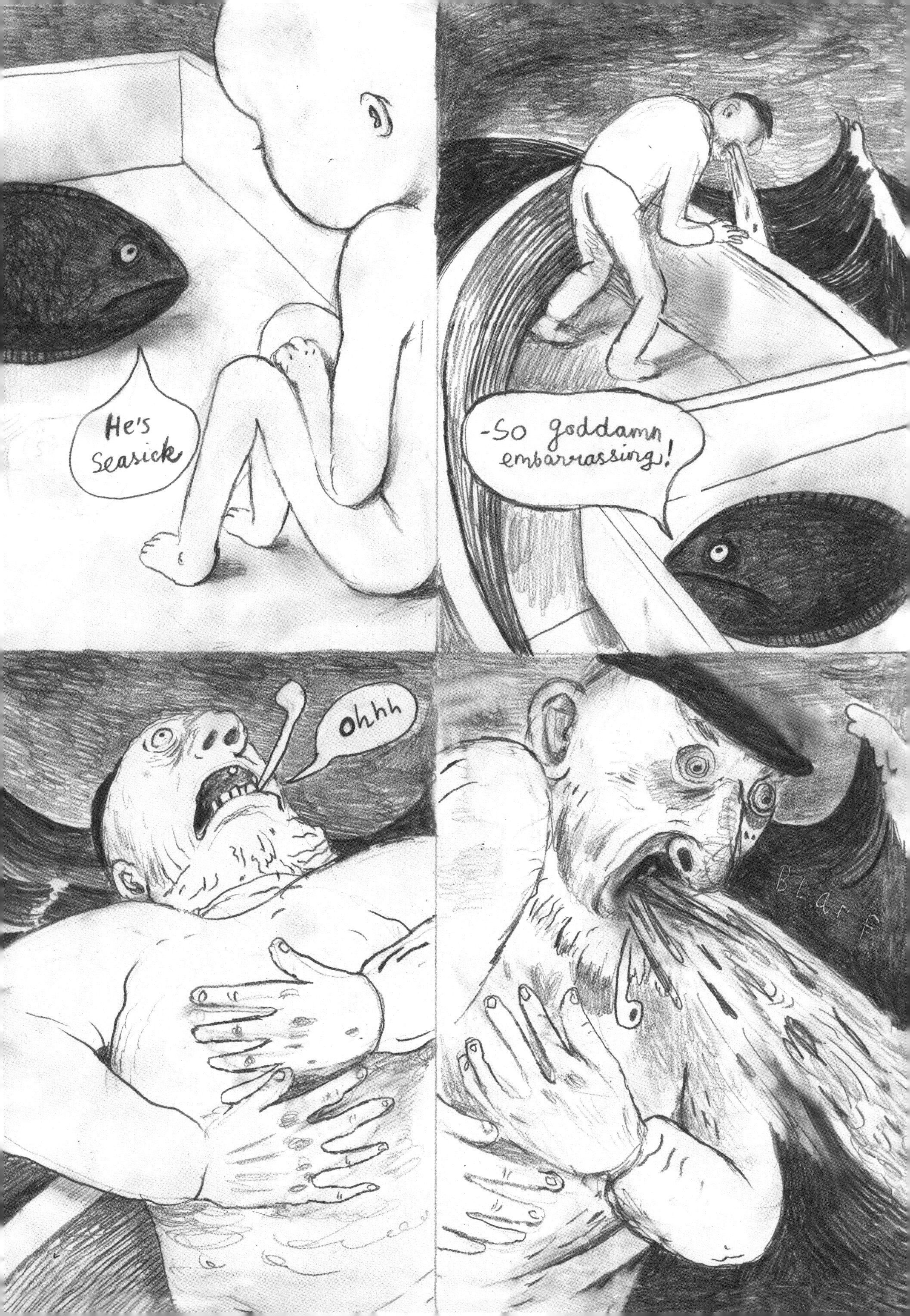
He's seasick
-So goddamn embarrassing!
Ohhh
BLarF

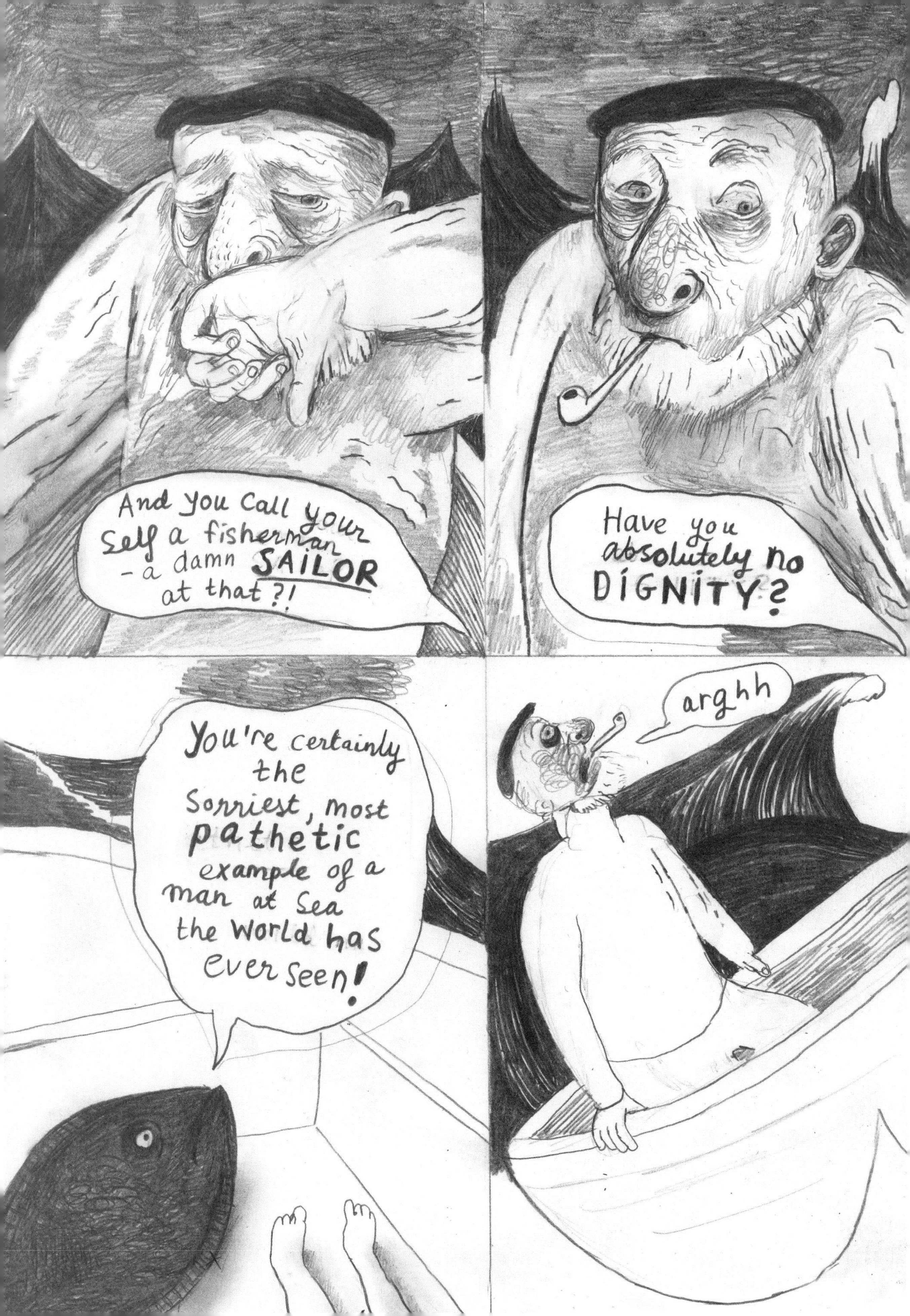
And you call your self a fisherman - a damn SAILOR at that?!
Have you absolutely no DIGNITY?
You're certainly the sorriest, most pathetic example of a man at sea the world has ever seen!
arghh

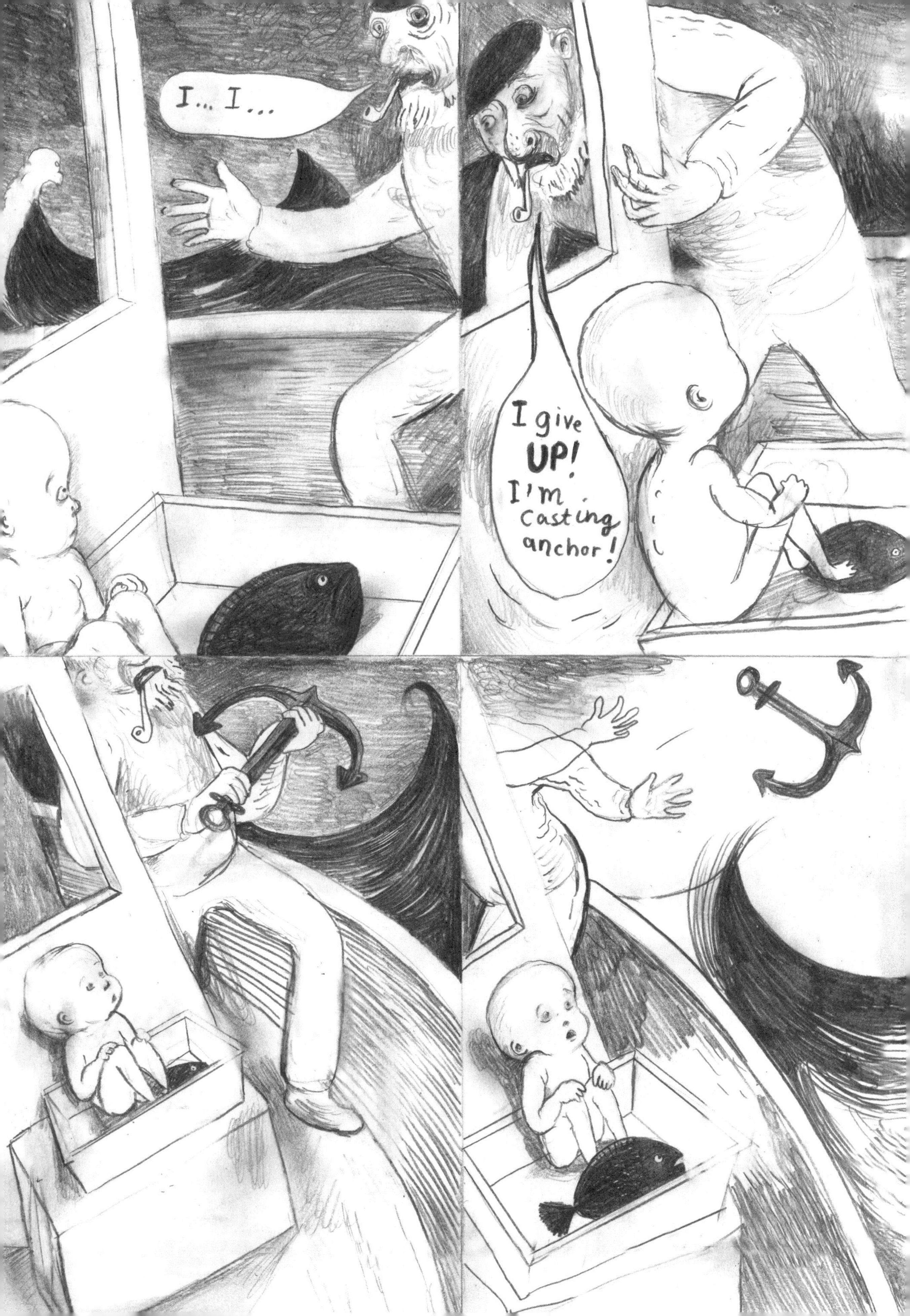
I... I...
I give UP! I'm casting anchor!

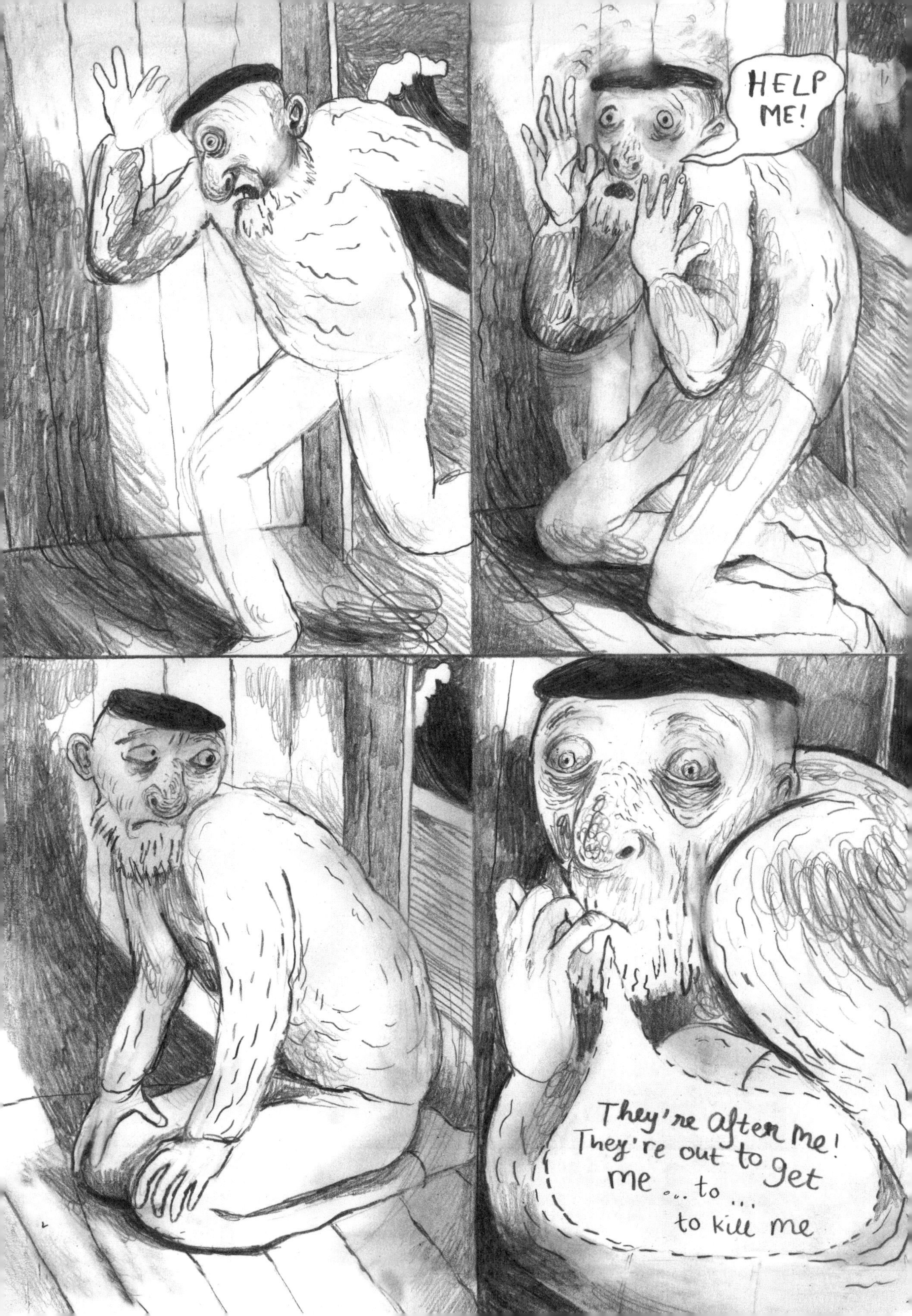
HELP ME!
They're after me! They're out to get me... to... to kill me

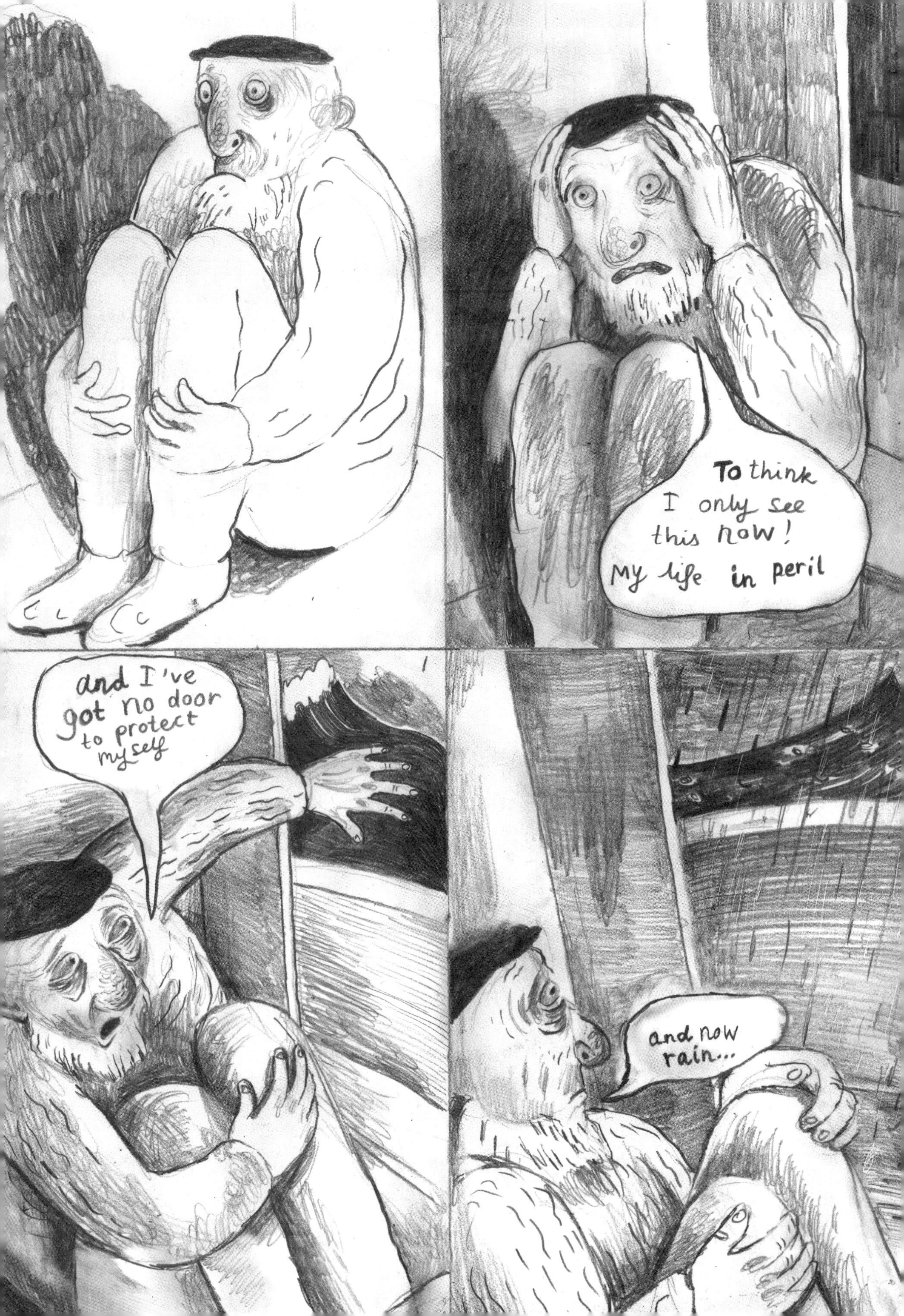
To think I only see this now! My life in peril
and I've got no door to protect myself
and now rain...

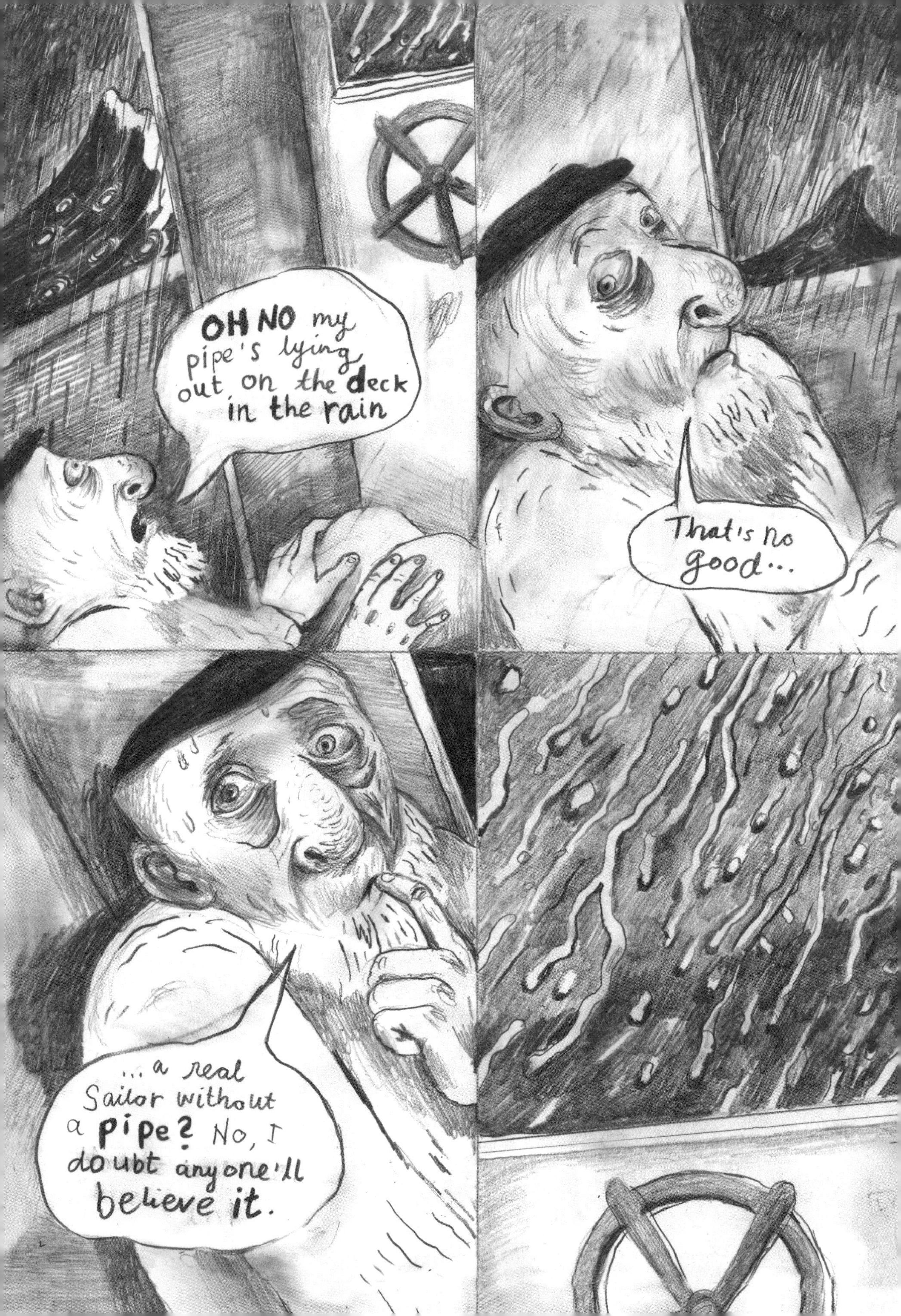
OH NO my pipe's lying out on the deck in the rain
That's no good...
...a real Sailor without a pipe? No, I doubt anyone'll believe it.

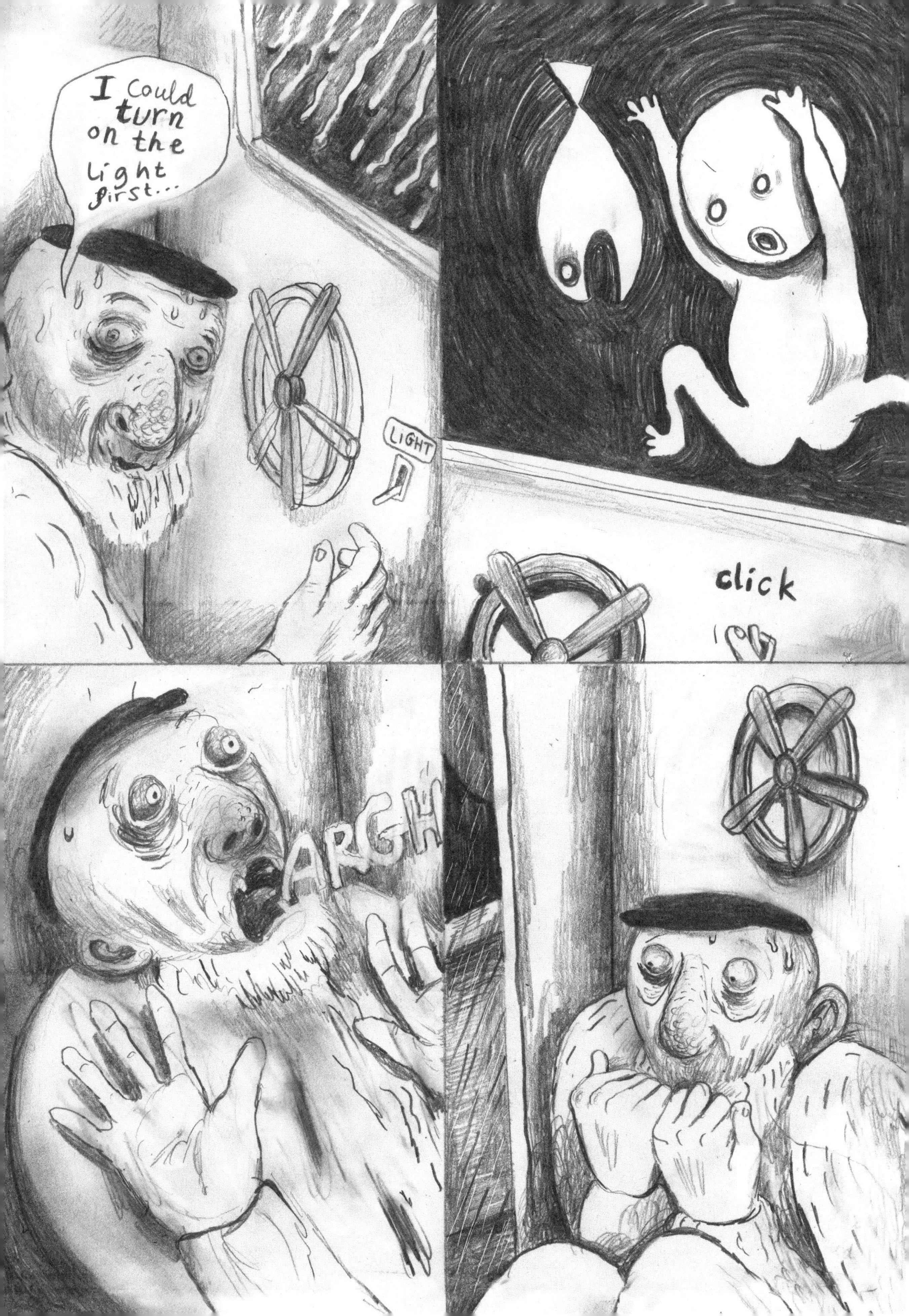

I could turn on the light first...
LIGHT
click
ARGH

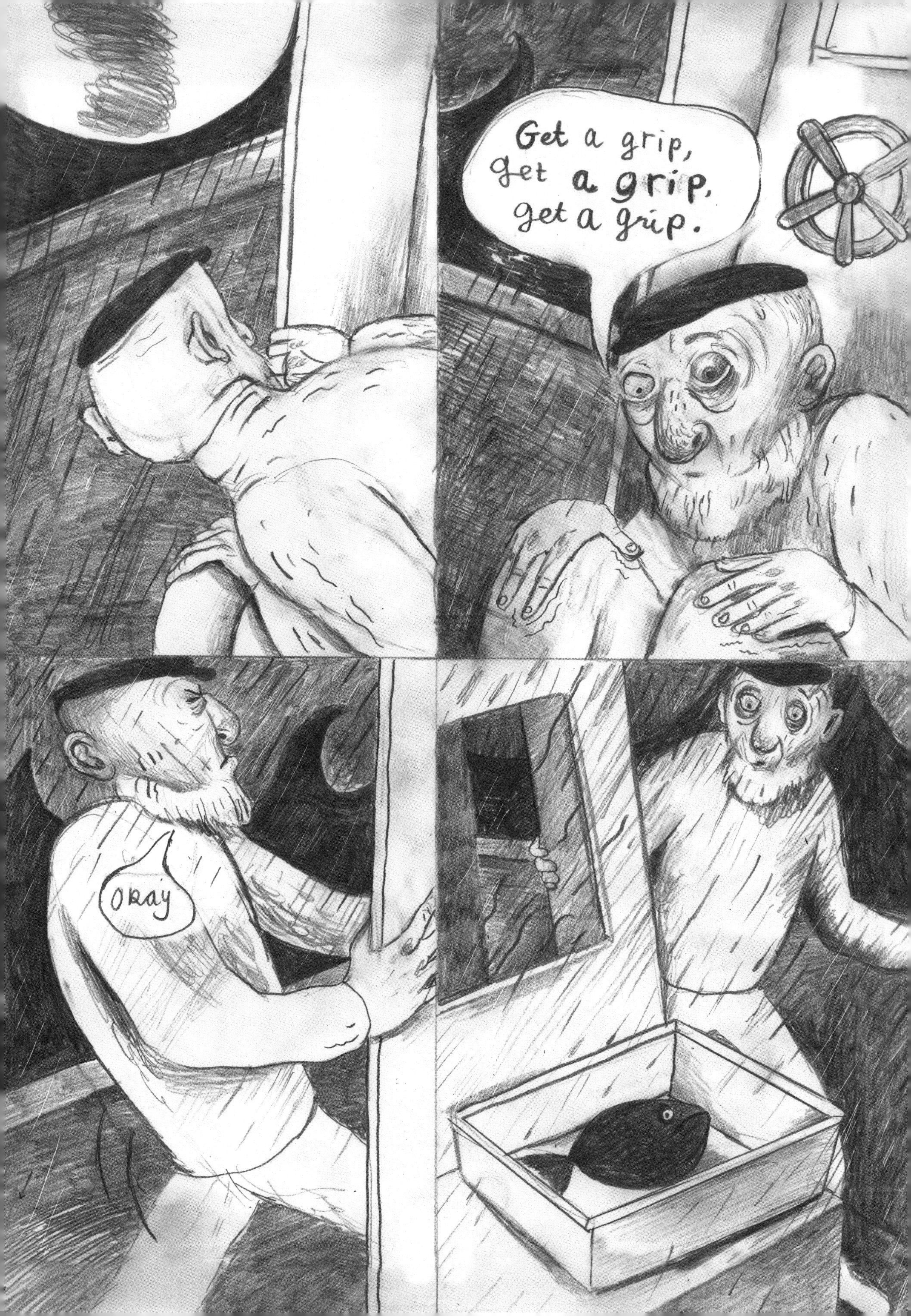
Get a grip, get a grip, get a grip.
Okay

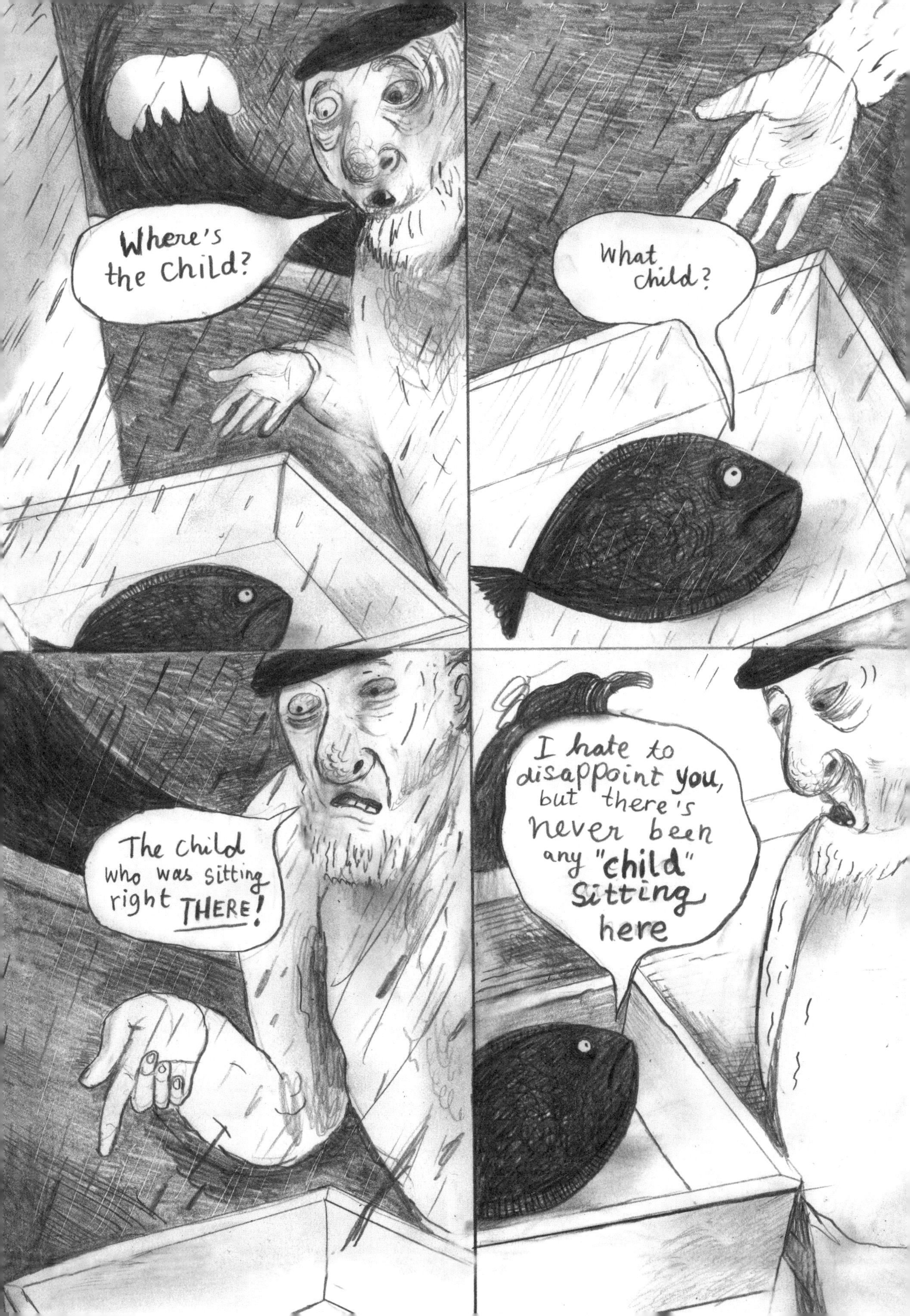
Where's the Child?
What child?
The child who was sitting right THERE!
I hate to disappoint you, but there's never been any "child" sitting here

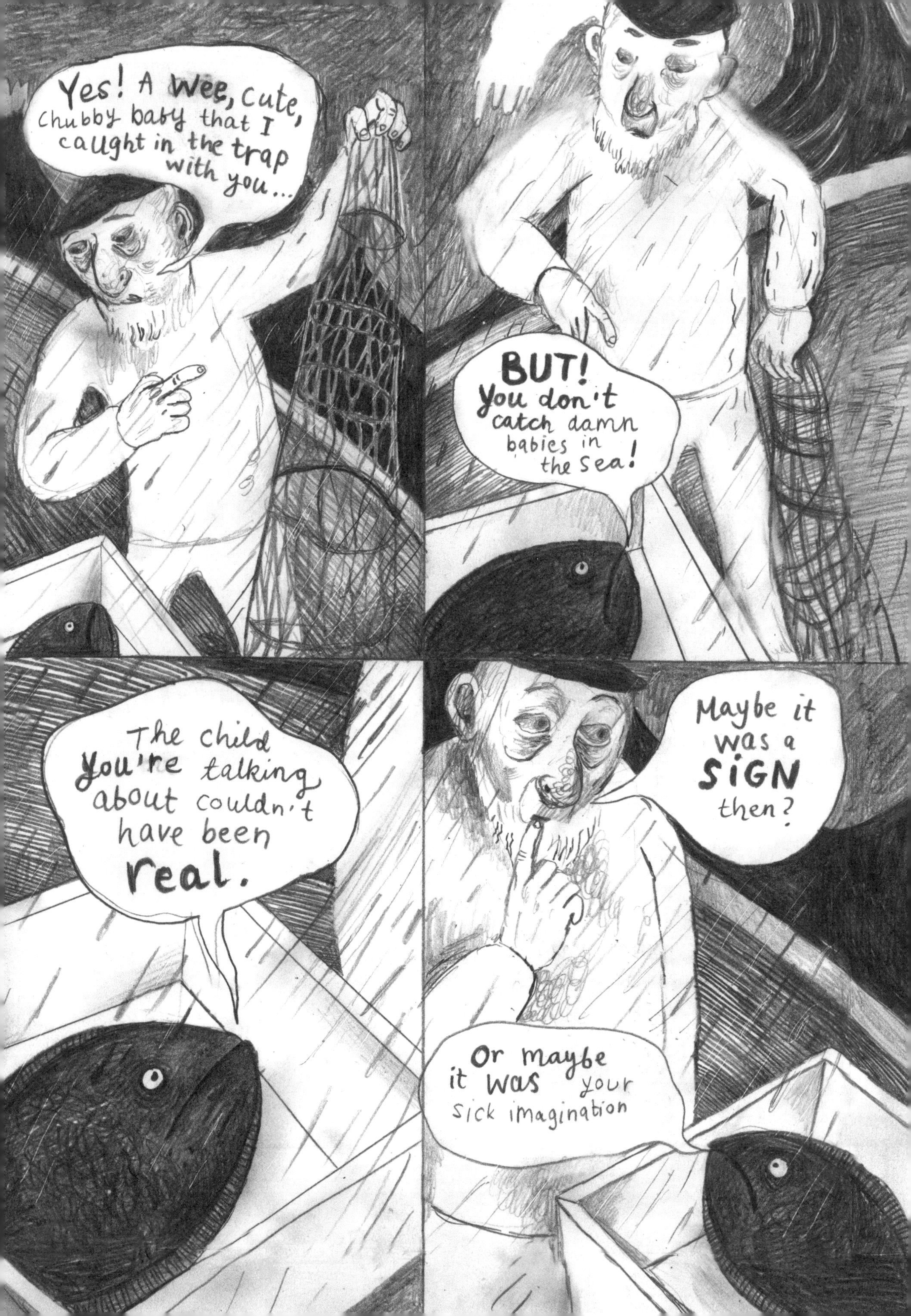
Yes! A wee, cute, chubby baby that I caught in the trap with you...
BUT! You don't catch damn babies in the sea!
The child you're talking about couldn't have been real.
Maybe it was a SIGN then?
Or maybe it was your sick imagination

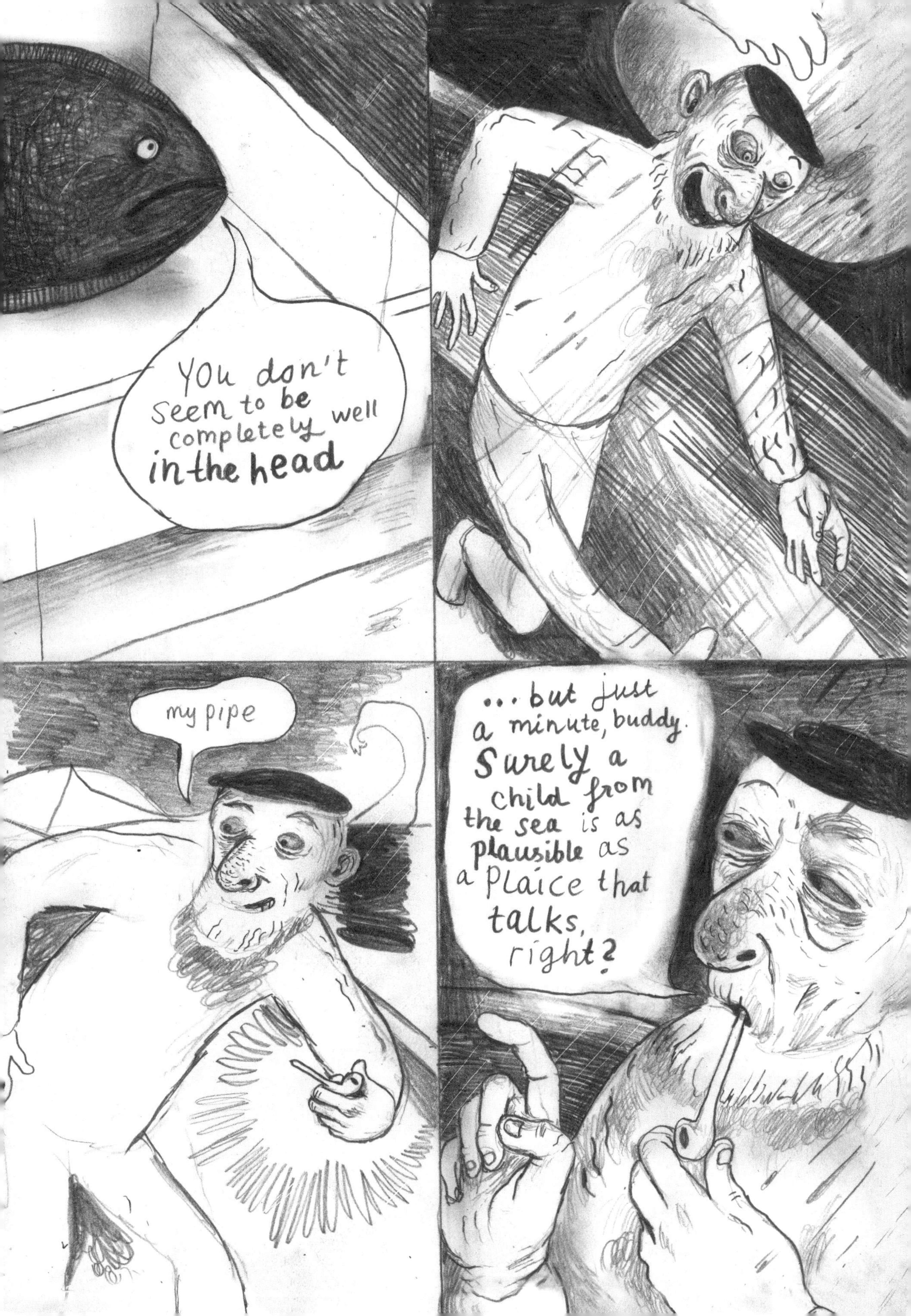
You don't seem to be completely well in the head
my pipe
... but just a minute, buddy. Surely a child from the sea is as plausible as a plaice that talks, right?

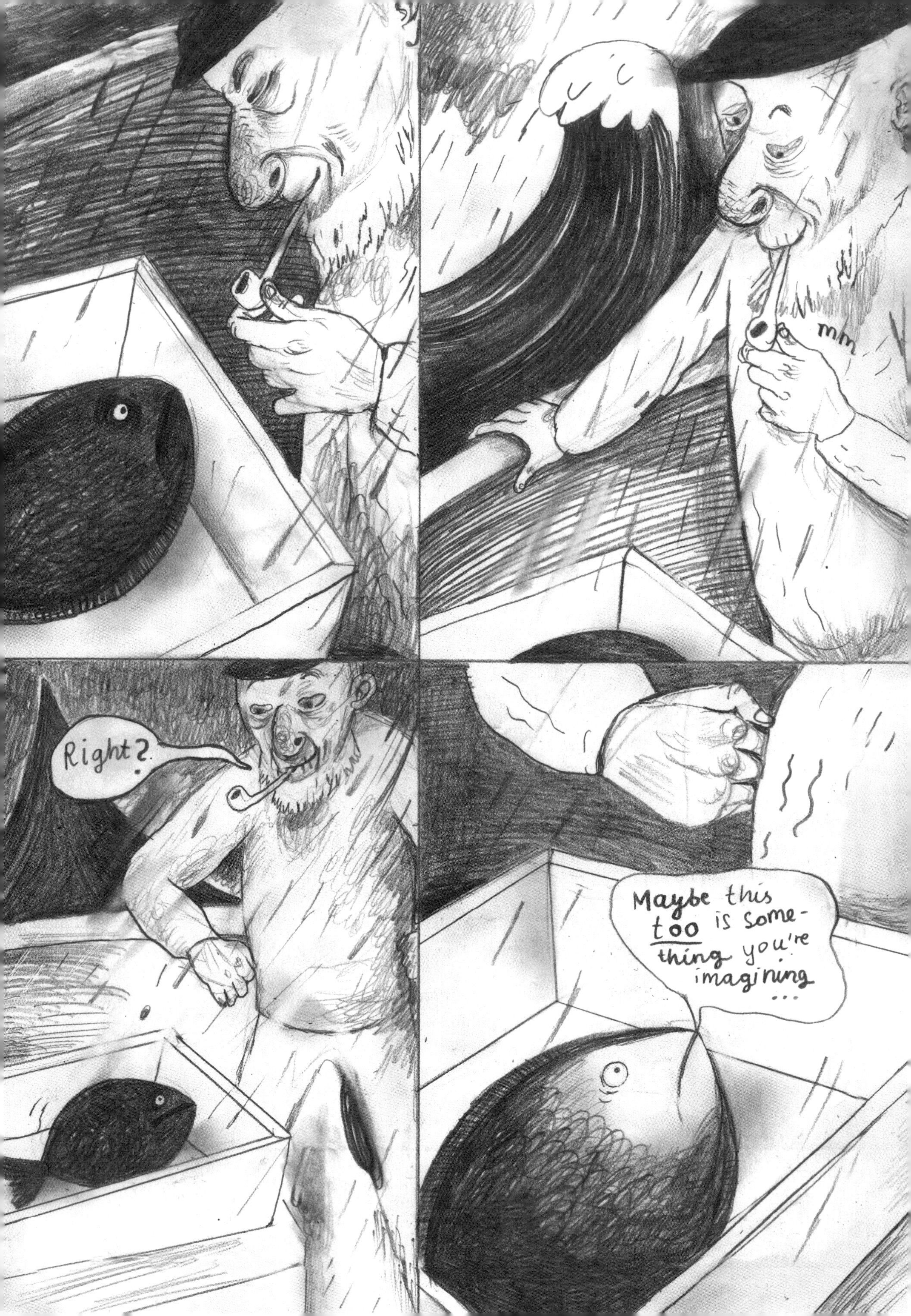
mm
Right?
Maybe this too is some-thing you're imagining...

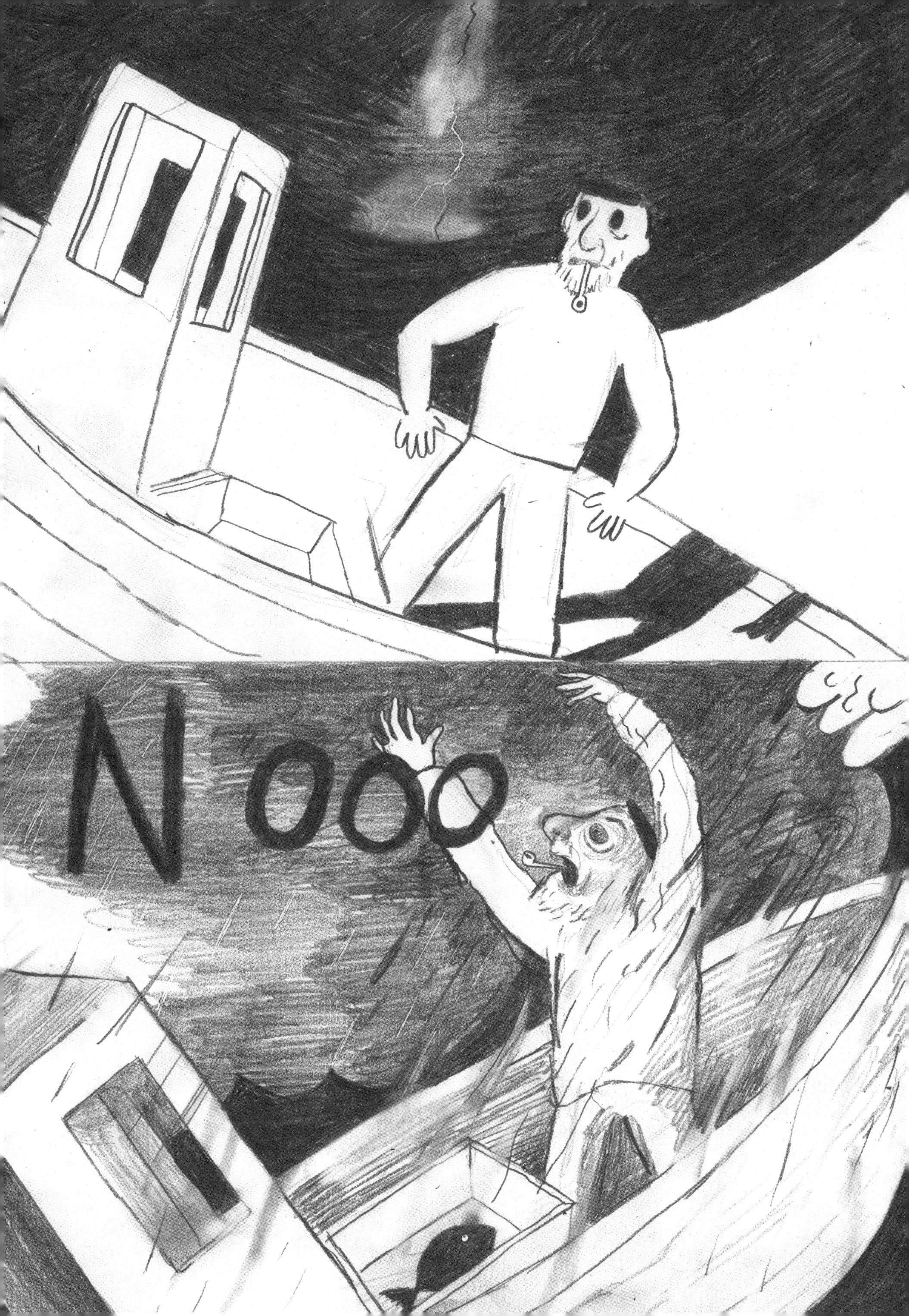
Nooo

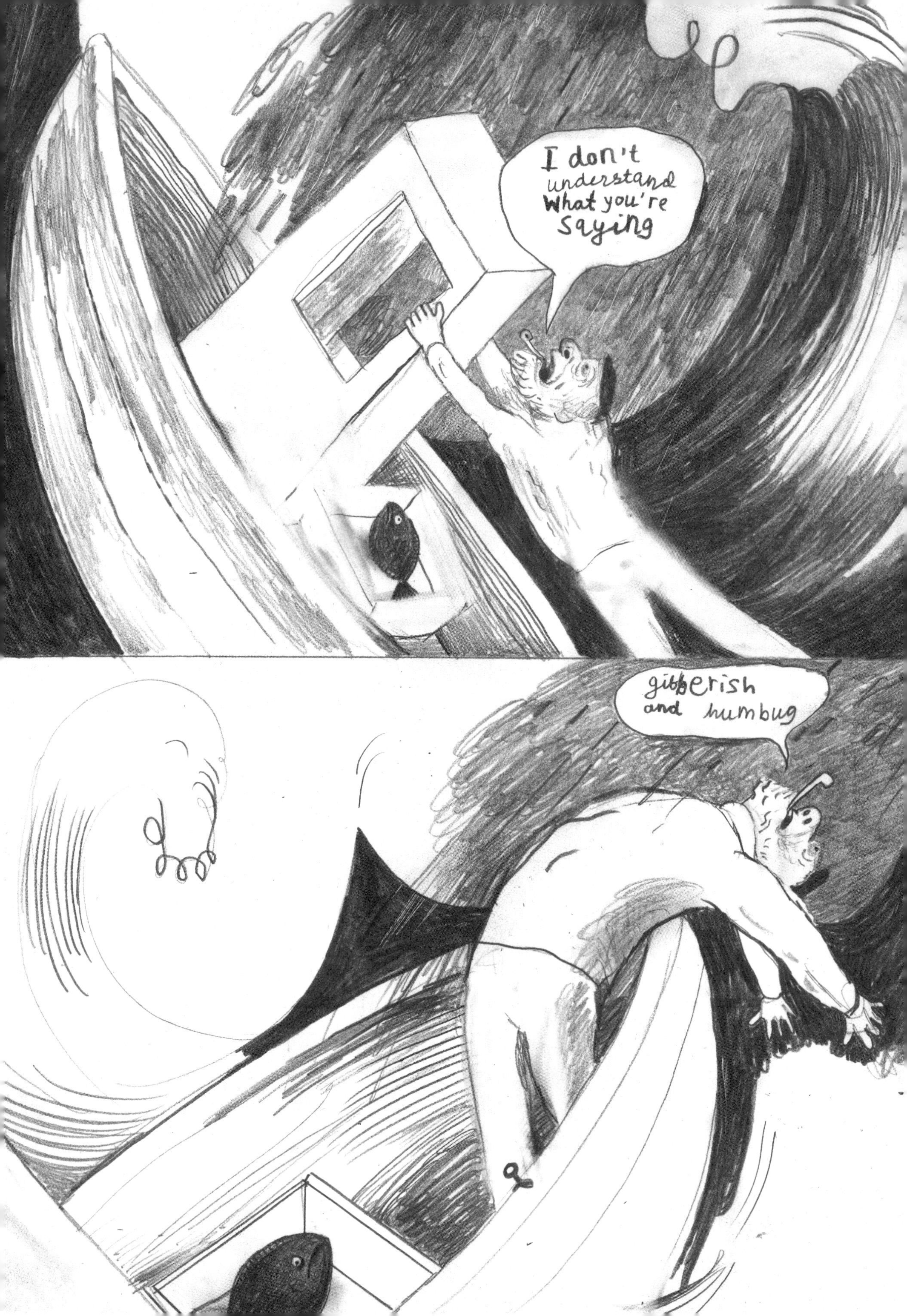

I don't understand what you're saying
gibberish and humbug

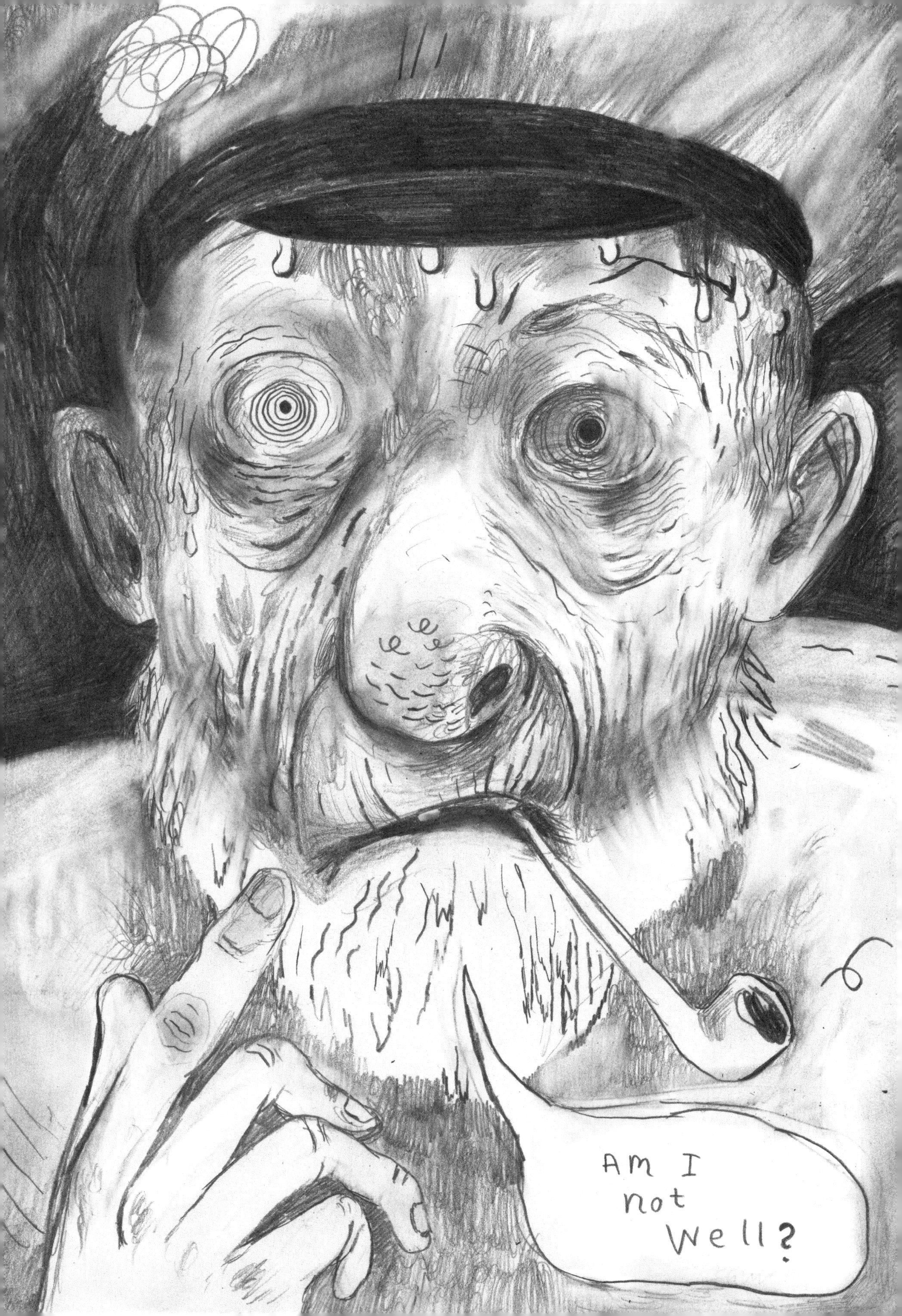
Am I not well?

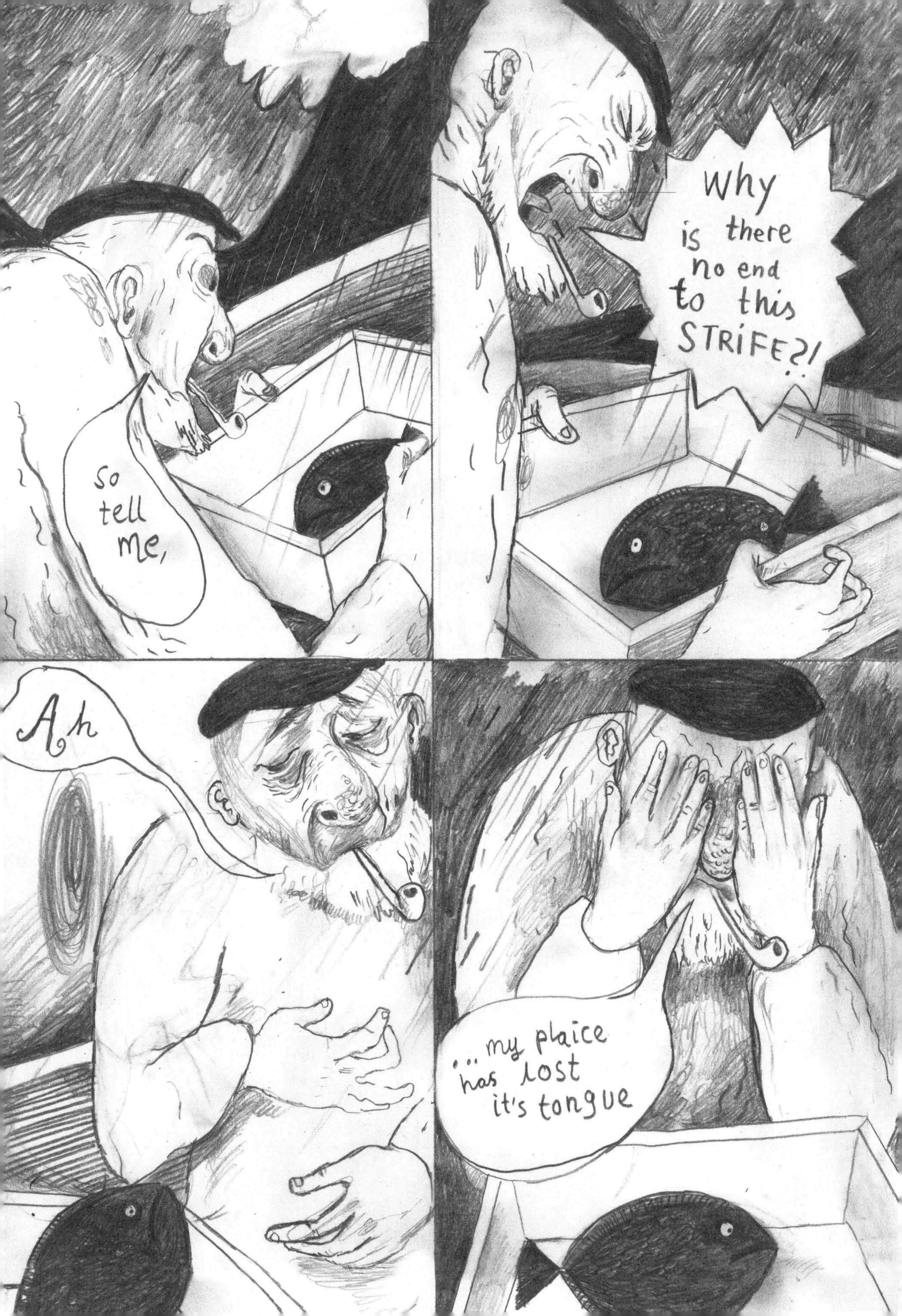
So tell me,
Why is there no end to this STRIFE?!
Ah
... my plaice has lost it's tongue

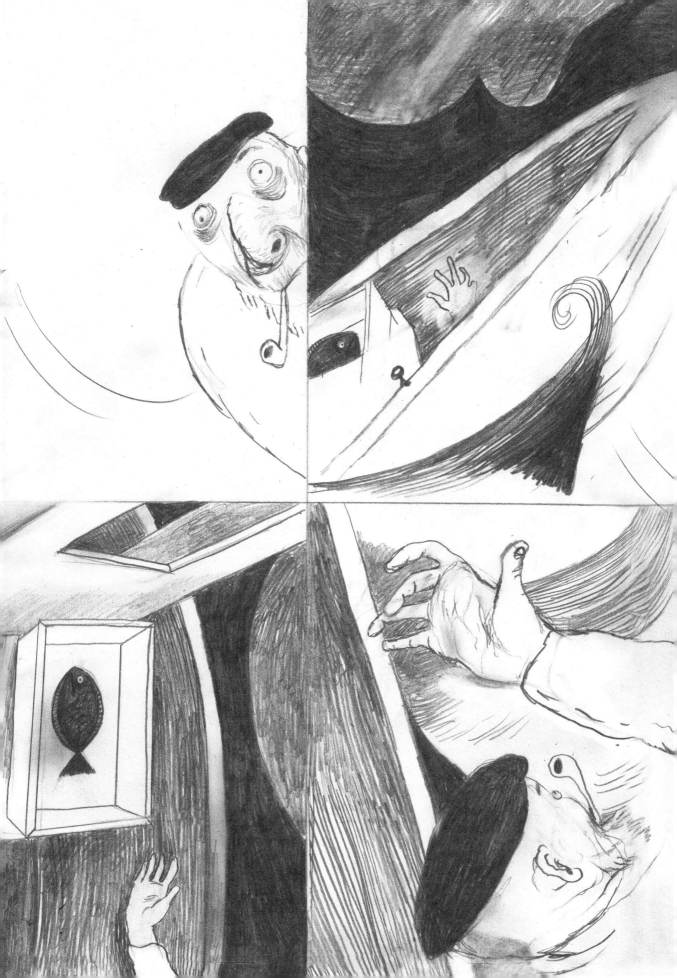

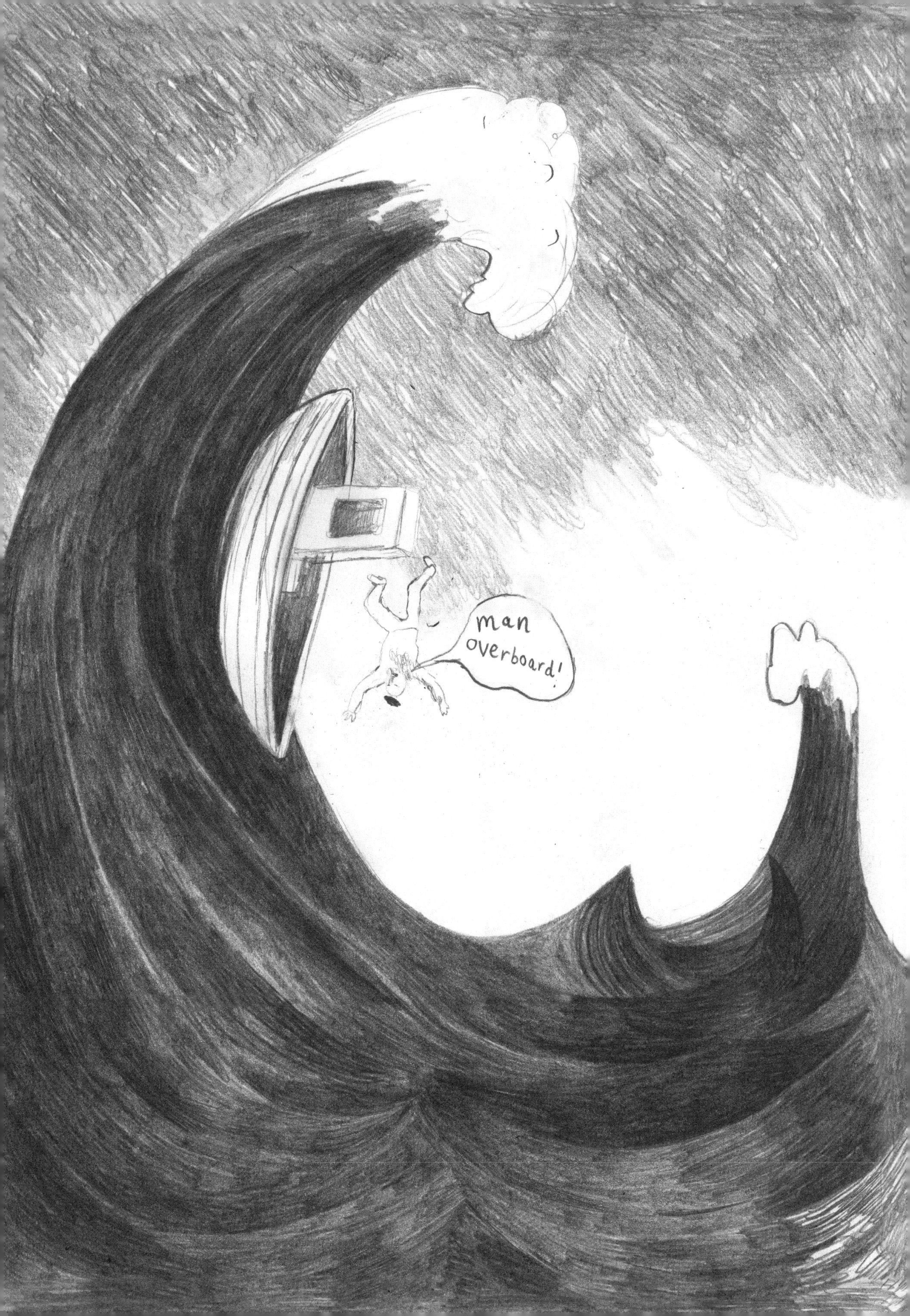
man overboard!

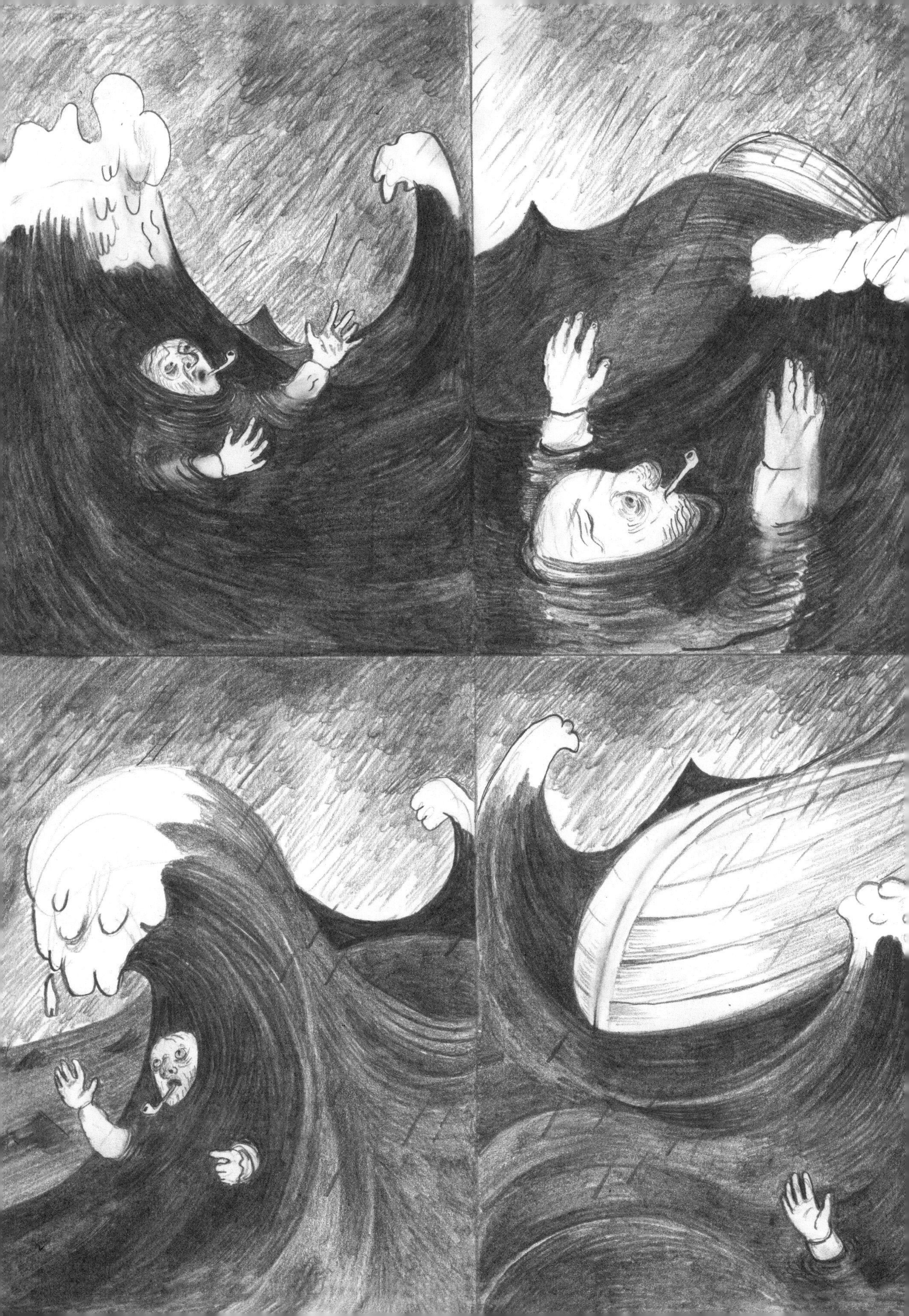

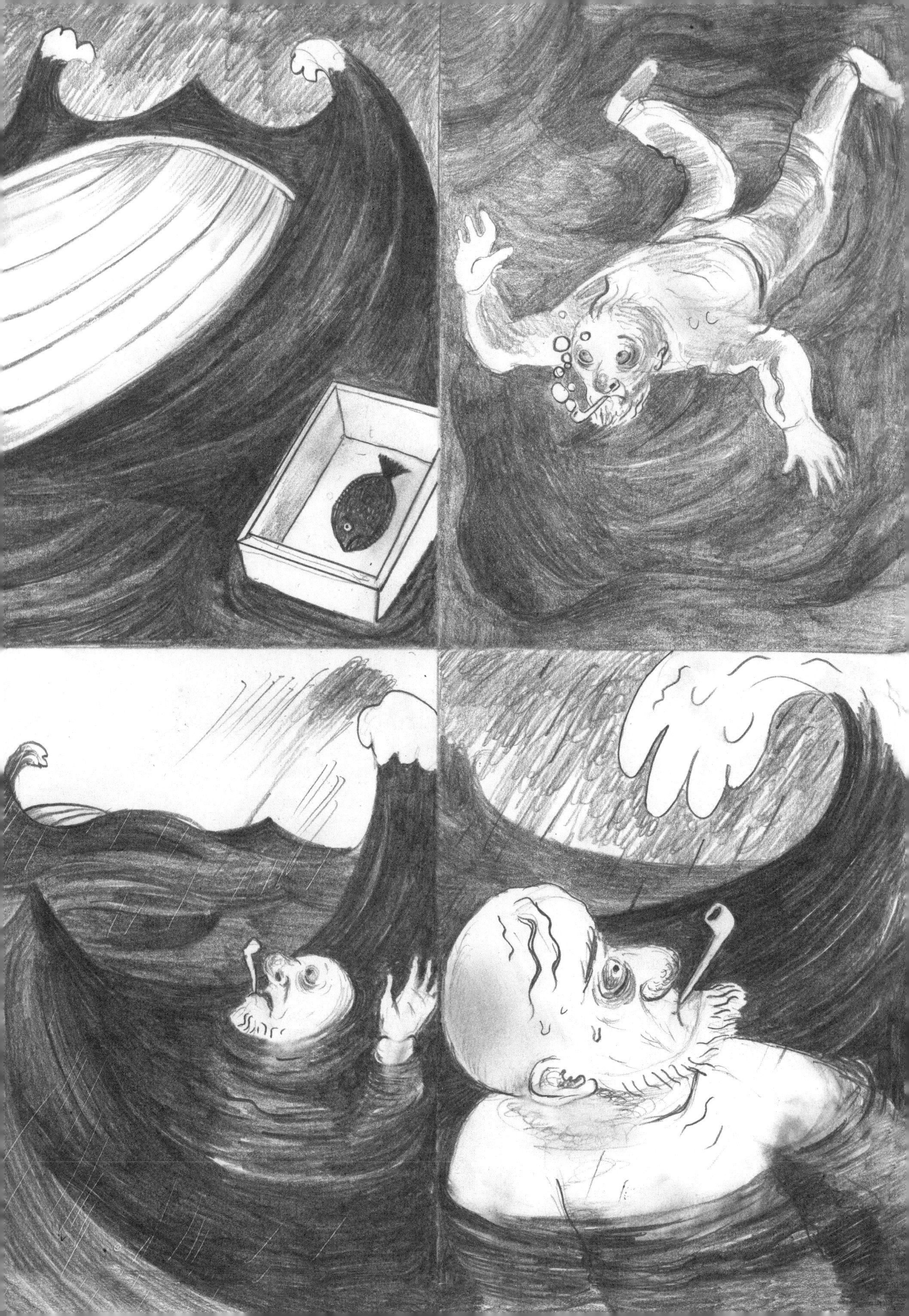

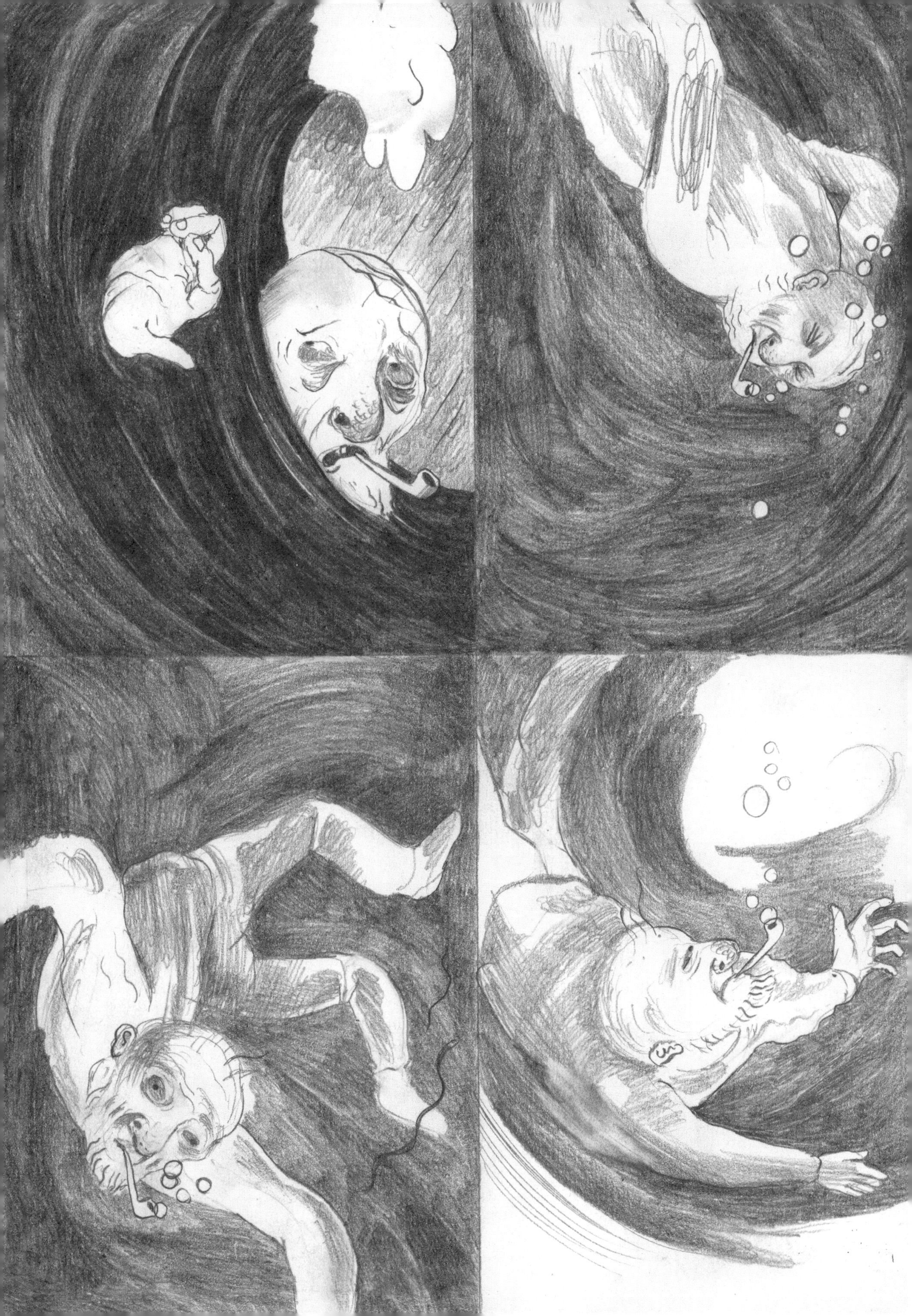

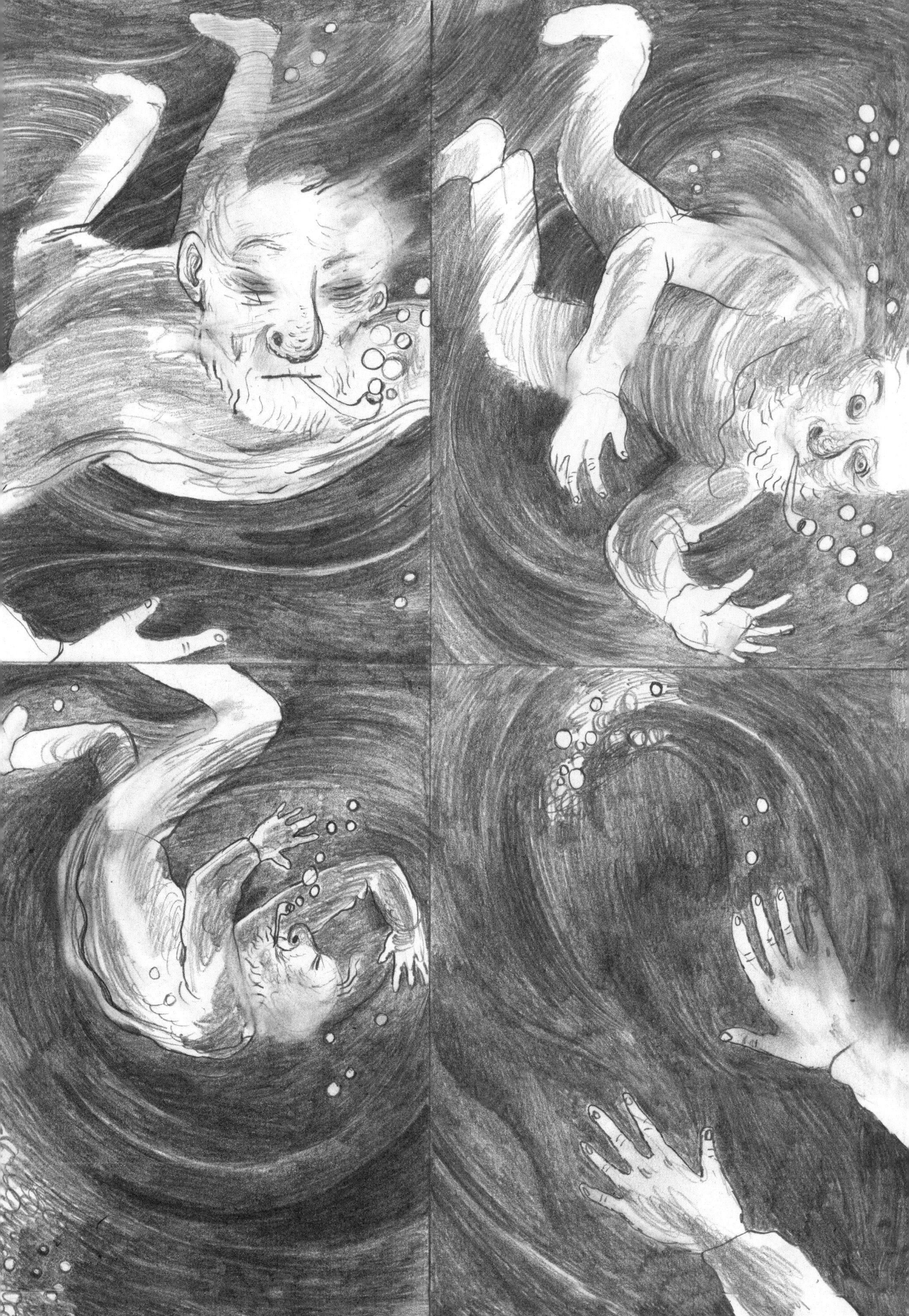

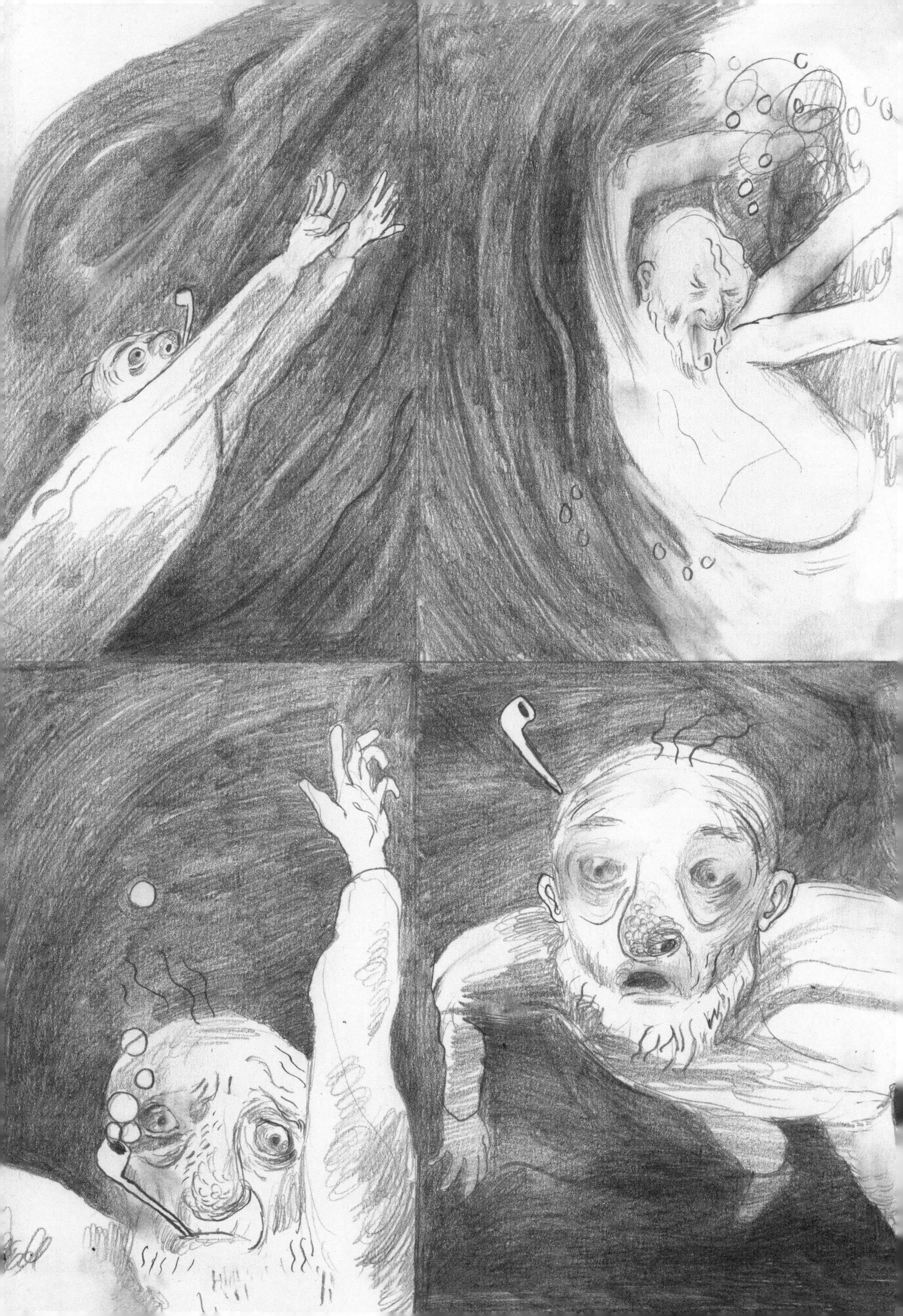

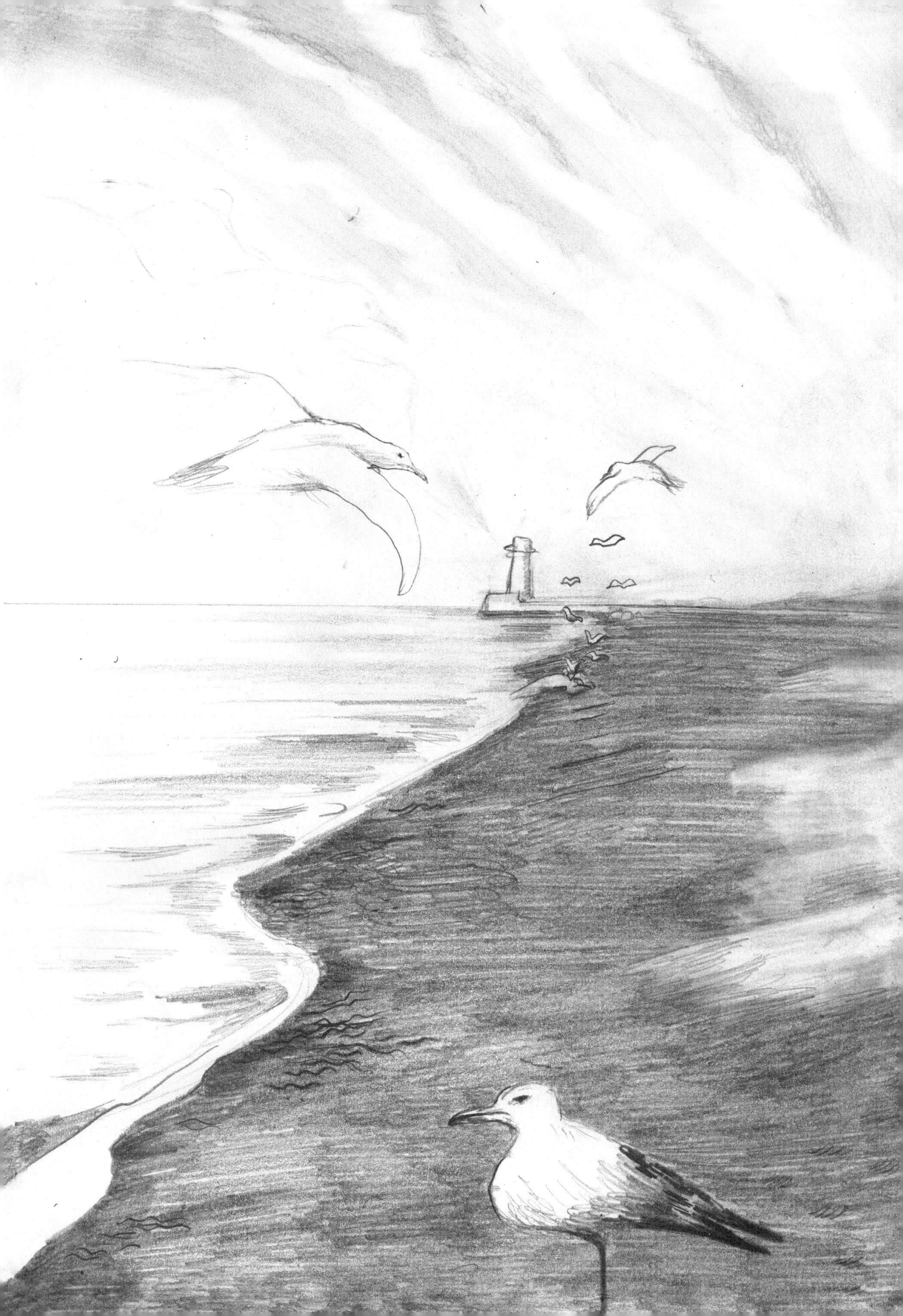

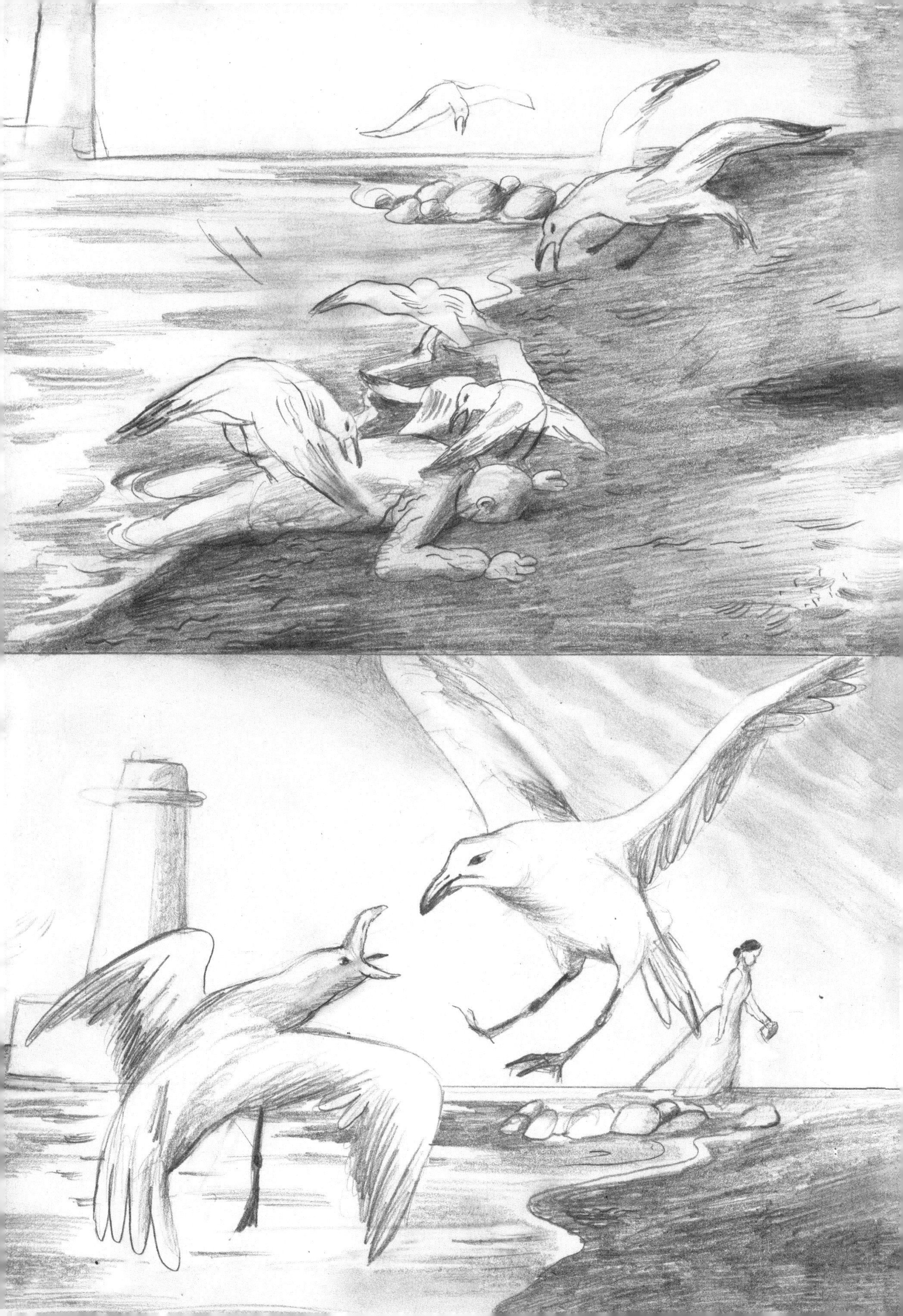

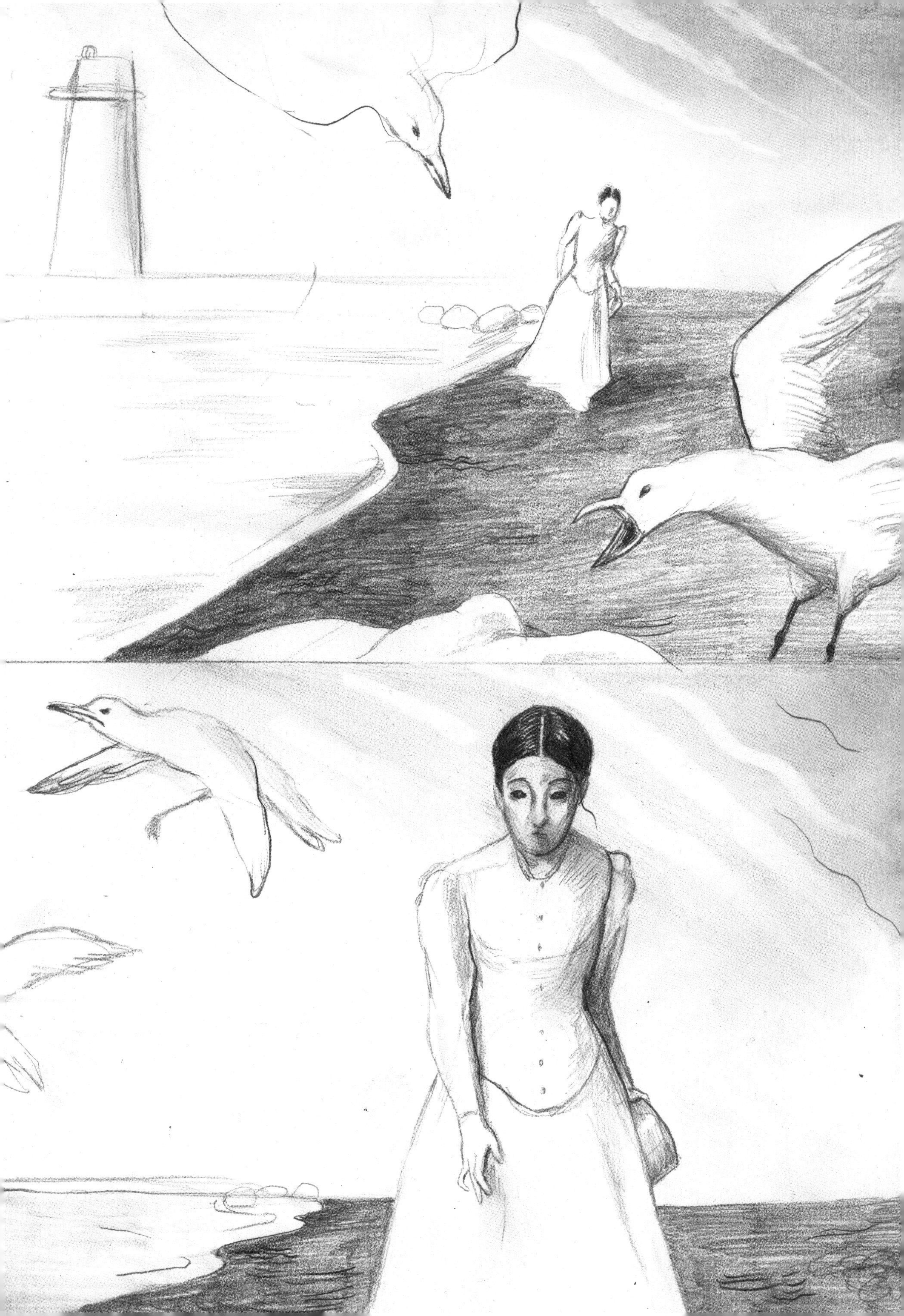

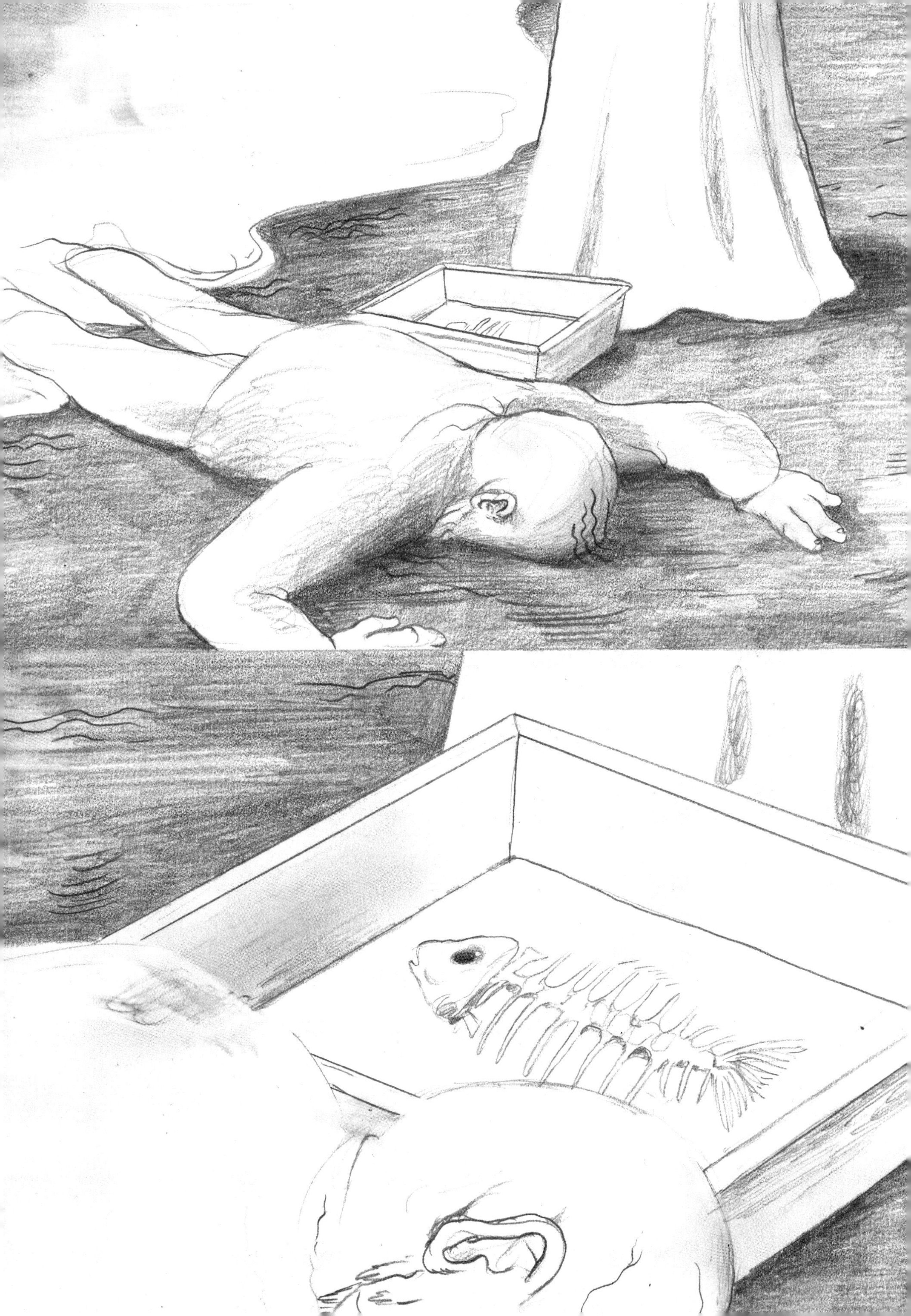

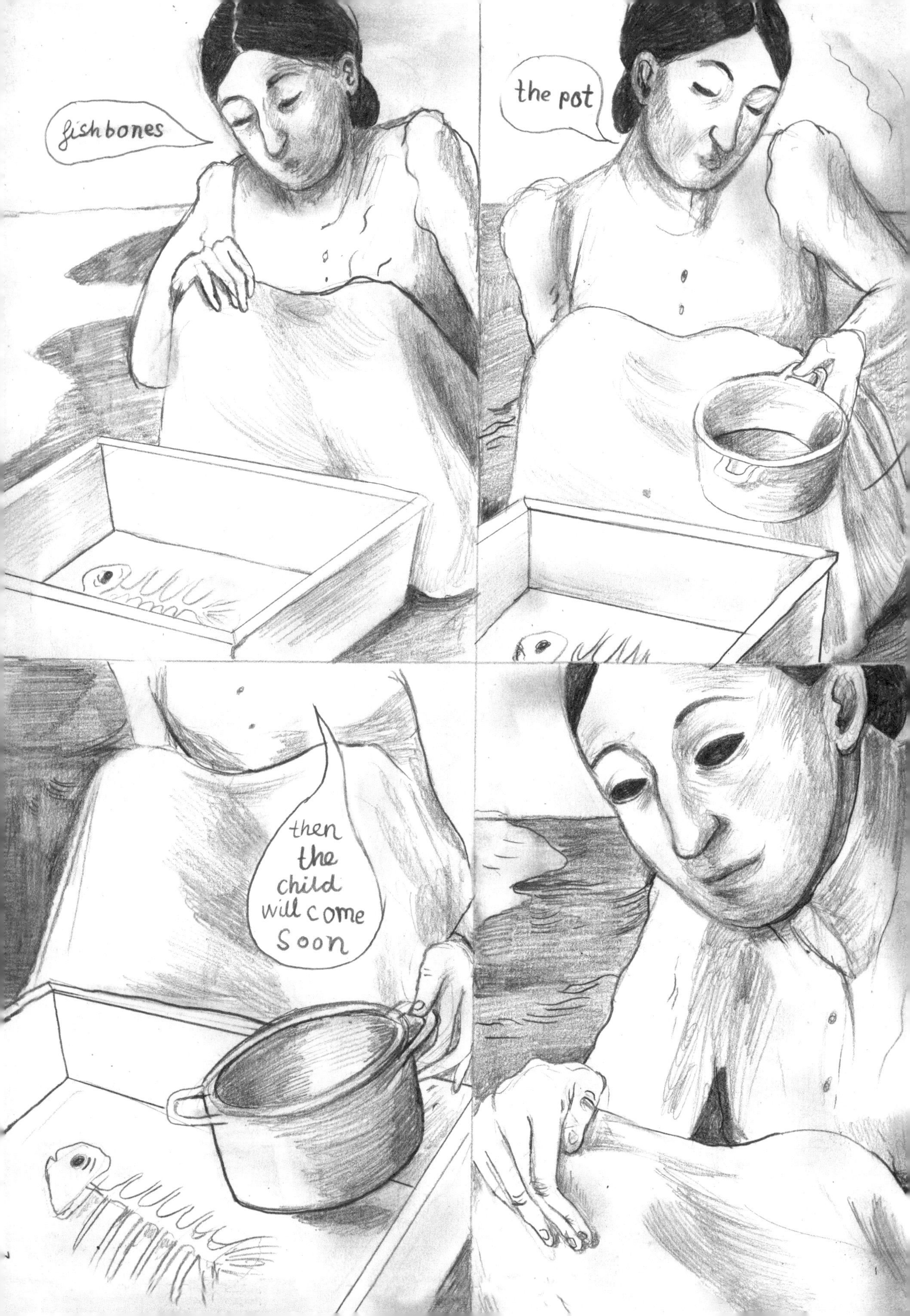
fishbones
the pot
then the child will come soon

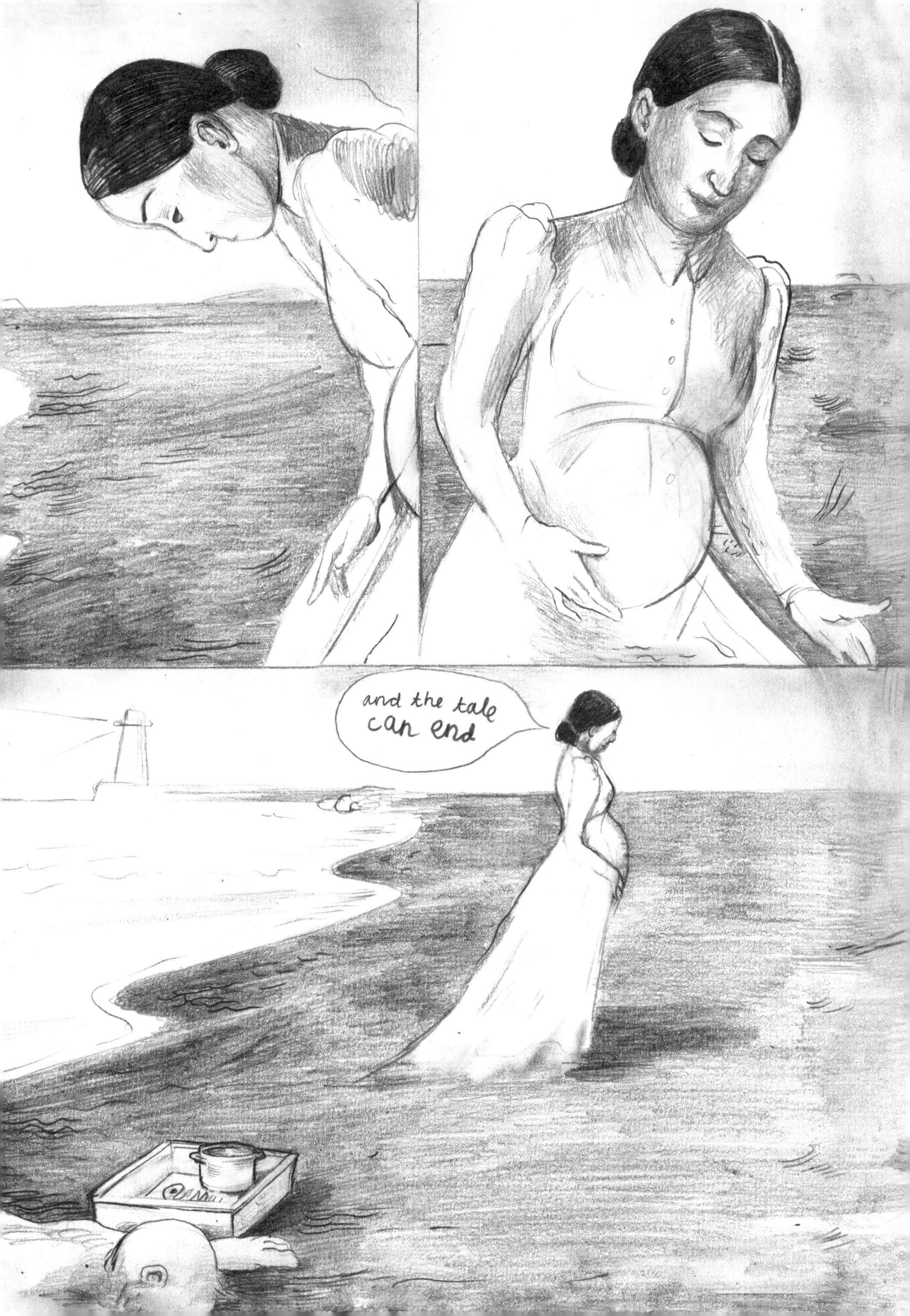
and the tale can end

Fantagraphics Books, Inc.
7563 Lake City Way NE
Seattle, WA 98115
www.fantagraphics.com

Translator: Misha Hoekstra
Editor: RJ Casey
Supervising Editor: Gary Groth
Designer: Keeli McCarthy
Production: Paul Baresh
Promotion: Jacq Cohen
Associate Publisher: Eric Reynolds
Publisher: Gary Groth

Published with the support of the
DANISH ARTS FOUNDATION

ISBN: 978-1-68396-149-9
Library of Congress Control Number: 2018936476
First Printing: 2018
Printed in Hong Kong